PERSONAL FOUL

MAGGIE RAWDON

PERSONAL FOUL

I'm her dirty little secret, the one she loves to hate.

She knows just what to say to cut deep, and I know how to press every single button she has. We hate each other, until one night after I lose the biggest football game of the year. When she offers the kind of mercy I need. It changes everything... until the next morning. Now I'm her dirty little secret, and she's avoiding me like the plague.

Which makes it difficult when we get partnered on a project and we're stuck on a couple's trip with our friends.

The tension between us is sky high. So I propose a way to lower it: enemies with benefits. One hotel room. A few days. A chance to let our little "hateship" run its course.

Except when it's unexpectedly cut short, I'm not ready to give her up. And I think I might be a bad habit she can't quit, despite how smart she is. But we have bigger problems, and both of our post-college careers are on the line.

NOTES

For content information: visit my website

ONE

Wren

THE BAR HAS BEEN ABSOLUTE HELL ON WHEELS TONIGHT. Half the customers seem hell-bent on driving me to the brink of insanity and the other half seem to think tipping is an invention best left to a previous century. The cooler has started leaking, one of the vents nearly caught fire because Tom forgot to properly clean it last night, and Stacey—one of my best servers—turned in her notice this week because she found a job that would pay her twice what she makes here and it meant she didn't have to rely on tips. I can't blame her, but I will miss her, desperately. Both in that she is a bright light on a dark night around here and because she is an incredibly efficient and upbeat server. Replacing her is going to be nearly impossible.

My phone dings with another text message. Liv asking if I can bring some ice to the party. It's less a party and more of a wake really. Moved from the football house to our house when it was obvious that we would be mourning the loss of our championship game rather than celebrating the win. It's heartbreaking, but between losing our star quarterback to injury and a host of other problems plaguing the team, it isn't entirely surprising.

The last thing I feel like doing tonight is going home to a bunch of drunk people toasting to a season that could have been, but I didn't really have a choice. Unless I want to stay upstairs at my grandfather's apartment where he'll keep me up half the night with his snoring. I'll probably get better sleep at home.

"Can you take this to table eight?" I hand off a plate of wings to Stacey who takes it from me and nods.

"Hey, sexy. I love that hair," one of the drunker patrons leers at me and tries to reach out and grab one of my braids before I pull away.

I have my hair up in two Dutch braids. It keeps it out of my face while I work, and it helps keep the tips coming, and god knows I need them.

"Another beer?" I point to his empty glass. He doesn't need one, but his friend has already admitted he's the DD for the evening, so I won't cut him off just yet.

"Yeah, sexy. And your number."

I smile back at him like I enjoy the comment and take his glass.

"Tom, could you put two more orders of chili cheese fries in for me please?" I call back to the kitchen before I head to the bar to fill up another glass with lager.

"Did you see the guy at table three? He's sexy as fucking hell," Tammy, who's old enough to be my mother even though we both pretend she's not, coos at a guy half her age across the room.

I glance up and see Mason and a couple of the other hockey players sitting at a booth there. He is hot, but he has also dated my roommate and best friend, which means he's off-limits for me. And while a couple of the other hockey players are equally delicious, I'm not about to dive into waters that murky. Especially since Mason and Liam, our quarterback and my bestie's new boyfriend, don't get along, to say the least. When I do date, which is rare, I like my men drama free.

I deliver the beer to the drunk guy and spin around to grab a couple of refills of water and pop to take the hockey table. A couple of them ask for the check and I nod. I check two more tables and drop off the round of chili cheese fries that are finally up. By the time I get back to the register the phone behind the bar is ringing, and there's only one person who still uses that line.

"Hi Gramps. What's up?" I tuck the phone under my ear while I run the tickets up.

"Hi Wren. I can't find the remote anywhere. Do you know where it got put last? I swear that Sherry is always moving it around. Like she's trying to hide it from me. Tells me I watch too much sports. As if there is such a thing as too much sports."

I chuckle a little to myself. "Did you check between the cushions on the recliner? And in the kitchen by the microwave?"

"No... hold on." I hear him set the phone down and shuffle across the apartment to look for it.

"Another beer?" A guy comes up and points to his glass.

I press enter to print the ticket and then take the glass from him, sliding it into the dirty bin.

"The winter lager, right?" I ask and he nods.

I spin the old wound cord from the vintage 80s phone around to my side and stretch over to grab a cold clean glass, and then slide back to the tap to pour it.

"Wren! Did you make the extra order of bacon this week?" Tom yells up to me.

"Yep! Back in the walk-in. Third shelf from the bottom on the back left. Can't miss it!"

"Thanks!"

"You still there, Wren?" My grandfather's voice returns to the line.

"Yeah, Gramps. Did you find it?"

"Yup, in between the cushion and the side of the chair. Must have lost it there when I took a doze earlier. Thanks, dear."

"No problem. Make sure you take your meds tonight, okay? I think you're due in about 30 minutes."

"Yeah. Sherry has a timer set for me. "

"Okay. Good. Love you and goodnight."

"Goodnight. Love you."

He hangs up the line, and I set the phone back on the receiver and turn again to slide the beer to the guy.

"That's some talent, managing the family and the bar." He smiles at me.

He's quite a bit older than me but cute.

"Thanks. I try." I smile back at him.

"I've been coming in here more lately and you're always here. You have a cot back there you sleep on or something? Never leave?"

"Something like that." I shrug, running another ticket for the hockey table as I talk to him.

"You ever go out to dinner? Or want company for it?"

I glance up at him and he gives me a sincere smile, and I almost want to agree, but I barely have time as it is and dating really isn't something I can find time for.

"I do, but I'm seeing someone currently." I give him a little smile, and shrug.

"Ah. I figured you probably were but couldn't hurt to ask.

Thanks for the beer all the same." He gives me a little nod and slides the money for the beer and a decent tip my way.

"Thank you."

I always hold my breath when a guy hits on me here. Usually, they're just drunk and aiming at the first woman they can see, but occasionally they build up our little chats while I serve their food, into something more in their head. And when I turn them down, it gets messy. Which is the reason I always lie and say I'm already seeing someone. But this guy is nice. I'll give him credit for that. I wish they could all be as easy as he is. Because while I love this bar and keeping my Gramps's dream alive is something I'm happy to do, some nights it's all a little much. And tonight has been one of those nights.

One that's going to continue I realize when I go to walk the hockey table's checks back and two of them are standing on top of the table pouring beer down two players' throats from a distance. I sigh and brace myself for the inevitable confrontation, glancing at the clock to see I only have a couple more hours left to go.

TWO

Easton

When I watch the ball slip through my fingers and hit the turf, it's like watching my entire future crash and burn. My future hopes for the NFL, my immediate hopes to hoist a trophy with my guys at the end of this season, my chance to prove that I'm worthy of the Westfield football dynasty. I feel sick the second it falls. Wondering if this is the end of it all. Wondering if everyone on this team is going to hate me as much as I hate myself right now.

Somewhere deep down I know it's not quite that fucking dramatic. There are a whole lot of things that went wrong during and before this game that led to me needing to make an impossible Hail Mary catch. But it was almost possible. So close I could taste it, and I fucking blew it. Fumbling the ball and our chance to win.

I can hear the crowd roar with disappointment. Boos and jeers echo throughout the stadium followed by the celebration from the opposing team's support section and band. Hearing their fight song queue up makes me feel fucking nauseous.

I'm reliving that same scene over and over again as I stand at this party. I'm not even sure you could call it a party. It's more like an excuse to get drunk and try to blot out the fact that after a fantastic season and somehow squeaking out enough wins despite Liam's season-ending injury, we still lose when it counts.

Everyone keeps reminding me it's not my fault. Could have happened to anyone. That's just how it goes sometimes. But that's not what it feels like. And I'm as fucking tired of the sympathy as I am of reading the commentary on the sports pundit websites.

I knock back another beer because I'm already too deep to drive and glance around the room to see where Waylon and Ben are. Another one of the redheaded sorority girls gives me a smile from across the room. She's already offered to be a consolation prize tonight, and I have zero fucking interest in it. I'm too depressed to fucking get it up, and even if I could miracle it out I sure as fuck don't want a consolation. I wanted the win. The trophy. The bragging rights. The better chance it would have given me to get into the pros.

I finally find the guys and Ben tosses me another beer, but I hand it back to him.

"I think I need the hard stuff. I'm fucking exhausted listening to everyone give me their fucking condolences."

"They're just trying to be nice," Waylon reminds me.

"Maybe. But I don't fucking care." I shrug. "Girls got anything hard? Bourbon? Whiskey?"

"There's a bottle of vodka and tequila in there. Gonna have to replace it though if you drink any of it."

"No problem." I grab one of the half-empty bottles and twist the top off and chug.

"Whoa. Slow down there, champ." Ben frowns at me.

"I shouldn't have fucking come. It's like a highlight reel of failure out here."

"You keep going that hard you're gonna have another unpleasant highlight reel." Ben shakes his head at me.

I shrug it off and wander out to the back porch where I can hopefully drink in peace. Their back porch is enclosed and heated—the place where they still do their laundry in the wintertime. I take a deep breath and another chug from the bottle, thankful to get two seconds of clarity. But that quickly turns out to be a failure because it's where I discover Liam and Liv and given the position I find them both in I groan and turn my back, and run a hand over my eyes.

"You two have to fucking put a sign on the door or some-thing. Give a fucking warning. Damn!" I feel my way back to the door and open it as I hear Liv giggling in the background and Liam grumping about something.

I know it's hypocritical of me to complain but fuck, I need a break tonight. A place to escape. And that's when I see the stairs. I know we're not supposed to go up there. That the whole upper floor is off-limits, but I feel like I'm part of the inner circle at this point, and given the circumstances they'll probably cut me some slack.

I hurry up them and find the door to Wren's room open. She's never here. Always works late nights at the bar, and some-times there's just a quick blur of her through the living room when she gets home in the wee hours of the morning. It's still earlyish right now. Which means I can't bother her by hiding out in her room for a little while. I can be in and out before she even knows, with the added bonus that I can sneak a look around her room.

I creak open the door when I get to it, half expecting her to be sitting on her bed telling me to go to hell. It's dark, and I flick on a light on the desk to partially illuminate the room. Posters line one wall, bands and what I assume are some of her favorite sports teams. There's a smattering of furniture; her bed, a bookcase, a dresser, and a desk and chair.

When I glance down at her desk, there's a handful of photos that have been printed out. A gorgeous woman sprawled out on a bed in hot as fuck lingerie. She's straddling a chair in others, and on the floor with the rain pouring down on her in the last set. I briefly wonder if this explains the lack of boyfriends in Wren's life and her absolute disgust in me until I look closer and realize the photos are *her*. I snatch them up, looking closer. Trying to reconcile the woman who tells me to go to hell on a regular basis with the one in these photos. I sit down on the bed and bust out the light on my phone, taking a swig of vodka to try and chill my fucking nerves because holy *fuck* is she a fucking knockout.

I'd always thought she was cute. She has a beautiful face and a cupid's bow mouth that most guys would fantasize about. But my favorite part of her has always been the way she uses that mouth to slice me in half while barely batting an eyelash. She's mean as hell and it's hot as fuck. We've had more than one argument while we were out with our friends that ended in me wanting to rip her clothes off and fuck her against a wall. I've wanted her for a while on the basis of that alone because I can only imagine how that attitude would translate in bed. I've been dying to fucking find out. But I had no idea this is what she looked like under all the ill-will and malice. *Fuck.* I shuffle through them again. No way am I going to unsee this.

I'm super curious why she has them. She doesn't strike me as particularly vain and if there's no boyfriend to send them to, there are limited other reasons. And now I'm starting to wonder if she has a secret double life we don't know about. Like I know she works at the bar, but she's there *all* the fucking time. What if it's code for something else?

I lay back on the bed and lay them out next to me, grabbing my phone to snap a couple of pictures of them. Is it highly unethical and a little bit of a dick move? Yeah. But I'm going to need to look at these again when I'm sober. Then I'll delete them and pretend like I didn't even know they existed. Except the temptation to taunt her about their existence is going to be sky fucking high.

I smile as I think about the kind of arguments I could start with her. The ways I could get under her skin. I close my eyes imagining it, telling myself I should really set an alarm so I'm out of here before she gets home.

THREE

Wren

When I get home that night, the house is overrun with people and I can barely get through my own front door. Part of the reason they moved the party to our place is because they expected there would be fewer people, not more, and I'm shocked by the turnout. I spot Liv from across the room, and mouth, "Holy shit," to her as I look wide-eyed at the massive gathering. She makes her way over to me, dodging bodies and drinks on the way, and helps me squeeze into the kitchen.

"What's happening?" I ask as I hand her a bag of ice I've brought home from the bar.

"I guess they all wanted to show support. For Liam and the guys and everything. They had a phenomenal season even if they didn't get the ending they'd hoped for." She gives a half smile and a small shrug, glancing over at Liam across the room.

"Well yeah, but damn. This is a lot of people. The house might collapse."

"Right? This is actually quieter than it was about an hour ago. They were spilling out into the yard then. I'm hoping people are going to start making their way out soon. Like go to a bar or go home, but they can't stay here. If they don't, I might have Liam or Waylon start dropping hints."

"Good plan." I nod, waving across the room to our other roommate Kenz who's sitting in her boyfriend Waylon's lap at the moment.

"Love you!" she yells and raises her cup in the air to toast me, and I yell that I love her too before I look back to Liv.

"All right, well I'm gonna go get changed and then I'll be down. Let me know what I can help with."

"Take your time." She shakes her head. "You just got off your shift. You deserve a break."

"All right. Well, I'll be back down in a bit."

I hurry my way up the steps, happy to get away from the crowds. The upstairs portion of our house has long been off-limits to party guests, complete with a rope we keep across the steps to deter people. So it's a good respite when I need a break from peopling on nights like this. And honestly, I hope I don't just crash and burn in my bed tonight because after the day I've had I don't know that I have either mourning or merriment in me.

When I get in my room, I toss my coat and my purse on a hook on the back of the door and pull my T-shirt off, trying to decide what I feel like wearing tonight or if I even want to bother with getting dressed up. This is probably another reason I'm single. I'm too tired to put effort into it.

"As much as I appreciate the view, not really in the mood for a strip show right now, Princess," a voice comes from my bed, and I nearly jump out of my skin.

I hit the light switch and look to see the tall muscular figure of one of my least favorite people sprawled out across my bed, thankfully still fully clothed and without company.

"Easton, what the fuck are you doing in here?"

"I needed to lay down for a bit and get away from everyone."

"In my room?"

"I knew you were at the bar, and it's not like Liv or Mac's rooms are safe. Don't need them stumbling in and starting to fuck in front of me. That already happened once tonight." His bicep is curled over his face and eyes, shielding them from the light in the room as he grumbles at me.

I'm curious but also don't know that I want to ask about the last part.

"Well, I'm home now so my room is no longer safe. Time to go."

"Why, you bring some guy home from the bar?" He pulls his arm back enough to peer at me from behind it. "'Cause I don't see anyone."

"No, but it's my room and I don't need you in it."

"Can you cut me some fucking slack? I don't want to go back down there. They're all trying to tell me how it's fine and it's not a big deal and how it was still a phenomenal season. Like I fucking want to hear all of that."

"So you mean they're being nice to you? What fucking assholes."

"I don't consider it nice to bring up the biggest fuck up of my career, but sure if you want to paint it that way."

"Get a grip, Easton."

"Poor choice of words, Princess," he fires back, sitting up slightly.

Oops. Not intended but I smirk a little at stumbling into another dig against him.

"Yeah. Would have been clever if it was on purpose though."

"That kind of cruelty is beneath you."

"This kind of wallowing is beneath you."

"*You* fuck up your career like this and tell me how you feel. When you accidentally set the bar on fire, you let me know."

"Well, we almost did today, actually."

"What?" He jolts again.

"Grease trap wasn't properly cleaned. It's been a fucking day. Hence why I don't want company."

"I don't want company either."

"Then get out of my room, Easton. It's that simple."

"I'm not company. Besides I'm too drunk to drive and the only place to go is downstairs."

"Then go sleep in your car or see if Kenz will let you hide out in the library up here."

"No thanks. Pretty comfortable here."

"And where am I gonna sleep?"

He looks around at the bed like he's judging it.

"It's what? A queen? There's plenty of room."

"Easton... like I said. Get over yourself and go downstairs with your friends. They want to support you. You made one mistake. That's not your whole career. It shouldn't have been down to that play anyway."

"It'll be on every tape the scouts look at. Everyone who hears my name is gonna think of that drop."

"Okay. So worst case scenario, no more football. There's just your entire trust fund and all your rich-boy connections to fall back on. It's a rough life, but I think you'll live."

"I want to earn my own living."

I give him a skeptical look because Easton does not strike me as the worker-bee type. More like the invest-daddy's-money or find-yourself-an-heiress type. Maybe if he bothered to put effort into commodifying all the looks and luxury he has, he could even have some sort of influencer career even without the football career to boost his name.

"Okay. Good news there too, you're also hot as fuck, and women across campus obsess over you. Find a sugar mama or you can start one of those sites where you sell naked pictures of yourself."

He gives me a sour look but then smiles.

"Is that what you're doing for extra cash these days?" He smirks, and I don't like it, at all.

"No. As you know I run a bar. That takes all my free time."

"So what are these then?" He holds up a handful of photos that he has next to him on the bed. They're from the boudoir photo shoot the girls and I had done a few weeks back.

Kenz had done it for Waylon, and Liv had done it to help twist Liam's arm. I had no guy to speak of, but I'd decided to go along for the fun of it. Thought it would be a fun confidence boost and something to look back on someday when I was older. In no version of reality did I imagine Easton Westfield seeing them.

"Were you fucking going through my things?"

"They were sitting out on your desk," he answers defensively. "You have half-naked pictures of women sitting out, guys are going to look."

"Guys aren't supposed to be in my room."

He smirks and runs his tongue along the inside of his cheek.

"I'm starting to think that's the reason you're twisted so fucking tight."

"You're an asshole. Give them to me." I reach across to grab them, but he holds them out of my reach.

"Nah. There's a couple in here I want."

"Very funny. Give them to me."

"I'm serious. I'll give them back if you give me the ones I want. I'm having a rough fucking week right now. Can't you have some mercy?"

"What the fuck are you going to do with pictures of me in my lingerie, Easton?"

He smirks, his eyes raking over me. "You really can't figure that out for yourself?"

"There are half a dozen women downstairs who are willing to be an in-the-flesh version of that for you. Give them to me."

This was our thing. Him teasing me about wanting to fuck me. Me telling him to go to hell knowing he has zero interest in carrying through. Barmaids with bitchy attitudes are not his thing. He likes them giggly, pliable, and already obsessed with him.

"But not you?" His free arm shoots out and wraps around my waist, and I feel a sudden surge of warmth and panic go through me.

Easton does not touch me. I don't touch Easton. He's like a work of art in a museum. Cold. Hard. Off-limits. Something to be admired and studied from a distance.

"What do you think...?" I glare at him, even though I can feel my heartbeat kick up a notch. Because Easton is in my room, on my bed, sprawled out, looking like a god.

"I think you want to fuck me. You just think it's beneath you."

Yep. That pretty much nailed it. Not that I was going to admit it.

"I think you think every woman wants to fuck you."

"Most of them do."

"It's nice that you're so humble."

"Fine. You don't want to fuck me. So then it's not a problem if I sleep in your bed tonight. You let me do that, I'll give you the pictures back."

I hesitate. But he's right. He can't drive, and I do feel the tiniest bit sorry for him having to relive his bumbled catch over and over again tonight.

"Fine," I agree reluctantly.

He grins wide and hands the pictures back to me, which I snatch from him immediately.

"I already took photos of them with my phone anyway."

"Easton, I swear if you did and you don't delete them, I will fucking throttle you."

"Good thing that sounds like fun."

And then, because the man has pushed every last button I have, I toss the pictures onto my desk and launch myself at him. I end up on top of him, and I get two good blows in to his arm and his side before he grabs me, tosses me on to my back and pins my wrists down above my head. A position he is very pleased with, as his stunned look morphs into smugness.

"I hate you *so* fucking much Westfield."

"Huh. That's weird. That sounded a whole lot like I want to fuck you *so* fucking bad, East."

There's a wicked grin on his face now as he studies me.

I choke out a laugh. "You wish."

"I do. So stop looking at me like that." His brow furrows ever so slightly.

"Like what?"

"Like you want me to fuck you. You do it all the fucking time when you think I don't see you."

"You're fucking delusional." I roll my eyes. Apparently, I've been too obvious. I try to keep my ogling discreet because I don't want him or anyone else to know. Because it's embarrassing as hell that I do actually have brains, sense, and reason on my side, and I'm still brought down by my baser impulses.

"Am I?" He pushes my wrists together and locks them both with one hand. Because his are huge. Part of the reason it was a fucking travesty he couldn't hang on to the dropped ball. Not that I'm going to say that. I'm a bitch, but not a heinous bitch, after all.

His other hand drifts down my side, over my bare skin, and teases the edge of the bra I have on. It's nothing sexy. And definitely nothing I planned for him to see. Just a good old trusty one I wear on nights I work for full support under my work tee, and I can't wait to hear what derogatory thing he has to say about it. How it compares to whatever the fuck all his high-end club girls wear for him.

"Let me take it off. I want to see you. Especially after looking at those photos."

"You just said you weren't in the mood for a strip show."

"I lied. I want you naked. I'll strip for you if you want. I've got a bottle of vodka up here. We can lay here and drink some." His eyes drift over my body as he talks. "Please. I need something to get my mind off all of this shit. I won't touch you if you don't want."

"What?" I ask, breathy and so fucking confused. If *I* don't want? But he wants? What in the hell is happening right now... There is no way Westfield is actually pleading with me to get naked.

His brow furrows and his eyes return to my face. "Never mind. I shouldn't have said anything."

"I need a shower," I say, and he releases my wrists.

I climb out from underneath him and stand again. I should walk away, hurry and shut myself in my bathroom far away from him and hope by the time I get out that he's gone. But I don't. I take a breath and look back at him over my shoulder. Braving out what I'm about to say, even though I know it's a bad idea.

"You coming?"

And the way his eyes go soft at the offer, I feel a flutter of something in my chest. Something that worries me. The rich boy is more dangerous than I gave him credit for.

FOUR

Easton

"WHAT?" I CAN'T BELIEVE I HEARD HER RIGHT.

"I'm not going to offer again. So you can either strip down and follow, or you can stay out here. I don't care." She makes her way to the bathroom on the far side of the room, and I follow her with my eyes for a moment while I try to make sense of what's happening. Because I think the little bird who hates me might be going soft on me, and that seems too good to be true.

I jump up way too quick for my drunk ass to handle, my head fucking spinning, and follow behind her to the doorway of the bathroom.

"Am I this fucking drunk or did you offer what I think you just offered?" I stare at her, wondering if she's going to try to land another blow against my ribs again for following her.

"This is a no-touching offer. It's just a mutual shower-taking offer. So you can sober up and I can get the bar smell off of me, and we can go to sleep."

"Is it a no-looking offer?"

"If you get in there with me, I'm definitely looking. You can decide for yourself."

And fuuuucckkk.

She looks back at me for a second before she turns the hot water on and then moves to take her shorts off. I stand there frozen, watching her undress. She wears this outfit at the bar all the time. Short shorts, a fitted T-shirt, and knee-high socks. She does her hair differently, but the braided pigtails she has currently are a favorite of hers. And I know she knows what she's doing when she wears them like that. I'm sure she rakes in the tips. I'd have fucking thrown a couple hundred her way on a couple of different occasions if I thought it would ever get her to look at me like something other than rich trash.

"You have to strip too, you know. That's part of the deal."

"Right," I mumble. Pulling my shirt over my head and tossing it on the counter as I go for my pants.

When I look up again, she's dropping the last of her clothes to the floor, and that's the same exact moment I'm wondering if I fucking fell asleep and am dreaming all of this. That looking at all those photos while I was laying in her bed has me conjuring up a fantasy where the woman who loves telling me to go fuck myself is not only inviting me to take a shower with her but has the kind of body that could only exist in my dreams. Like she was written just for me. But when I climb into the shower after her and feel the water hit my body, I know it can't be. It's real. I just still can't make sense of it.

She stands to the side of the water, undoing the braids in her hair, and I want to reach out and touch the other one. Undo it for her. Undo her. Fuck, but I can't because there was a strict no-touching order. So instead I lean back under the water, letting it roll over my body and I close my eyes for a second, trying to focus on the sound of it rushing to help me think straight.

When I emerge again, she's staring at me, her eyes drifting over my body, nearly every dirty thought she's having transparently on her face. And I clasp my hands over my face and push the water back through my hair to keep from smiling. One that makes it obvious how much I know she wants me. One that will trigger her bad fucking mood again. But I can't help it, because the girl who fucking hates me also wants me and it's satisfying as fuck to finally have that information for sure.

"You're hogging the water," she complains, and I smirk, letting my eyes rake over her and taking in this wet dream before I sidestep her and switch positions. Her shower is big enough for both of us, but just barely.

The water swirls through her dark blonde hair, dripping off the ends where it's tipped with teal, something she'd done as part of her support for our now-dead hopes at the championship. And it cascades down over her breasts, rivulets of water parting for her nipples and crashing to the floor beneath us. Her waist nips in and then the curve rounds out again over her hips, and thick thighs. I've stared at her legs a lot when she works in her tiny shorts, but nothing compares to this view.

"Your body is fucking insane," I mutter, studying her curves, wanting to run my hands over them. "You're built like something out of a fucking fantasy."

She scowls at me.

"What? I said something nice." I'm clueless as to why this is her reaction.

"You said something bullshitty. Don't do that, or there will be a no-talking rule too."

"That wasn't bullshit. That was fucking honest."

"Spare me the fucking Westfield charm, okay?"

"Princess, I don't have the energy tonight for charm. And if I did, I wouldn't use it on you because I don't think you're capable of being charmed."

She smiles a little at that, and I raise a brow.

"That's better."

"That's how you want me to talk to you?"

"It's how we are normally."

"We're not normally naked."

She shrugs as if it's a fair point but also one she doesn't care about.

"I'm not one of your girls. So don't talk to me like I am."

"I'm well fucking aware."

"Good." She dips her head back and then turns around under the water. "Switch."

I move as she asks, and she grabs her soap and puff and starts soaping herself up. Acting almost as if I'm not even here. As if she doesn't care. And I don't like that one fucking bit.

"Why *do* you have photos like that?"

"Why shouldn't I?"

"Doesn't really seem like you. And to my knowledge, you don't have a boyfriend you're taking them for."

"You don't know me, Easton."

"I know enough."

She gives me a dismissive glance and then runs her hands down her thigh, bending to get to her knee and calf. The humidity in the shower is fogging the glass and surrounding me with the scent of her peach bodywash.

"You have a double life? Secretly a cam girl on the side?" I prod her as she goes for the other leg.

"Yes, that's it, Easton. You've caught me out. I'm secretly a cam girl. Making loads of money. I just sling beer at a bar on the side for funsies."

"I mean you're doing a pretty good impression of one right now."

"I'm taking a shower." She gives me an annoyed look.

"While I watch you."

"Then don't watch."

I let out a choked laugh. "Princess, I'm already making a mental fucking recording of all of this."

She flashes me a look and then returns to soaping herself up.

"Are you always this crude?"

"No, but you said no charm."

"Those are my options? There's no middle ground?"

"No, Goldilocks, there's no middle ground."

She flips me the bird as she reaches around to soap up her back.

"You want help?"

Her eyes flutter up to mine, and I can tell she's thinking about it. Can tell that she wants me to and that she might even let me. But a second later she looks away.

"I've got it."

And I resist the impulse to fight her on it. Too worried I'll say the wrong fucking thing because as much as I'm not kidding about the charm being off tonight—I'm too drunk, too angry, too tired to fucking try—I don't want to completely fuck this up.

Instead, I just keep watching her as she lathers her hair up with her shampoo, running her fingers over her scalp as she works the bubbles. And I wonder if she knows about my voyeuristic tendencies and is playing this all out on purpose, or if this is just a happy coincidence. My guess is the latter because I doubt she cares enough to pander to me.

"What?" she gripes as she looks up at me again.

"Just enjoying the view."

"Don't make me regret pitying you." She gives me a little dark glare.

"Is that what this is? A pity show?"

"Isn't that what you asked for out there when you were pleading with me to take my clothes off for you?" She gives me a sassy as fuck look. "Switch"

I run my tongue along the edge of my teeth, grinning as we switch places, and she nearly grazes my body with hers.

"I can tell what a miserable experience this is for you by the way you can't stop staring," I taunt her.

She glares at me and slides under the water, turning to get the soap off of her skin and out of her hair. Pretending to be too busy with the task to bother responding to me. She turns her back to me, leaning over to grab something from the corner of the shower and the sight of her sweet little hourglass frame and perfectly thick ass and thighs is too much. I have fucking limits, and she's pressing on them.

When she stands back up, I lean over her, one arm over each of her shoulders as I brace my hands against the tile.

"Just admit you want me and let me touch you."

"You wish," she huffs back at me over her shoulder.

And you know what? *Fuck it.* It's true.

"I do wish. I wish for a lot of things. You want me to go first? I'll tell you. You drive me fucking crazy. The way you run your fucking mouth. The way you treat me like I'm trash that's beneath you. You push all my fucking buttons. It's fucking hot as hell. Some nights I have to go home and shower and think about what I'd do to you if you gave me the chance. And I wonder what you'd say if you could see me sliding my hand over my cock while I think about you naked and wet underneath me. What you'd think if you knew how many times I'd come that way wishing it was you there with me. That sometimes when I come like that, I say your name. Just praying that someday you'll let me touch you, kiss you, worship you until I know exactly how hard you'd come on my cock."

Her hand slides up the wall, coming within an inch of mine almost as if she might touch me.

"Your turn, Princess, unless you're too fucking scared."

FIVE

Wren

My turn. My turn to confess the fact that I think about Easton way more than is healthy or normal. Something that no matter how things go from here on out it's going to be compounded by whatever this is we're doing. Because now I've seen him. All of him and that isn't something I'll forget. I don't think it's something anyone forgets, and it explains why so many women are desperate for repeat sessions with him. And while it's occasionally a thing he does, you pretty much have to be a unicorn for him to consider it.

"Princess..." he repeats, his tone impatient.

I turn around to look at him, and it's a mistake. The look on his face, so fucking serious and intimidating, his body like this with all his muscles fucking taut, the way he makes me feel small under his gaze. It does things for me. It does things *to* me. And it all means I should run. But the reminder that this is a limited-time opportunity makes me embrace it.

I let my eyes wander over him while I tell him the things I shouldn't. The things that will only blow his ego sky high, and we all know it's too high to begin with. But since he's wounded tonight and I feel for him because the weight of the game is on his shoulders when it shouldn't be and now the blame will be too... I'm going to let him have this thing, and then pray that he's merciful enough to return the favor and forget it tomorrow.

"Sometimes I think about pushing you until you slam me up against a wall and fuck me hard. What you'd say. If you'd tell me how much you wanted me. If you'd be any good in bed at all or if you'd be just another one of those rich fuckboys who doesn't have to try. If you could even make me come."

I tear my eyes away from his body to meet his face, and the way he's looking at me right now could cut glass.

"Let me touch you, Princess, and I'll give you all of that and more."

"Touch me then," I dare him.

I expect to be slammed up against the tile. For him to be rough and unrelenting, punishing me for all the times I've been an unrepentant bitch to him. So when his hand goes to the side of my face, gently running his knuckles over my cheek and then threading his fingers through my wet hair, I freeze like a deer in headlights.

He tilts my head back, and stares at me for a second, studying me like he's trying to puzzle something out. I wish I could read minds in this moment and know what he's thinking. He narrows the gap between us, bringing his face so close to mine.

"I'm glad you wasted time getting clean, Princess, just so I can get you dirty as fuck." He smirks and a moment later his lips are on mine.

He kisses me in long slow strokes that are soft, almost careful, and incredibly fucking calculated. The boy has had lots of practice, and that combined with the fact that he has lips that are way too lush to be a football player's means I'm slowly losing any will I thought I might still have to resist him. Because my body does not care that he's an asshole or the campus manwhore or that he will do nothing but gloat about this for all eternity. My body just knows he can deliver on promises, and I need it tonight.

So I stop fighting him, and I kiss him back, letting his tongue dip inside and run over mine, letting him kiss me like he wants to convince me how much I want him, until I press for more, answering him with rougher strokes of my own until I nip at his lower lip and he pulls back and raises a brow.

"You in a hurry?"

"Don't waste your time trying to seduce me. Just fuck me."

"Don't try to bait me into rushing. You want a quick lazy fuck; you could have taken some guy home from the bar. You wanted me."

"Only because you were conveniently located and asking for it."

A stuttered laugh comes out of him, like he's surprised but amused at my response.

"Yeah, well, all the same. You're fucking *me* tonight." He uses the leverage he has to push me against the tiles, and I stare up at him. And fuck he's beautiful, distractingly so.

"So then fuck me. I don't need all the rest. I told you that I'm not—"

Before I can finish the sentence, his lips are on my throat and his hand slides over my breast, pulling my nipple between his fingers and pinching just enough that it sends a bolt of pleasure and a tinge of pain through me. He slides his thumb over it again, like he's trying to soothe the pain he caused before he moves to the other and repeats the same measures.

"Fuck," I curse and start to slide down the tile a little, but he slides his leg between mine and his hand wraps around one side of my throat, pinning me in place while he nips along the underside of my jaw. His other hand cups my breast again, rolling the tender tip between his fingers until he has me in such a fucking state that I rock against his leg for friction before I realize what I'm doing. Until a little sound of satisfaction rumbles out of his mouth and against my throat, and I start to stand up straight again. But his hand tenses around my throat. Not enough to hurt but enough to grab my attention.

My eyes drift to his, and I'd swear they changed color. Darkened three shades from their usual pale green, because of the way his lashes are low. The way he looks at me, I worry for my own sanity.

"Don't stop. Grind that sweet little cunt on my thigh. I want to feel how desperate I make you."

"Fuck you."

He grins. "Patience. I told you."

Then he pinches my nipple again, hard, and a little gasp pops out of me, and I rock forward as the tingling sensation it leaves in its wake blooms to pleasure.

"You like that?" he mutters against my skin before he skims his teeth over my neck and then brings his mouth to mine, kissing me again with renewed fervor.

I pull away, turning my head, annoyed that he thinks he has my number. "You're boring me."

"Am I?" He slides his hand down between us, reaching between my legs, and dragging two fingers along my center before he holds them up for me to see. "That why you're so fucking wet? Because I'm boring you?"

I raise one shoulder half-heartedly, "That's from looking at you. Not from anything you're doing. I have no trouble admitting you look incredibly fuckable. It's a shame you don't have the talent to match."

An incredulous sound leaves his throat, and he lets go of me, and I slide down the wall just the tiniest bit where he'd been bracing me. He shuts the water off and opens the door to the shower, reaching out to grab the towels that are on the rod there. He tosses one to me and uses one on himself.

It all happens so fast that I can barely register what's happening. Apparently, I've pushed him so far, he's just done with me. Which is going to be very unfortunate for me if it means it costs me the chance I had tonight with him. I doubt I get another. Especially one like this where he practically begged me.

I towel off in the silence, a little shocked and unsure whether to speak again. But the quiet beyond the slow drip of the showerhead is suffocating.

"That it, then? All you've got?" I goad him again because I have no other alternative in me.

He tosses the towel he's using to the floor. Then he grabs me, tossing my towel down, and hauls me up with one fucking arm carrying me back into my bedroom, and tosses me down on the bed.

I start to sit up, but he climbs on top of me in one swift move, pinning my legs between his thighs. He reaches over my head, grabbing one of my pillows and rips the end off of one of them.

I let out a little shocked growl sitting halfway up and looking back at my pillow. "What the fuck are you doing?"

"I bought them. I'll use them how I want. And I'll get you more if you can fucking behave," he grumbles at me, his brow furrowed and his whole face a mess of disgruntled irritation.

He wasn't wrong. He had technically bought them. They're the ones he got me after he'd sent Waylon up here to my room thinking Mackenzie was here when in reality it was a trap that Holly had set for him. Trying to convince him to be with her instead of Kenz. It failed miserably, but the trail of body glitter Holly had left in my room had left me more than a little pissed. So he'd sent me four sets of sheets to replace the ones he'd helped damage. Ones far nicer, and much more luxurious in their thread count, than anything I owned before them. I loved them, but I wasn't going to let him know that.

"What are you doing with it anyway?" I ask, looking at the sad torn edge of my pillowcase.

"Blindfolding you," he says it so matter-of-factly I'm still somewhat confused when he starts to wrap the fabric around my eyes.

"What?" I ask softly, but I feel the whisper of apprehension slide down low and pool into desire at the thought of not being able to see where he'll touch me next.

"You can talk your shit, Princess. But you're not gonna fucking lie to me." I can feel him tighten the knot at the back of my head and the room which was already dim descends into darkness.

"Sensitive I'm using you for your body now?" I smirk.

"Just helping you focus on what's important."

"Gonna gag me next?" I taunt, but I'm a little worried that I've given him an idea as soon as I say it.

"No. Your mouth is one of the best parts of you."

And if the statement hadn't silenced me, his mouth would have because he's back to it again, kissing me in a way that makes it impossible to focus on anything else but him, and the way his body brushes over mine. I feel his knuckles dragging their way down over my stomach, sliding lower and lower until he parts me. He starts stroking me softly in rhythm with his mouth, the pads of his fingers teasing the sides of my clit, giving me just enough to want more.

He releases my mouth and kisses his way down my throat and over my chest, never missing a beat of his rhythm, and then takes my nipple in his mouth, running his tongue over the tip until I arch my back up off the bed. He grazes his teeth over it, and then moves over to the other, sucking harder until I start to feel the edge of pain. I gasp a little and he releases it.

"You're beautiful," he whispers against my skin, kissing a trail to my stomach.

"Don't," I warn.

"Don't what?" His fingers slide south, slipping inside and stroking me.

"Start with the charm," I fight to say the words against the hint of a moan I'm trying to stifle.

"That all it takes to charm you? Some asshole telling you you're beautiful? You're fucking the wrong guys, Princess."

"And you're the right guy?" I laugh, but he swipes his thumb over my clit, and it takes the breath out of me.

I feel his weight shift over me, and his breath down my neck. Knowing his eyes must be watching me but not knowing how or where makes me shift a little under his touch.

"You tell me, Princess. Because you hate my guts and yet you're naked and underneath me right now, moaning and writhing while you clench around my fingers. Feels like this little cunt of yours is starved for some good cock. So am I the right one or not?"

I hesitate only for half a second before I admit the truth.

"Yes."

He kisses me then, rough, less practiced than before and I kiss him back. It feels like a pact. Like we've both agreed to do something that we both know is terrible and a very bad idea, but we can't back out now.

"I'm gonna get a condom. Ass up, face down for me when I get back, Princess," he bites out before he jumps off the bed.

SIX

Easton

I watch her as she does what I asked while I roll the condom on, how compliant she is with the request, how eager she is to have me inside her. The way she looks with the long line of her back extended and her round ass in the air. Waiting for me. Waiting for the guy she hates so much that she literally berated me tonight before we got in the shower. I don't know what the fuck we're doing exactly, but I'm not stopping either.

It's been such a long time since I wanted a woman this badly, so long I can't remember. I don't know if it's my fucking ego that needs her to want it as bad as I do or something else. Can't figure out why I'm so focused on her in particular when she's right, there are a dozen other girls who would be in my bed in a second if I texted them. But I can't help myself. I want what I want.

34

"Easton?" she asks, turning her head, still blindfolded, toward me.

The sound of my name on her lips with her looking like this pours gasoline on the fire.

"Yes," I say, finally crossing the room to her again, climbing back on the bed and kneeling behind her.

"Fuck me. *Now*," her voice laced with impatience.

I want to argue. There are so many other positions I want her in. So many other ways I want to touch her, take her, have her, so I can feel like I got the full experience before she tells me how much she hates me again. But I can't. I don't have the willpower. Not tonight.

So I slide inside her, inch by inch, while I grab her hips and she pushes back against me, a little gasp comes from her when I'm all the way in. And I can't help but groan when I feel her clench down on me.

"You feel so fucking good, Princess. So-fucking-tight," I grit out.

I test her once, sliding in and out slowly, and she moans softly, almost inaudibly. Pulling one of the pillows she has closer and burying her face in it. I smirk because I imagine the conversation we're going to have about this later. One where she tells me she could barely feel it, that I imagined things, and I remind her of how much she moaned every time I moved.

I run my fingertips over her hips as I start to rock into her, setting a rhythm as she starts to counter me in shorter strokes. Her hands tighten around the edges of the pillow, gripping it as I take her faster and harder.

"I want to fucking hear you." Because I don't want her to deny me this. I know she'll never tell me in plain words, but she can at least give me this.

She shakes her head and then buries it again, instead rolling her hips and urging me on to a quicker pace.

"Let me hear you."

Silence.

"Please," I try.

"No," she says defiantly, and it's the last straw.

I pull out of her and flip her over with a gentle force that surprises but doesn't hurt her, pulling the blindfold off in the process. She stares up at me, mouth slightly open in shock.

"What the hell?"

"Do you wanna fuck or do you wanna fight? Because at a certain point it's one or the other, and I need to know what we're doing here tonight."

Something flashes across her face followed by another little look of defiance, but she finally mutters, "Fucking."

"Good." I smile at her. "And is my cock somehow underwhelming to you?"

"No." Her eyes drift down my body.

"Then let me know when you like something."

"Your ego—" she starts.

"This isn't about my ego, Princess." I kiss the edge of her jaw, and my hand slides down the side of her breast. I can't help touching her. Her body is so fucking gorgeous and soft. I run my thumb over one of her nipples again and her lashes lower. "This is about you letting me know when it's good for you, so I can make it better."

Her eyes raise to mine abruptly, like that's not a thing she expected to come out of my mouth.

"That's what I need tonight. The only thing I want. Is you coming hard, okay?"

She nods, her eyes looking heavy and her tongue darting out over her lips. Her brow furrows a little like she's still unsure.

"Do you want me again?"

She nods.

"Then tell me how."

"Against the wall. Hard."

"You like it rough?" I grin a little at her.

"I like the idea of you rough." She gives me an answering little smirk and fuck it hits me in the chest. The way she says *you*. The way her eyes light. *This fucking girl*. Fuck.

"See; that so fucking hard?" I kiss her lower lip for a second before I haul her up to her feet with me.

"Yes. A little part of me dies inside every time."

I shake my head, laughing a little as I walk her back against the wall.

"Then we better make the way you come worth the sacrifice," I mumble as I pull her up into my arms and she wraps her legs around me.

She's still wet for me, maybe even more so now and I slide inside her, still slow because she's so fucking tight I'm afraid I might hurt her.

"Fuck, you fill me so well," she sighs against my shoulder, her arms tightening around me.

And the words go straight to my fucking gut, twisting, making me harder, making me want.

"I'm pretty sure you're just that fucking tight," I mutter against her neck as I start to kiss her and rock into her.

"It's so fucking good. You are so fucking good..." she mumbles, and her fingers wander up and down my neck as she talks, sliding into my hair, and twisting the ends. "Harder though. Like you hate me."

I pick up my pace, thrusting into her harder and faster. Digging my fingers into her and using the wall as leverage to take her deeper until soft whimpers start coming out of her that threaten to take me over the edge way too fucking early. Fuck this girl is dangerous.

I turn us, setting her down on the edge of her dresser as a

few things crash to the floor, so I can free a hand to run my thumb over her clit, circling it and dragging out a few moans from her in the process.

"Louder, Princess. I want to know if you want more."

She does as I ask, increasing her volume just as I hear footsteps in the hall. I put my hand over her mouth, silently motioning at the noise, and stilling as we both listen. The floorboards creak as someone walks into the room next door. The little library that Mac keeps up here.

She shakes her head and rocks her hips, moving to the edge of the dresser. I frown at her, as the movement almost makes me groan out loud. She grabs my hand, pulling it from her mouth.

"Don't stop," she whispers.

"They'll hear." I know she'd care if they found us like this. She'd hate it.

"Don't stop. I need it."

I thrust into her again and the dresser rocks with the movement, rattling things she has on top of it and making another one fall to the floor. I give her a wide-eyed look and she laughs. And while I don't particularly care about being found fucking her—I might even like it a little—I do care about who it is that finds us. Because there's a big difference between it being Liv or Liam, considering he's told me to think with my fucking head and not my dick when it comes to her, I can just imagine how it'll end.

Someone coughs and walks back close to the hall again, the creaks in the boards giving away their location. And suddenly I feel a tug, and Wren is taking us both to the rug on her floor, pulling me down on top of her and smiling up at me.

"If they open the door, they still can't see us down here. Right away at least. Now fuck me." She grins.

"Are you sure this isn't just a ploy to fuck me on every

surface in here?" I tease her, staring at the way her eyes light, the flush on her cheeks, and the way her plush little mouth quirks up at the corners when she looks at me.

She gives me a little shrug and half a smile.

"It's my fantasy we're playing out, right?" she teases me back, and the sudden change in warmth in her tone fucking hits me hard. Like she's reached into my chest and lit something on fire.

I slide inside her again, not wasting any time, fucking her hard. Her leg wraps around mine, and she runs her fingers down my side. She looks gorgeous underneath me and for a second I almost feel like I'm dreaming again because it doesn't feel real. Doesn't feel possible that she could be soft and sweet, whimpering under me like she needs me.

"Fuck, you're so good, East. So fucking good," she praises, and I wish that I could freeze this moment and replay it. Make sure I fucking heard her right. But instead, I lean down and kiss her, taking her mouth with mine and trying to seal the feeling of this moment into my memory. One I can pull out the next time my ego is this sore.

Her fingers drift to my back and on the next deep thrust, she digs her fingernails in and rakes them up.

"Oh fuck, Princess. Do that again," I groan.

And she listens, digging deeper this time, and I see a little ghost of a smirk cross her lips as she does it. Then she nips my shoulder hard, letting a little bruise bloom in its place. Her smile widens. Like she likes the idea of having marked me for her own and fuck, she just keeps hitting every little fucking kink I have without even trying tonight. I take her faster then, needing more of her.

"I'm so close. Just a little harder. You feel amazing," she mumbles in-between moans, rocking her hips up to meet me with each thrust, and I slide my hand up her side again, teasing her nipple under my thumb. Her hand runs down my forearm and grips me gently, pulling my hand up to her throat.

"Like before," she whispers, her eyes soft, looking up at me with something more than lust in them, and it fucking twists me inside again.

I tighten the grip on her throat just a little, just enough that she can feel it. Staring down at the image it makes, sends a searing sensation rolling through me. Because I know she's trusting me. Letting me take control and knowing I'll give her what she needs. I stroke the side of her throat with my thumb, and she closes her eyes, biting down on her lip as she starts to come for me.

"That's it, Princess, come for me. You're so fucking sexy. So fucking good I can barely stand it..." I mutter as my own release starts to hit. It comes in hard waves, racking my body and making me feel spent and fucking exhausted as I finally pull out of her.

I toss the condom and collapse next to her on the ground. Both of us are quiet and breathing hard. I'm a sweaty fucking mess. I can't remember the last time I ended up on the fucking floor having sex. As I glance around the room it looks like a fucking tornado hit it. Between the scattered clothes and towels trailing out of the bathroom, the shit we knocked onto the floor, the torn fucking sheets. We've managed to practically destroy her room in a matter of minutes.

"What's funny?" she asks, curiosity in her tone.

"This." I wave my finger around in a circle and she glances around.

"Oh god."

"And you thought if they opened the door they wouldn't know." Another wave of laughter hits me.

"And I'm too tired to care now." She sighs and pulls herself up to her knees.

I want to reach out and touch her. Kiss her. Fuck, I think I might even want to cuddle her. But all of it sounds dangerous, so I keep my hands to myself.

She opens a dresser drawer and pulls some clothes out, standing and heading toward the bathroom. She grabs my clothes and sets them outside the bathroom and pauses just before she shuts the door.

"I'm gonna get cleaned up and dressed and then go to bed. You can still stay if you want, or this is your opportunity to not be here when I get back."

She doesn't even bother to look back at me, so why I stay and climb into bed instead of taking that opportunity, I don't know. Probably has something to do with the way the little spur of wings in my stomach refuses to fall flat even after that dismissal.

SEVEN

Wren

THE NEXT MORNING WHEN I WAKE UP, THE SUN IS already pouring through the windows, and I blink as I take in the room. It's a mess. Things are scattered, sheets and pillows are on the floor, and I feel my heart skip as I wonder what the hell happened while I was sleeping.

It's wonderment that lasts all of a few seconds before I remember exactly what happened when I wasn't sleeping. *Easton.* Easton fucking happened to me. I have no idea how I made such a stupid decision, especially since I didn't even have alcohol to blame it on. Just loneliness and a long week. And Easton—looking and talking the way he does.

Then I realize I don't remember him leaving my room last night. He was in bed, back to me when I got out of the bathroom. I assumed sleeping off the rest of the alcohol. But surely, he's the kind of guy who sneaks out in the wee hours of the morning to avoid the whole morning-after conversation, right? He probably ran home with as much regret as I have right now way before I ever woke up. Something I will silently thank him for.

Except I don't even have to look over, because I can feel his warm body inches from mine. The soft rise and fall of his chest as he sleeps. Shit. Shit. *Shit.* I am not prepared for any morning-after run-in with him.

I slide my way out of bed, praying he doesn't wake yet until I can come up with a plan. I need to know what time it is. Figure out whether or not the girls are up. Because the last thing I want them to find is this... Him in my bed, my room looking like we had insane fucking sex, and me, I am sure, looking like I was on the receiving end of it. Another flash of us together last night pops into my head, and I wince.

I grab clothes out of my dresser on the way, eager to get out of my PJs and dress again before he wakes up. I make it to the bathroom and quietly latch the door shut, leaning against the counter. I snatch my phone off of it to see that it's already late morning. Which means there is zero chance everyone else isn't already up in the house. How the hell am I going to get him out of this room without them finding out?

The panic swells in my gut. I can already see their faces staring at me as we walk down the steps. Mac and Liv looking worried as hell. Like I've finally cracked. I can hear the lecture Liam is gonna be giving if he finds out we hooked up, telling Easton that he should be smarter than to put his dick anywhere near this friend group. Ben might even judge me for this one.

I hear a rustling in my room, and I assume that means time's nearly up for me to face whatever the hell Easton's going to say to me. I'm sure it'll be something smug and rude. Like it always is. But I can endure it. I can be just as smug and rude.

After all, this is a two-way street. We'd both been epically stupid last night.

I run the water, pretending like I came in here for a reason besides a panic session, and then open the door. He's sitting up, his hair messed and dried to one side like he slept on it funny. His gorgeous perfect chest and abs are on display, the sheet around his hips, draped over his lap. I can't believe I slept with him. It is not fair that this is how he wakes up in the morning. He scrubs a hand over his face and then looks at me, cracking a wide grin. And I'm surprised when it's boyish, almost flirty, rather than his usual arrogant one.

"All right, Princess, tell me, did I just have the *best* fucking dream, or did any of that actually happen?"

And he's talking way too loud in an old house where people are presumably awake and have ears. I rush over to him and clamp my hand over his mouth. His brow raises and then slams down, furrowing as I put my finger to my lips.

"It's late morning. Guarantee they're already up. So try to be quiet," I frown, and then to illustrate my desperation I add, "Please."

He nods his annoyed understanding, and I release my hand.

"We have to figure out how to get you out of here," I whisper conspiratorially.

"Through the fucking door and down the stairs—like a normal fucking person—would be my choice." The playful tone he had a moment ago is gone.

"Right. Because they won't have any questions at all."

"Princess, my car is parked outside. I never said goodbye to anyone. There's only one room I could possibly still be in in this house. I'd put 100 on the fact they've already puzzled that one out."

Shit. He has good points.

"Then we need a story."

"Yeah? Well, there were several last night. Pick one," he sneers.

Why? Why was I stupid enough to sleep with this fucking man. Of all the men in the world.

"You came up here to get away from everyone. You were drinking and passed out up here. I found you when I got home, and I let you stay because we were both just tired. Woke up late for the same reason."

"Oh good one. And the claw marks on my back and the bite mark on my shoulder? Did I also wrestle a feral raccoon that snuck in?" He's up out of the bed, putting his clothes back on now.

First, goddamn this man is gorgeous. Like, unfairly so. Seeing it all again compounds how much I want him. Second, *holy shit* did I do a number on his back. He deserved it, but still, the evidence is a little hard to look at in the daylight.

"They're not going to see when you have a shirt on."

"I live with Waylon. I go to the fucking gym with them and change in the fucking locker room."

Wow is he grumpy this morning. I'm not sure if it's me, the hangover, or some combination that is putting him in this mood, but that part at least is decidedly unsexy.

"Then tell them it was one of your sorority girls or groupies. I don't care as long you don't tell any of them about last night."

He puts his shirt on, pulling it down and smoothing it out. But he doesn't say anything. Doesn't promise me he'll keep it to himself. And that makes me nervous. I don't want to be another on his long list. I don't want other people to know I made that particular list.

"I'm serious. They can't know. That includes Waylon."

I worry he'll tell his roommate, even in passing, and

Waylon keeps nothing from Kenz. You tell one of them, you're telling both of them. And I do *not* want Kenz to know.

His back is to me, but I see the moment he straightens his spine, and stands a little taller after I say it. And I brace myself because he's going to taunt me. I can feel it coming on.

"I heard you," he says, and then he turns around, a little smirk on his lips. "And don't worry, Princess, your dirty little secret's safe with me."

I expect more. I wait for more. Something rude. Something cruel. But he doesn't say anything else on the subject. His face relaxes like he's morphed into whatever the next chapter of his day is.

"Can I use the bathroom before I go?"

"Yeah."

He disappears behind the door a second later. And apparently that's it. End of discussion. Surprisingly easier than I expected, and I guess that's a good thing.

I bend to start picking up some of the things that were knocked to the floor, the photos, a few things off my dresser, and the bottle of vodka he'd been drinking from. It was Kenz's, and she was not going to be thrilled about that. I toss my clothes in the hamper and then set to work on the bed, smoothing out the sheets and putting the pillows back in order.

He re-emerges and looks refreshed. His hair back in some semblance of order and his clothes a little straighter. He still looks like he had a rough night but now it looks more like it was the result of too much alcohol and not from fucking me rough on every surface in this room.

"You coming down?" he asks gruffly as he heads to the door.

"Yep. Just need to put this away."

He glances at the room, and then at me, picking the last few things up off the floor that we'd knocked over. He looks like he's about to say something but then thinks better of it. And while

I'm curious what it was, I'm thankful he doesn't try to press my buttons this morning.

A moment later, I follow him down the steps and sure enough, our friends are downstairs at the dining room table. Drinking coffee and eating donuts that someone picked up, while they slowly start picking up the mess left over from the party.

"Seriously, what even is this?" Kenz holds up a cup that contains a putrid green concoction that's slightly foamy.

"I don't think we want to know. Here, give it to me." Waylon takes it from her and grabs a bag of trash as he heads outside.

When we reach the bottom of the steps though, all eyes and heads snap in our direction. And I'm just begging the universe that I can manage not to blush here. Or look as guilty as I feel.

"Good morning!" Liv gives me a wild smile.

"Good morning!" I smile back at her and layer on a dose of cheeriness I don't feel. "Please tell me that someone got the double chocolate donuts. I need one."

"Two in that box." Ben points and I grin at him.

"You're the best!"

He smiles back at me but then his eyes drift over my shoulder, to the broad and broody man behind me. His brow raises in question, and I wish I could see East's face. Make sure that it is serene and sleepy, and not smug and self-satisfied.

I can feel the tension mounting in the room as I move the boxes around to get to the donuts I want. The ones that are gonna fill my mouth so that I can't possibly talk or elaborate on why I'm coming down the stairs in the morning with the six-foot-four tight end who hates my guts.

"Please don't fucking make me be the one to ask," Liam grumps from the far side of the table and I tense as I go to take a bite of the donut.

"I got pissed about the game again. Drank a shit ton. Passed out on her bed, and she let me stay 'cause she was too tired to argue with my drunk ass. That satisfy you or you wanna interrogate her on whether or not I snore?"

"Oh, I can answer that. He does. Loud as fuck. Through the walls." Waylon smirks as he comes back into the house.

"You really want to talk about things that are loud as fuck through the walls?" East gripes back at him.

"I know you're jealous of my abilities, bud. I told you, all you gotta do is ask. I'm happy to give tips." Waylon slaps him on the back as he walks by.

Easton's lip pulls up into a sneer, his eyes drifting up like he's remembering something, and I pray, hope, and beg with every silent ability I have that he doesn't take that bait. Because I have no idea what Waylon's abilities are, but East's need zero improvements. A fact I wish I didn't know for certain now.

"I'm gonna head out. See you all later." He turns and heads for the door.

"Do you want a donut for the road?" Liv calls after him.

"No thanks." He shakes his head but gives her a little smile, and she smiles back at him as he disappears.

She sighs, "He's really having a hard time."

"Well people kept trying to give him encouragement last night, and he wasn't having it." Liam shakes his head.

"I mean, not exactly a thing you want to be reminded of over and over again." Ben tilts his head.

"How did he seem to you?" Liv looks at me and unfortunately, I've just swallowed the bite of donut I took so I have to answer.

"He seemed upset but okay. He's Easton. I'm sure he'll be fine once he fucks a couple of sorority girls." I shrug and then take another bite of donut, so I don't have to answer follow-up questions, desperately hoping that sounded as nonchalant as I mean it to be.

Because I don't like the way I feel a little dip in my stomach at the thought of Easton with a couple of girls. And given the mood he's in right now, I'm sure that's exactly what he'll be doing tonight. He is who he is. There can't be a repeat, and I can't be sitting here hoping for anything else.

EIGHT

Wren

A WEEK LATER AND CLASSES ARE BACK IN SESSION, AND we've just gotten partner assignments for my capstone marketing class. I stare at the name in the email my professor has sent me, one outlining a semester-long project and I laugh. Hard. Because it's ridiculous. Because otherwise, I would cry. I've done something terribly wrong, karmically speaking, because there is no way on earth this is just happenstance. No possible way that I get paired with Easton fucking Westfield by chance.

The idea of spending an entire semester having to spend nights and weekends working on a project with him is bad enough, but that the project has a direct effect on my post-college career prospects is untenable.

We haven't seen each other or spoken since the incident, and the last thing I want to do is be forced to strike up conversations on a regular basis for this. I could just see his face now. The knowing little smirk. The way he'll taunt me for falling straight into the Easton trap. For having no excuse for why I was so reckless. And I don't want to see his face, because it will remind me of all the things we did. What he sounded like. What he said. The inevitable daydream where I start reliving it all. No. I was not doing that.

I also didn't need a rich fuckboy jock putting my entire future in jeopardy because he cares more about parties and jersey chasers than this grade. What is he even doing in this class? It's high-level advertising and a public relations seminar. It's designed for people who plan to have a post-college career in it. Which I do. But Easton is, for all his other downsides, a phenomenal tight end for Highland State and one of Liam Montgomery's favorite targets in the end zone before he got hurt. And with a brother playing in the league and a father coaching in it, Easton's NFL prospects are still rumored to be pretty damn good even with the mishap. And even if they aren't, it's obvious from the way he throws money around at parties and clubs that he doesn't need a job or a career anyway. Stock investments. Portfolios. Private clubs. Those are probably his future.

So there is no way this class assignment is going to stand. I'm going to have a discussion with the professor. I'll leave out all of Easton's off-field antics and my general hate for him. I'll take the high road and focus on the practical aspects of this partnership not meshing. There is no way his extracurricular schedule and my work schedule are ever going to allow us to work together. As it is, even with our friends being as close as they all are, I see a glimpse of Easton on rare occasions. Usually, as he's headed out to a club, I'm headed up to bed. Minus the one occasion he was in said bed.

We don't have time to work together. It's just that simple. And my professor, if he's worth his salt, will see that problem easily fixed by pairing us with different partners.

I close out the email and grab my bag off my bed, so I can head downstairs for breakfast. I already hear the sounds of my roommates, Liv and Kenz, chatting and making coffee. The smell of caffeine in the morning is just the thing I need after the long shift I worked last night.

When I hit the kitchen, Kenz looks up and smiles at me for a second before it falters.

"Uh oh. What happened? Shitty customers last night?"

"Bad tips again? Those assholes." Liv shakes her head.

"No. An email from our professor about a group project. Well, a partner project."

"Oh god. I hate those so much. Every single time I get partnered with some jerk who could care less about the assignment and just scribbles something down at the last second."

"Yeah, those are the worst. I hate having someone else I don't know has influence over my grade. It's a special kind of torture," Liv adds.

"Yeah well, I do know them. And that's the problem."

"Oh. Who is it? Do we know them?" Kenz looks at me as she adds another splash of creamer to her cup.

"Easton."

Liv and Kenz burst into laughter at my expense, and I glare at them both.

"You're not helping." I pour my coffee with a heavier hand than usual and skip the creamer and sugar. I'm gonna need the fuel to steel my spine on this conversation.

"Oh come on, he's not that bad. He's... East but it's not like he's a slacker or anything." Kenz comes to his defense.

"Isn't he? I've never once heard him talk about homework

or grades or anything other than partying and football. I don't even know how he's in this class. Another jock privilege, I guess. Do whatever you want because the athletics department says it's okay."

I love sports. I practically live at a sports bar. I can recite stats in my sleep. Before I worked too many hours to do anything else, I even used to coach girls' soccer. And at one point, a long, long time ago, I had dreams of playing in college and the pros. But even I can acknowledge that sometimes the system is rigged.

"Be nice, Wren," Liv chides me from across the kitchen counter.

"I'm nice to people who deserve it. And Easton does not deserve it after... everything."

I had other reasons to dislike him, beyond being disappointingly fantastic in bed. I really did.

"Well... he means well most of the time. I think." Liv hedges.

Means well is doing a lot of heavy lifting. Easton had nearly doomed Mac and Waylon's relationship when he set up one of the jersey chasers in my bedroom to seduce Waylon, and while he had sort of helped Olivia and Liam finally come to terms with the fact there was something more than friendship between them, he'd done it by locking them out on a rooftop patio. And both times, I was responsible for trying to extricate Waylon and Liam from their fate. I managed to rescue Waylon. Liam on the other hand was, uh, already too far gone with Olivia. I shake my head trying to get the images of the two of them that are burned into my brain, thanks to Easton's handiwork, out of my mind.

"Does he?" Kenz raises a brow, and I'm glad I at least have half an ally in her.

"His intentions are good, at least for him." Liv shrugs.

"'For him' being the operative part of that sentence. And whatever the case, I don't want to be stuck on this project with him. I'm hoping the professor is going to let me switch partners."

"Did you talk to East about it?" Liv questions.

"No. Why would I talk to him? He doesn't care who he has as a partner. In fact, he could probably find someone who would only be too happy to do all the work for him."

Liv and Kenz exchange glances.

"What?"

"Nothing." They both say in unison and return to sipping their coffee.

I eye them warily but put my empty cup in the dishwasher rack and start heading for the door. If I get to campus early, I can get to the bookstore to buy the rest of my books before it gets too wild.

"I'll see you all later!"

"Bye! Have a good day!" they call after me.

I STAND AT THE PROFESSOR'S DESK AFTER CLASS, WAITING in a line of students to discuss the prospect of not having Easton as my partner. I'm honestly even willing to go it alone if it means not having to work with him. I glance down at my phone, hoping this little conversation isn't going to take too long because I need to get to the bar within the next hour to relieve Kelsey from her shift. I need to put the order in for this weekend's food, and I need to contact the freezer repair guy to check the broken gasket on the door before the health inspection people show up unannounced and have my head for it. And I need to put in another beer order because we are running low on several kinds, and I do not need cranky customers for this weekend's big hockey game.

"So I see we're paired together for this," Easton's voice breaks through my mental laundry list.

"Yeah, that's what I'm going to talk to the professor about," I say without looking at him. I really wish he would just have gone to the gym or his next class or wherever else he needs to be. I do not want to see him.

"What do you mean?" A tone has entered his voice, and I finally turn to look at him. It's a mistake because he looks especially good today. Don't get me wrong. I hate him, body and soul, but the boy is pretty. The money means he dresses well, he grooms well, and he has all the swagger that comes along with it. I hate it, but I also kind of like it. A little. And now that I know what he looks like with it all off? *Doom.* It spells doom. This is why I can't be around him.

"I have an insane schedule. Between classes and work, I don't have spare hours. I'd prefer to work on this project alone. If he won't allow me that as an option, then I at least want to be paired with someone with less... extracurriculars." I straighten my spine, trying to increase my five-foot-eight stature to something a little taller. Something that might match his stupid height and build.

"Football's over. I have plenty of free time."

"I assume you have The Combine to train for, and all of your many *many* parties and club openings and whatever else you do." *Whoever else you do.* I keep that last part to myself because I refuse to be jealous over him. I had a one-night stand. A thoughtless ill-advised one-night stand. But nothing I can't handle.

"I have stuff going on. But this class and this project—it's a priority for me." His jaw takes on a hard set like he's offended by what I'm saying.

"All the more reason for us not to work together if we're both taking it seriously."

"Why?"

"Because we can't stand each other."

He stares at me for a moment, his brow furrowing, like I've said something strange.

"I don't have a problem with you."

"Well, I have a problem with you."

"Why?"

"Why? Are you serious?"

"Because of the night of the party?"

That's what we're referring to it as? Okay then. Before I can even formulate a response though, we're at the front of the line.

"And how can I help you this morning?" The professor looks up from his desk and his eyes bounce between us before returning to the papers in front of him.

Shit. What was I going to say? I had a whole speech planned and then I talked to Easton. And everything went blank. This is exactly why it won't work. *Right.* Why it won't work. That's what I need to get this professor to understand.

"Um yes, we were just wondering if it would be possible to reassign our partnership."

"Why?" The professor glances up at me with a look that says I'm irritating him.

"Well, I work very long hours outside of class time, and Easton has a demanding schedule as well with prep for the draft. So us finding time to work together will be next to impossible."

"In the real world, you'll have similar problems to negotiate."

"I understand that, of course. But I just don't even know when we'll be able to make time. Even if we try."

"Part of the challenge of the project is interpersonal communication and coordinating your schedules to make it work. It's what a real job in this field will require. Along with long hours and unusual time frames. If you're already struggling with that aspect, you may want to rethink taking this class."

"No. I mean, I need this class, and I am certainly up for the challenge. I just—we—" I struggle for the right words. "We also have a history that will affect our working relationship in a way I think will be untenable."

The professor sighs and his eyes flick up to Easton, and then back to me. A look like he knows exactly what the problem is.

"Are you former paramours?" he asks at last.

"What? Absolutely not!"

I look to Easton, waiting for him to deny it but he just smirks. The professor looks between us again.

"Unless you have documentation from the university that there is a reason that it would be unfavorable for you to work together, then that's not sufficient either. Again, in the real world, you'll have to work with people who you may believe to be unsavory characters or may have disappointed you in the past. It won't change the fact that you'll be partnered with them or have them as a client, and that your work will have to rise above it."

My heart sinks because I realize I'm going to be stuck with Easton. This guy will not be moved.

"Is there a documented reason the two of you can't work together?"

"No, sir." Easton shakes his head, a faux look of seriousness crossing it.

"Then let's consider this matter settled."

"Thank you," I say softly before turning on my heel and doing my best not to storm out of the lecture hall.

I can hear Easton trailing behind me, and I feel like it's going to be a matter of seconds before he gloats about how ridiculous I am.

"So when do you want to meet up to go over the requirements? I figure the sooner we can pick a project and nail down the details, the better."

"Why are you even in this class?" I huff.

"Because I need it to graduate."

"Which matters so much when you're just going to go straight to the NFL."

"There's no guarantee of that. Especially not after the way things ended."

"Right, and you definitely need the money. Not like you own a car that would be a normal family's take-home salary for three years." I turn and glare at him.

His reaction is unreadable. His face an emotionless mask. I imagine he thinks I'm another hysterical female angry that he didn't text after we slept together. He probably has lots of practice with this scenario.

"Do you want me to come to your place tonight?"

"No. I work."

"What about movie night?"

"It's movie night, and it's one I want to see."

"We can meet before."

"I have a bunch of errands to run when I'm off my shift that day."

"After the movie."

"It'll be late."

"It won't take long to discuss the basics." There's an insistent tone to his voice. Maybe he does care about this project.

"Then text me, and we'll discuss it there." I shrug and start to walk off. Whatever gets me out of this conversation right now. Away from him. That's what I need.

He doesn't call after me or follow, so I take a breath and decide to be thankful for small mercies.

NINE

Easton

"Have you ever had a hookup that haunted you?" I ask as I sit down on the couch next to Waylon and grab a slice of pizza from the box.

Before Mac, Waylon used to fuck around almost as much as I do, so I'm hoping he can give me some perspective on my Wren situation. Because fuck if I can stop thinking about her.

It's never been an issue for me before. If I liked someone well enough, if the sex was good, I might hookup with them another time or two, but I have definitely never spent my waking hours fantasizing about them the way I did with her. I thought that maybe it'd just been because I couldn't have her, but now I have, and I just want more. And she wants... nothing to do with me. Which is only compounding my problem.

"Besides Mac, you mean?" He raises a brow in question.

"Yeah."

"No."

"But she did?"

"Fuck yeah. She was all I could think about. I mean I wanted her before, but after... Fuck. That's how I knew for sure I was gone on her. Why?"

Well, *fuck*. That sounded familiar.

"I just had a hookup recently. And it was good, really fucking good. Unexpected. I mean I thought maybe we'd have some chemistry. I'd been interested for a bit but, fuck, this girl just like... every fucking kink I have, every single thing I like, her body... all of it."

"Sounds like a unicorn."

"Something like that. I can't get her out of my head though."

"So see her again. Aren't they usually begging you for a second round anyway?"

"Not her."

"What'd you fuck up?" Waylon gives me a surprised look as he takes a sip of his energy drink.

"I don't fucking know."

Not entirely a lie. I don't know, but I can guess. She doesn't want the association. She's smart, driven, independent. I know Mac and Liv count on her for advice, that she's the brains behind their little trio. The idea that she would end up in bed with me even out of pity seemed so impossible I'd never thought what the reality and the aftermath would be like.

"Well, step one. Figure that out. Step two, fix whatever you fucked up. Knowing you, you blew the aftercare portion of the event and she thinks you're an ass."

"I didn't. She did," I say defensively, and immediately regret it with the way Waylon's eyes snap over to me.

"How did she blow it?"

"Basically told me to fuck off," I grumble.

"Then it was before that. Did she get off?"

"Yes, she fucking got off." I glare at him.

"Are you sure? Mac says women can be excellent at faking it. Not that I would know." A little smarmy grin flits across his face.

"I'm fucking positive. If she hadn't, she would have told me. Trust me."

"That doesn't sound like your usual type." He looks over me like he's trying to puzzle it out.

"She wasn't my usual type, no."

"Then maybe don't go out of your lane."

"Out of my lane? Because Mac was in yours?"

"East, man, I don't know how to say this without being a dick but I'm going to try. Yeah, I wasn't exactly Mac's type but we kind of had a thing going. I knew on some level she liked me. I knew I wanted her. Not just for a hookup. You're... not really the kind. I'm not saying you can't be. I'm just saying, don't go chasing after this girl if all you want is another hookup. She sounds like she has her reasons for moving on, and unless you have solid ones for her to want to revisit things with you—you're both better off going your separate ways."

It hits me a little in the chest to hear him say it so plainly, but he had good points. The only problem is I think I might want more than a hookup. I think I might actually want her to see me as something beyond that which is terrifying as fuck.

TEN

Wren

I'm staring at the ice cream bars in the store when I come to from my latest daydream about Easton. I throw the freezer door open and grab one of the boxes, tossing it into my basket, and practically slamming the door shut again. I cannot get the man out of my head, and now knowing we are going to be stuck together for an entire semester. It's fucking terrible. There's no way for me to avoid him.

I don't want to think about how he felt, how he kissed, how he talked, or how he fucked me. I don't want to think about how I want him to do it again. I don't want to think about what a bitch I was to him after. And worst of all, I don't want to think about the fact that I can't avoid him forever because we still have to work on this project. Although, thankfully, he has been quiet the last several days, and I've skipped that class this week because I had to work an extra shift.

Tammy was sick. One of our two dishwashers was on the

fritz. My blow dryer and my vibrator have broken this week. And if one more thing goes wrong, I'm going to scream. Which reminds me, I need to pick up replacements. Thankfully we live in the modern era where I can get my ice cream bars, blow dryer, and vibrator replacements all at the same big box store. Along with the latest historical romance movie and candy. Because *fuck it*. It has just been that kind of week.

I stand in the condom aisle, grabbing a pack because what I really need more than a vibrator at the moment is a one-night stand. Something to erase Easton from my memory. Except that's work, a lot of small talk I don't want to bother with, and hours spent weeding out a decent one-night stand prospect from the dozens of would-be, could-be jackasses on a dating app. All things I don't have time for. But I'm still an optimist so in the basket it goes. I grab one of the cheap vibrators too because replacing the one that broke is not going to be an inexpensive affair, and I do not have the money right now.

"That one's not as good as this one."

Holy fuck. I am hearing *his* disembodied voice give me advice on vibrators now. I need help. Maybe a trip to the grippy sock ward. This is getting out of hand.

"It's worth the extra money, just saying. Although... it looks like you're having quite a fucking night tonight there, Princess." He leans over, staring into my basket as he tosses the one he just pulled off the shelf into it.

No.

Nope.

Not Happening.

This is not happening.

But when I look up, it's definitely him. Definitely his smug little grin. The smell of his fucking cologne drifting over me and perking up all my nerve endings. All the ones that remember what it felt like to kiss him, touch him, fuck him. *Fuck.*

My brain struggles to comprehend how I'm going to get out of this one with any dignity at all intact. I start by pulling the box he's just thrown in out, setting it back on the shelf silently. A small grin on my lips as I do it.

"I'm surprised you're willing to admit vibrator expertise. It takes a big man to admit he's not enough for a woman. I'm impressed you have it in you to set your ego aside like that."

He grins back at me, even wider than before.

"My ego comes from being able to get women off. Reliably. Often. How that happens doesn't matter to me so much as the fact it does. But you *know* that."

Well *fuck.* What's the retort to that? I don't know.

"Well, I'm good. But thanks anyways for the advice." I move past him because I need to. I need acres, miles, continent's worth of distance from this man.

"You missed class." He's behind me, following me.

"I had to work an extra shift. One of the servers was sick. I told you; I have no free time, and sometimes that includes during class."

"When do you want to meet about the project? We still need to finalize an idea. I have a few."

"I don't know. Text me. We live in an era where we don't have to be in person to work on this. It's lovely. Means we don't have to see each other." I pick up my pace.

"Wren." He stops and says my name loudly, turning several heads in our direction in the process. More attention is the last thing I need.

"What?" I snap, turning on my heel. "I've had a long week. I have to make several other stops before I can go home tonight. I'm tired, and I don't want to talk about the project right now. I told you, just text me, okay?"

"Okay," he relents, frowning.

I hurry on, desperate to get away from him because the last thing I need is any more encounters that fuck with my head.

I GET HOME FOR THE SECOND TIME TODAY A COUPLE OF hours later. I dropped my groceries off the first time and then ran back out to check on the bar and visit the local restaurant supply shop before I could come home for good. I'm so excited because we're watching a new movie that's just come out on streaming, and Liv is cooking her homemade chicken dumplings tonight along with strawberry cake.

I set the wine I picked up on the way back on the table. It's the cheap kind, but we've grown to love it, and I desperately need a girl's night tonight. Good friends and food are what I need right now. Something to give me a break from this hellish week. Which is why when I hear the distinct sound of male voices in the living room, my heart sinks.

I'm happy for Kenz and Liv. Truly happy. They deserve men like Waylon and Liam who worship the ground they walk on and make them a priority. I'd done my best to help get them together. But I, as their single best friend, wish that occasionally they would be a little less coupled up. I missed my girls' nights. Especially girls' nights in after a week like this one where I want to unload about everything including my Easton encounter. And now I'm just going to be the awkward fifth wheel, curled up on the chair in the corner while they both snuggle their boyfriends and sneak off early to bed.

The frustration in my chest grows, clawing its way up my throat until I almost feel like I might cry. But I won't. I can't. At least not in front of everyone. So I take a deep breath and run up the steps, pretending like I need to hurry to take care of something.

"Wren? Is that you?" Liv calls after me from the kitchen, but I just keep hurrying my way up the steps.

"Yep, talk to you in a minute!" I call back down.

"Okay but—"

I don't hear the rest of what she says because I'm already in my room, shutting the door behind me and collapsing into a heap against the back of it. Finally letting the tears come because I am a mess right now. Exhausted. Worn out and more than a little frazzled. And I don't want to take that out on my friends. It's not their fault. I know if I had said something, Kenz and Liv would have made sure it was just us tonight and done whatever I need. But I feel weird asking, and I don't want to be that needy friend who just seems unhappy all the time.

I draw my knees up to my chest, tipping my forehead down and take a deep breath. I can pull it together. I can get through this week. I need to stop overreacting to things like this, but it's just one more straw on the heap right now. I stand and stretch, reminding myself that next week I have two days off in a row and can get caught up on school and things around the house. I can probably even squeeze in some binge reading.

Then I see a box sitting on my bed. It doesn't look like anything that would have come in the mail, and I didn't order anything that I could remember anyway. A piece of paper is folded under it, stationery from my desk. I frown and pull it out.

"To make sure your downtime is effective. Have a better week."

I don't recognize the handwriting, but the second I open the box I know who it's from. Apparently, since I wouldn't take his advice, he made sure the advice came to me. Then I feel the panic creep up the back of my neck because *he'd* been in my room again.

It didn't look like anything had been touched.

Except he didn't need to touch anything to find more humiliating things to add to the list. Because bras and laundry are scattered on the floor, random notes are pinned to my wall, and my room in general just looks like chaos. Like I live here in fits and starts because it's true. I hate it. I hate that he's seen the mess. That he's had an inside look he has no business having while I'm melting down this week. And right now I hate Liv for being so fucking happy that she can't think of us unhappy people long enough to realize we're a mess right now and don't need witnesses. I toss the box on the desk and curl up on the bed.

I must cry myself to sleep because a knock on the door wakes me up.

"Yeah?" I ask.

"It's me," Kenz's voice comes through the door.

"Come in."

I hear the door creak open, and she crosses the room, and I feel the bed dip under her weight.

"Are you coming down? Dinner's ready."

"I don't think so. It's been a long week, and I just want to sleep."

"But we're watching that new movie you wanted to see."

"I'll just watch it by myself sometime. You guys can do your couples thing, okay?"

"Okay. If that's what you want," she says quietly. "Easton's here though. He might like it if you came down, so he doesn't have to be the fifth wheel."

I inhale sharply. I hadn't imagined that he would still be here. In the scenario in my head, he dropped this box off and left. Knowing that he's still in the house makes my stomach somersault. A feeling I don't want to think too much about.

"Don't women just magically appear next to him? Maybe he can conjure one to keep him company."

Kenz laughs at that and runs her hand over my back. "Okay. Well, I love you. I hope you feel better. If there's anything I can do, just let me know, okay?"

"Okay." I nod, burying my face further into my pillow.

A few minutes later my phone dings with a text.

EASTON

Please don't make me be down here with them alone

Sorry. Not in the mood for couples tonight

Can I come up then?

I stare at my phone for a good minute, because I'm torn. My initial reaction is fuck no, but then I pause to think about it. Part of me actually wants him up here. At least arguing with him would distract me from my pity party.

EASTON

I have an idea for the project

The follow-up text comes a second later. I still don't feel like talking about project stuff, but he's going to be relentless apparently until we hash it out. How strange is it that I thought he was going to be the slacker and now I'm the one avoiding the project?

Okay

ELEVEN

Easton

I'M SURPRISED. I'D EXPECTED A NO, ALONG WITH A STRING of expletives or an explanation of how much she hates my guts. Because that's exactly how she's acted since the morning after. Like us fucking somehow doubled her animosity toward me instead of reducing it. But she actually agrees and now I have to figure out how to go up there without attracting too much attention. Our friends will definitely not want me up there alone with her. I'm a menace to all women apparently, even smart ones like Wren who find me repulsive, and our interactions have caused our whole friend group to be wary any time the two of us are together. If they knew we'd fucked, it would only underline their apprehension. Fuck, I'm not even sure I should go near her.

The movie is well into the opening scene though. Waylon and Mac are busy making out and trying to be sly about it, and Liam is whispering something in Liv's ear so if I'm quiet, I doubt they'll notice my exit on the other side of the room. I get up slowly, practically tiptoeing my way out like a teenager sneaking out in the middle of the night, making a quiet ascent up the stairs. I rap my knuckles lightly on the door to her room, and she calls out for me to come in.

She's curled up on her bed, leaning against the wall and staring at her phone. She looks like she's been crying, but I doubt she'll like it much if I point that out. It's good info to have because now I know I'm essentially walking into a lion's den unprepared when said lion is cranky as fuck and wounded on top of it. I might have been safer downstairs.

"Hey," I say, sitting down on the edge of the bed, noting that she found the box I left her because it's been moved to the desk. I'd hedged my bets buying it for her, but hopefully, she took it in the spirit it was intended—a peace offering.

"Hey," she responds softly, setting her phone down, but still not looking at me.

"So I was thinking about the project," I charge forward to try and avoid awkward silence. "And what if we did your bar?"

"What?" She frowns, her eyes finally meeting mine.

"I assume it's struggling. I've been in there enough times to see it could certainly be doing better, and you're working with a skeleton crew half the time which I assume is also not what you'd be doing if you had a healthy balance sheet."

She doesn't answer, but I assume the lack of correction is an admission of sorts.

"But the food is good. The place is nice; comfortable, plenty of screens, good atmosphere. It's even a decent location close to campus. Which makes me think it's the marketing that could be improved."

"I mean there is no marketing. I don't have a budget or the time," she notes defensively.

"So now you would. And you've got access to all the data we'll need to make a compelling case that it's successful."

"*If* it's successful."

"It will be," I say because I have more than a few ideas that I think could bring the place back to life.

"We'd need a budget, and I don't have it."

"I'm willing to put money into this if it means we get a real example out of it."

"I don't want your fucking charity, Westfield," she snipes at me.

"It's not charity, and it's not for you. It's for this project, your bar would just happen to benefit from it. This project is important to me, and your bar would be perfect. You could be anyone, and I'd still offer the same. I told you. I want this interview as much as you do," I argue, trying to cut off her objections.

She stares at me for a few minutes, and then past me at the wall. A soft sigh and a slump of her shoulders have me thinking she might be seeing reason.

"It's not the worst idea in the world," she says quietly.

"There's only one problem I see that we need to hash out first."

"What's that?"

"You giving up some control, and letting me do my half of the project. It'll mean looking at your books and using ideas you may not like."

Her nose scrunches and I watch her sit a little straighter like she's about to argue, but she stops.

"Yeah. I guess that's true."

"So, is it a deal?"

"I want to sleep on it. But probably."

"You mean you want to come up with excuses not to do it."

"I didn't say that."

"Yeah, but you know it's a good idea. You just don't like it for whatever reason you don't want to admit is the real one, and so you're going to try to think of alternatives."

"It's a good idea, and I hate it. I need to sleep on it to try to convince myself to do it despite the fact my gut reaction is hell no."

"Why?" I'm honestly puzzled.

"Because I can't stand you, Easton. And the last thing I want is you bumbling around my bar and swinging your fucking AMEX around telling me how things should be done. Is that not obvious?"

"Why have you hated me? I mean I can guess why now, but before the night of the party?"

"Are you serious?"

"Yes."

"You've been nothing but shady as long as I've known you."

"Shady how?"

"Waylon and that sorority girl? Olivia and Liam?"

I sigh and shake my head.

"I was just trying to play matchmaker. I'm not saying I'm fucking good at it, but you're seriously going to fault me for that? That's not something you've done with them—the whole dinner at the bar with Waylon and Mac?"

"Matchmaker between Waylon and that harpy?"

"Think about it from my perspective with the knowledge I had at the time, yeah? From where I was sitting Mac was jerking Waylon around left and right. And he was totally fucking broken up over her. Meanwhile, Mac was at her ex-boyfriend's place. There weren't a lot of reasons for her to be there besides fucking him or other shit that was going to fucking hurt my friend. And Holly was in love with Waylon. I get that to all of you she was the fucking enemy, and honestly, after the deceitful shit she pulled I don't blame you. But she just kept telling me how much she loved him and how she wished he would notice her. So I thought fuck, why doesn't he go for the girl who actually wants him rather than the one who's just using him to get her ex back. I thought a little push would help him move on. I didn't know he'd told her no. I didn't know all the details of what went down between him and Mac until later."

"I guess that makes some sense." Her eyes meet mine for a second before they dart past me and over my shoulder. "But Olivia and Liam?"

"I know you're not actually mad at me for that one. We all knew those two needed to fuck it out. Again, I was just giving them the opportunity to move forward."

"By locking them out on a balcony in the freezing cold?"

"Yeah, well she didn't waste much time warming them both up, did she?"

Her eyes narrow and her lips press together in a distractingly sexy way. One that reminds me of what she looked like underneath me. All this talk about our friends fucking it out reminds me of how much I want a repeat session with her.

"Let me make you come again," I blurt out.

"What?" She looks at me like she misheard me.

"You're stressed. An orgasm usually helps. And I'm here." I try to smooth it over.

"What are you—"

"We can start slow. I don't even have to touch you if you don't want." I cut her off. I don't want to have a discussion about why it's a bad idea. Or why she thinks the last time was a mistake.

Her eyes flick up to mine. "How do you imagine making that happen?"

"You'll see," I whisper, hoping that she's gonna cave to it. I can tell she's thinking about it. That she wants to, even if she does hate me deep down.

"Okay," she relents. "But only because I'm curious."

"Didn't like it?" I stand and point to the box, where it's been tossed on the desk and the note is crumpled next to it.

"Your arrogance that you're better at selecting vibrators for me?"

"Like I said, you seemed stressed. I wanted to make sure you could relax. It was a peace offering."

When I turn back around, she's put her phone down on her nightstand, and she's eyeing me like she's still not quite sure if this is a good idea. I know she's trusting me just by letting herself be as vulnerable as she has been so far tonight. I didn't expect that to happen. I'd just been hoping for her to talk to me again. The silence between us was killing me. Making me want to ask questions like a needy asshole about what went wrong and if she really hated me this fucking much.

But now that I know she's this stressed, crying this much. I just want to take the edge off for her. Give her something else to focus on for a while. And I'm fairly certain as far as she's concerned this is all I'm good for.

I sit down on the edge of her bed and put the vibrator on the nightstand before I turn to her. Her eyes dart to mine, and I can see the anxiety dance behind them.

"I won't touch you unless you tell me to. And I'm not here for me, okay? I don't expect anything from you."

"I hope you're prepared for a whole lot of nothing."

"If all I get tonight is to watch you for a bit, that's plenty."

Her lashes flutter like I've said something she didn't expect, and her face softens just the tiniest bit before she gives a smartass little smile.

"Am I getting a taste of the legendary Easton charm again?"

I know what she's doing. Putting distance between us. Trying to keep a wall up.

"No, is that what you want?"

"No," she whispers quietly.

I reach out and run my fingers down the line of her jaw. She's fucking stunning. A smattering of freckles on her nose and gorgeous cupid's bow lips make me want to kiss her again. I press my thumb into the indent of her lower lip before I lean in, slowly in case she wants to stop me.

My eyes go to hers to look for permission but hers are already shuttered, her head already tilting up, so I close the gap and take her mouth, softly at first, teasing her with short shallow kisses before I press for more. And she answers me willingly. Teasing me with the tip of her tongue before she lets me have more.

And fuck. Just everything about her turns me on. She makes me want so fucking much. But I have to keep this about her. Walking the line so that I don't ask for more than she can give. Because she is never vulnerable, least of all around me, and I don't want to fuck it up.

I release her mouth and trail kisses down her jaw and neck. Taking a breath because what I'm about to do next is either going to doom me or give me a fucking shot at getting her to open up.

"Have you thought about me since?" I ask quietly.

"I don't know. Does it matter?"

"Yes. I can't stop thinking about it," I confess.

"I'm sure," it's a huffed exasperated whisper.

"It's true. I wasn't lying when I said I was trying to memorize it all. It plays like a fucking loop in my head."

"Don't patronize me, Easton. I know you don't—"

I swipe my thumb over the indent in her lip again and stare at it.

"I think about what your fingernails would feel like digging in my back again. All the other positions I could have you in. All the other ways I could make you come for me."

A little breath rushes out of her, and her eyes go to mine searching for a moment like she wants it to be true. She presses her lips together, kissing the tip of my thumb. The little gesture kills me. Makes me think of all the things I want to do to her. The ways I want to make her see I can be what she needs.

But I don't. I grab the vibrator off the nightstand and flick it on, the little hum breaking the silence in the room. She's dressed in an oversized sweater layered over leggings; the material so thin I bet I could see through it in the right light. Which is a blessing and a curse in the current situation. I slide the vibrator between her legs, hovering just above and withholding contact.

I wait for her to argue. To stop me. To give some kind of pushback, but she doesn't. So I press it down and her eyes flutter closed, and she rolls her lip in between her teeth. A little whisper of a breath escapes her lips and she might be the sexiest thing I've ever seen in my life. I wish I could capture this moment to rewatch later. I'd replay it every fucking night.

"That feel good?" I ask softly.

She nods but doesn't speak, her eyes still closed. But she spreads her legs an inch wider, tilting her hips, and I have to stifle the smirk I feel coming on. So I talk to her instead, to distract myself and keep her focused.

"It's hard not to touch you. Now. At the bar. When I'm out with our friends and you show up and tell me how much you hate me. Fuck, when you do that, it makes me want to press all your fucking buttons. I've missed seeing you though."

A breathy moan pops out of her mouth and goes straight to my cock. I'm so fucking hard I can barely stand it, and the second I finish her off I'm gonna need my hand to take the edge off.

"And I've seen you for a while. Way before that night. Watching you work, in those fucking knee-high socks with your hair up like you always have it. Watching you put all those assholes in their place and running it like you own it... It's fucking sexy as hell. I go home and fantasize about what it would be like if you ever told me you wanted me again. All the ways I could make you come."

She leans back and twists the corner of her pillow in her fist, her head tilts back, her teeth biting down hard on her lip. I give her more pressure with the vibrator and kiss my way up her neck until I reach her ear.

"I need you to come for me again. I need to hear it. I'm addicted to the sound of you, Princess."

Another soft moan escapes her lips, and I swallow it up as I kiss her, her hips rocking against my hand and the vibrator as she comes hard against it. I can feel the heat of her against my knuckles and fuck if it isn't a form of torture that I can't touch her.

As she rides out the last of it, I flick the vibrator off and set it back on her nightstand. I kiss the side of her jaw one last time.

"I'll let you get some sleep," I say quietly as I get up off the bed.

"Where are you going?" It's soft and it doesn't sound like her when she speaks. A breathiness and a want to her voice that I didn't think I would ever hear from her.

"Home... to take a shower," I say pointedly as I grab the door.

Her eyes rake over me, and she starts twice before she finally speaks. "Thank you."

I smile because I can't help it. "Goodnight, Princess."

TWELVE

Wren

Kenz, Liv, and I all pack up our laptops and books at the library. We'd been studying and doing research for a couple of hours, trying to keep each other accountable and get caught up. Liv's phone lights with a text and she grins.

"The guys want to know if we want to go get dinner with them," she explains.

She looks up to see our reaction, and I sigh a little internally. I'd been hoping to go out to dinner with them to chat and catch up post study session. The conversation was much less interesting with the guys around.

"I'm down." Kenz smiles.

"If you don't mind the fifth wheel," I say quietly, tucking my laptop in my bag. Liv nods and texts Liam back before she finishes cleaning up her area.

"Hey. You're not the fifth wheel. You're the main wheel. If anything Waylon's the fifth wheel." She gives me a sincere look.

I smile back at her because I know they genuinely care, and it's not their fault they're all happily paired up. They'd tried to get me to date. Offered to hook me up with guys they knew, many times, and I'd always said no. I don't have time to date. I have the bar. I have school. That's all the hours in the day minus sleep. And I needed my sleep.

Liv looks at her phone when it lights up again.

"Liam says to warn Wren that Easton is coming too."

I don't like the way my stomach does a little flip at his name. The way flashbacks of him and me invade my senses.

"It's fine." I shrug, trying to be nonchalant.

"He's coming around a lot lately..." Kenz flashes me a look.

"Unfortunate by-product of being stuck on this project together."

"Is that all it is?" Liv tucks her phone in her jacket pocket as we start to walk out.

"What else would it be? Westfield charm doesn't work on me."

I haven't told them anything, and I don't intend to. They don't need to know that I have those kinds of lapses in judgment. They rely on me to be the sensible one.

"I mean it wasn't Waylon's charm that worked on me." Kenz raises a brow at me.

"Waylon is a sweet guy with lots of positive qualities who you just happened to like arguing with. Easton has zero positive qualities, and all we do is argue."

Zero that don't involve sex, anyway.

"Hey now. That's not fair. He's got them, they're just buried under a lot of arrogance," Liv says defensively. I think she's the only one who's got a soft spot for him, in the same way any mom does for their black sheep kid.

"And I'm not looking to excavate layers of bullshit to find

them," I snark, hoping that it'll put a close to this conversation that I don't want to be having.

Kenz snickers and links her arm with me as we walk out to Liv's car to head out for dinner.

WHEN WE GET TO THE RESTAURANT THE GUYS ARE already there and have a table for us. I get stuck sitting next to Easton as the couples cuddle up around the semi-circle booth.

"No Ben?" I ask as I sit down because I'd much rather be sitting next to him right now.

"He was meeting up with someone," Waylon answers.

"That's too bad." I set my bag at my feet and do my best not to look at Easton.

"Don't tell me *you* have a crush on him now." Waylon shoots me a look.

"Wren doesn't have crushes on mortal men, honey. Her crushes are Fitzwilliam Darcy, Alexi Lalas in his prime, and Harrison Ford in his Indiana Jones days," Kenz muses to Waylon

"Alexei Lalas over Tim Howard?" Easton asks.

"I like redheads," I respond in a clipped tone because I really don't want to discuss my taste in men with Easton. Especially when lately he's top of the list.

"Oh, right. I forgot Jamie Fraser." Kenz's lips turn up in a bemused smile.

"Do you want to talk about your crush on '90s Kevin Costner?" I narrow my eyes.

"Let's not and say we didn't." Kenz flashes me a look.

"Costner? Really?" Waylon shoots her a look of disbelief.

"He had a surly vibe that was hot in the movies he did then, okay? The characters. Not him."

"Personally I prefer '90s Brad Pitt," Liv chimes in.

"The fuck you do," Liam grumbles before he captures her mouth with his and we all have to look away because my god those two do not stop with the PDA these days.

"Did you get coverage to go on the ski trip?" Kenz turns back to me, giving us something else to focus on.

"I did. I managed to line up some backup help. So long as none of them has to call off or bail at the last minute, I'm coming." I smile at her because I'm excited about the mini vacation we're taking.

That's one of the benefits of Highland State, in addition to Spring Break we also get a week off in the winter. Even though it's technically a ski vacation, I plan to spend most of it curled up in front of a fire with a book and hot cocoa with a view of the mountains.

"Speaking of, I booked our hotel rooms," Easton glances down at his menu as he says it.

And I'm surprised he was given that task over someone like Liv.

"Yeah? Anywhere good?" Kenz asks.

"Yup. Called in a couple of favors and got us a great deal at an exclusive resort," he answers and that explains why he was given the task. "Only problem is that it's couples only."

I frown, because he knows damn well I'm planning to go, and while he and Ben could probably call up jersey chasers for the occasion, I don't have the same kind of roster at my fingertips.

"How's that going to work?" Kenz frowns, and I'm thankful she asks so I don't have to.

"You and Waylon. Liv and Liam. Ben and his friend Chelsea. Me and Wren."

"What?" I say a little too loudly. So loudly that it even stops the Liv and Liam make-out session happening on the other side of the table.

"I'm not about to take one of the other girls and have them thinking we're on some romantic vacation, and I assumed you didn't have anyone," he answers, like he's only talking to me. But I'm very aware we have the attention of the table.

"That's a big assumption. One you should probably ask about first."

"I also figured it'd give us a chance to work on the project while you were off work." His eyes flick over me like he's assessing something.

"She needs real time off. She's had a long fucking month," Kenz corrects Easton, and I want to thank her for it, but he's right that it would give us some much-needed time to get it started.

"Well, it would give us some time we don't normally have, I guess. But I'm not sharing a room with you. I'm not gonna be sleeping on the couch while you bring a parade of snow bunnies in."

"One, it's a couple's resort so you have to share a room with someone. Two, it's a couple's resort, so there are no single women."

"You're gonna go a fucking week with no pussy?" Liam laughs. "I'm taking bets now on how long it takes him to fuck off to one of the lodges to get some and then disappear for the rest of the trip."

"I'll put money down on that," Waylon chimes in.

"See, he won't even be in the room very much Wren. So you'll have it all to yourself," Liv smiles at me, and I grin back. Hoping that it looks at least a little sincere.

"I can fucking go a week without. Fuck," Easton gripes.

"Since when?" Waylon's eyes dance with laughter.

"I have on several occasions when I needed to focus or

practice more, thank you *very* fucking much." Easton's voice has a defensive edge to it.

"Whoa, no need to get your fucking panties in a twist." Liam raises a brow at him like he's out of line.

"Then shut the fuck up, yeah?" He flicks them a surly look and glances down at his menu again.

"As long as there's a pullout couch or an extra bed or something... fine. Just let me know what I owe, okay?" I glance over at him because as much as I don't like him, I don't like that he seems genuinely upset at the comments being made about him. I feel weirdly defensive of him, and I have no idea where that's coming from. I'll have to put that on the list of things to investigate later.

His eyes meet mine like he's equally unsure about the way I'm caving suddenly. They search my face for a second, something there I can't quite read before he nods.

THIRTEEN

Easton

"WANT A RIDE HOME?" I ASK AS DINNER ENDS, AND KENZ follows Waylon to his truck, and Liv and Liam discuss going to his place.

I figure she's going to say no because she avoids me like the plague, but I know the walk from here to their house is a long one and it's freezing outside. She might have Liv drop her off anyway, but I'm going to offer.

"If you don't mind." She shrugs.

The easy way she agrees surprises me and my eyes flash to hers. That's twice tonight that she's gone along with something I suggested, and I'm not sure what it means. If maybe, just maybe, she's going a little soft on me.

"You don't have to though." She suddenly looks sheepish like she's said something wrong.

"I want to." I look away from her as I put my coat on

because I don't want to smile or do anything that's going to spook her and make her bolt.

We walk to my car in silence, the snow is starting to come down, and it makes the entire world seem whisper-quiet despite the traffic and voices in the distance. I unlock the car when we get there and almost go to open her door before I think better of it. I know she'd hate that sort of chivalry and I'm not about to give her an opening for another argument. Especially since I can tell from the look on her face, she already has things she'd like to say about the car.

"You can change the temp and the seat warmer however you want." I point to the controls, and she gives me a little smile in return.

"Thanks."

"No comments, huh?" I give her a teasing glance.

"Nope. Keeping them to myself. Liam and Waylon gave you enough shit tonight."

"You don't have to stay with me if you don't want on the trip. If you've got someone, I can rebook the rooms," I say as I kick the engine into gear. But fuck I hope she doesn't have anyone. Because I want this girl to myself right now, and having her alone for several days at a couple's resort in the mountains? I might actually convince her she doesn't hate me as much as she thinks she does.

"It's fine. I don't mind. As long as I don't have to see shenanigans, and assuming you didn't like... book the pent-house, and now I've gotta figure out how to sell a kidney to pay for my half of the room."

"Yeah... I think it's only going to be like $200 for your part. I'm happy to cover it though. It was my pick." It's a lie. The room was more than that a night, far more than that. But I'm not about to tell her, because I want her to go and enjoy it for once. Without the constant stress that surrounds her. If I can give her a few days off from it, it's more than worth the money.

"I can cover $200. It's not a problem," she answers.

"All right. As far as the rest, I actually wanted to talk to you about that. Just not in front of them…"

She glances over at me, and I can feel her eyes on me as I drive. Trying to keep mine on the road even though I'm distracted by the fact she's next to me. I'm not really prepared for this conversation, because it's not one I've ever had before.

"Thank you, by the way for not saying anything to them. I just know they would all have big opinions about it, and I don't want to hear them," she says quietly.

"Right." I stiffen a little because the tone in her voice makes me feel like she regrets it. And I'm about to do the thing I hate doing—talking about it. "Do you regret it then?"

I can see her look over at me abruptly again like she can't believe I just asked that.

"No… but I… It's awkward now, right? We had the whole frenemies thing down pretty well, and now it's muddy. Now we're frenemies with sexual tension or something."

I laugh because it's not a terrible description of where we're at. "Fair enough. I had another idea though."

"What's that?"

"Frenemies with benefits?" I smirk.

She doesn't answer for a beat, and I look over at her briefly. She looks pensive like she's mulling it over.

"We could try it while we're on the trip. We'll be alone. They'll be off doing their couple thing half the time and won't bother to pay attention to us. So it wouldn't be hard to keep it from them."

I feel like a devil sitting on her shoulder, luring her to a fate she doesn't deserve. But fuck, I want more of this girl. I want a chance to have her without worrying about our friends being downstairs or in the next room. I want a chance to spend time with her alone.

"Why?"

Well that was a new fucking question. No woman has ever asked me why they should fuck me before. I thought all of that was pretty self-evident, especially when she's already tried it once. So I guess I need to figure out what her specific objections are because I thought I'd already covered them.

"Why not?" I turn the question back on her, and I hear a little sigh like she doesn't love it.

"Because it's a romantic couple's resort, right? Won't that be weird? Like we're cosplaying some kind of fucked up relationship... or a hateship or something? And I don't want to pile on after Liam and Waylon, but you're more of the hit-it-and-quit-it than the return-for-more type Easton."

"A hateship sounds pretty hot actually." I try hard not to smile because I can tell it's not the time.

"Be serious."

"I am. And I've already come back for more. So I've already proven you wrong there."

"I'm pretty sure that was just you wanting to be right about the vibrator."

I let out a choked laugh.

"I already knew I was right. That was about you looking stressed and me wanting to help you relax."

"What would this trip be about?" she asks just as we pull up to her house, and I put the car in park and turn to look at her.

"Testing the hateship out. I think it could be fun."

"And when it's over and we have to come back to reality?"

"We figure it out when we get there."

She presses her lips together and shakes her head, "It must

be nice to get to live like that every day. Figuring things out as you go. No worries."

"Okay, worst-case scenario. We hate it. We hate each other. And we're right back where we started. You already said this limbo was awkward, so problem solved."

"What happens when you get bored on day two and bring a threesome back to the hotel room, and now I'm hiding in the bathroom just to get some peace and quiet?"

"The only way I bring a threesome back is if you decide it's something you want to try. I'm not gonna get bored. I have fun with you, even when we're arguing. And the sex the other night? That was the best sex I've had in a long fucking time. I'm pretty sure if I wasn't drunk and you weren't just throwing me a pity fuck it could be even better."

"It wasn't a pity fuck."

"It was. You're normally too smart to fuck guys like me. But you already made the mistake, so might as well keep making it for a while and enjoy it, right?" I grin at her. It hurts a little to admit the truth, but she and I both know it.

"Maybe."

"Besides, you know they're all gonna be fucking like crazy. You really want to be the only one going back to your room early at night by yourself?"

"This is a crazy idea. We don't even like each other." She shakes her head and looks out the window.

Except. I think maybe I do like her. At least, I'm sure I don't hate her anymore. But I'm not about to tell her that and blow this hateship up when it's the only thing that has her vaguely interested.

"I didn't say anything about you needing to like me. It might be better that you don't. You just have to let me make you come like the other night. And you like that, right?" I let my hand ghost over her thigh, and it drags her attention back to me.

Her eyes follow my hand, up my arm until she catches my eyes with her own.

"Yes."

I drag my knuckles under her chin when she starts to look away again, bringing her eyes back to mine.

"Then just think about it. Okay?"

She nods, and I brush my lips over hers. She gives me a soft tentative kiss in return. One that's unsure and careful. Almost like she's worried about something. I wish I knew what she was thinking. Wish I could reassure her that I only have good intentions where she's concerned. She pulls back after a few minutes and turns her head to look out the window.

"I should go inside. I've got a paper I need to finish."

Right. Real life. Things to do. Which reminds me of the project I should be working on with her, the one that has a decent say in our futures and should probably be more of a focus on my own to-do list. The one she now keeps jumping to the top of.

"Okay. We also probably need to figure out a schedule for the project."

"Right. I need to send you some stuff for that. Or I don't know, maybe we can meet at the bar? I can give you the stuff you wanted to look over and you can have some cheese fries while you work. Maybe a beer if you're good." She grins at me.

I can't help but smile back.

"Sounds like a plan. Just let me know when a good night is."

"I'll text you tomorrow."

"Night, Princess."

"Night." She looks over me one last time as she climbs out of my car.

FOURTEEN

Wren

I CAN'T STOP THINKING ABOUT HIM. THE WAY HE TALKS TO me. The way he kisses me. The man is on replay in every corner of my mind. And I can't decide if I love or hate it. We've already met up once this week at the bar to discuss the project, and he started going through the books and previous promotional events we've done. He gave me a few suggestions that were outside the box that we could try, and I'm not sure how I feel about them yet.

Time is ticking down to the trip though, and I need to figure out how I feel about that. If I'm going to agree or not. I'd been working when I saw him at the bar and didn't get to talk to him much, but before he left, he'd dragged me into a dark corner and kissed me hard up against the wall. Asked me if I needed anything else to convince me to take his offer up for the weekend away, and I told him I was still thinking.

Which was true. Because I know what I want, there's just a

little nagging voice in the back of my head that keeps reminding me that it's a bad idea. That whoever this Easton is, he won't last.

Then, like he knows I'm thinking about him my phone dings with a message.

EASTON
How's the debate going?

About the bar?

About us

I stare at the word us. I would never have used the word us in a sentence to describe Easton and me, but here we are. I play stupid because I feel a little well of panic and lust every time I think about the two of us.

What about?

EASTON
The hateship. You in or out, Princess? You're torturing me. We leave in a few days

It sounds like playing with fire

I like playing with fire. And I definitely like every time I play with you

My stomach does a little somersault. His admission makes me feel like maybe, just maybe I'm not totally alone in this hateship. A few days, running around pretending like Easton and I are actually a thing. It could be fun. It could take the edge off—in general, and about the way I feel about him. If we can drop the tension between us several notches, it'd probably make this whole project go easier too. Maybe we can stop arguing every five seconds. Maybe I'll figure out that he's actually terrible in bed and the one night we had was a fluke. But if it had been just a preview, I am doomed.

Then I think about what our friends would say if I could ask their advice. And I guarantee they would hate it. Tell me it's a bad idea. That I'm going to get hurt. That we are just going to fight more as a result. But I'm not worried about getting hurt. I know who Easton is. I know what he does and doesn't bring to the table. I'm not worried about catching feelings where he's involved. And he definitely doesn't have to worry about me having feelings for him. He's a walking red flag, an entire collection of them really, and feelings are not involved. So why resist the attraction if there's no real risk...

Okay. I'm in

EASTON

See you Saturday then, Princess

LATER THAT WEEK KENZ, LIV, AND I ARE ALL PACKING FOR the trip, bouncing back and forth between each other's rooms trying to decide what to take and what we're going to wear. We're currently in Liv's room while she tries to pick a couple of dresses for when we go out to some of the nicer restaurants, and she's modeling them for us in between discussions about how much skiing we're actually going to do versus shopping, eating, and generally being lazy couch potatoes.

"You know it doesn't matter what you wear, right? This dress or the last one, he's going to be obsessed with you no matter what. And you look gorgeous in everything," I say, shaking my head as I smile at her fourth dress.

"I just want to make sure I look good. I know he's Liam, but he still makes me kinda nervous you know? In a good way." She smiles back.

"We know." Kenz winks at her.

"Are you also bringing a war chest of sexy dresses?" I look at Kenz.

"I have a few."

"Do you want to borrow some?" Liv looks at me.

"For what purpose? All the taken men who will be at the resort?"

"I mean we're going to go out to dinner and do some sightseeing. There might be a cute single ski instructor at one of the lodges eating dinner. He sees you in a dress from across the room..." Liv starts daydreaming for me out loud.

"You're assuming she won't spend the first half of this trip murdering Easton and the second trying to find a place to bury him." Kenz laughs and then turns to me. "You know if you do need to bury him just let me know. I've listened to enough podcasts now. I've got tips."

I laugh. "I'll be sure to do that."

"Are you sure you're okay staying in a room with him?" Liv asks.

"Yeah. He's mostly harmless when he's not irritating me," I lie because I'm not about to admit all the ways Easton gets to me.

"If you need to swap or anything, just let us know. Once we're in, I doubt they're checking rooms or anything," Kenz offers.

"I appreciate it. But hopefully, he'll be off busy doing his thing, skiing and screwing snow bunnies in their rooms, and I'll get to enjoy the room and catch up on some reading and sleep."

I am a lying liar who lies to my best friends because the only thing I want Easton screwing is me. It's all I can think about when I have a moment to think. To the point where I'm starting to question my sanity. And I have a full-blown problem on my hands too because when we put a pause on our fighting, he's easy to get along with. He's funny and kind of... sweet? I don't know what to make of any of it. I hate that feeling.

———

WHEN I GO UP TO MY ROOM LATER TO FINISH PACKING, I see three dresses laid out on the bed. Including one that's short, sexy, and black. I can guess who put them there.

"Just in case, you know." Liv winks at me from the door frame.

"In case of a sexy single ski instructor run-in?" I smirk.

"Or a sexy tight end." She shrugs, and I feel a tug in my chest at the mention of him.

"Yeah, I don't think so..."

"Like I said, just in case. That's all." She grins and then takes off back to her room.

I stare down at the dresses and decide to bring them with me. It couldn't hurt to have them on hand, especially if Liv and the rest decide they want to go somewhere fancy. And maybe, just maybe a little part of me wants to impress him too. If I'm going to do this whole hateship thing, then I might as well go all in on it.

FIFTEEN

Easton

We're having a guy's night, watching a playoff game, eating wings, and drinking beer at my place for once. It's a nice break from the football house where everyone and their mother comes passing through, disturbing the replays and commentary. Liam, Waylon, and Ben can be trusted with the responsibility, which is why it's just the four of us.

When half-time comes, we all move to the kitchen to refill on food and drinks, and that's when Liam decides to start his shit up.

"You really think you can keep it together for a whole week with her in your room? Without the two of you arguing or you doing something stupid like waking her up by fucking two girls in the bed next to her?"

"I'm fucking certain I can handle a week. Why do you always doubt me?"

"Because I know you."

"She and I are already partners on this project and have to spend a ton of time around each other anyway. We have to adapt to the circumstances, and I don't think we're fucking it up so far."

"There has been a downturn in arguments lately." Waylon gives me some credit.

"And no ulterior motives?" Ben eyes me because Ben knows me better than Liam. Where Liam is worried that I'll be an asshole and fuck it up, Ben's worried I'm going to fuck her. Literally. Too bad he doesn't know that already happened.

———

LATER THAT NIGHT AS BEN GETS READY TO HEAD OUT, I stop him. Liam's already left and Waylon is busy getting ready to go see Mac, so I have a window where I can try to talk to our resident expert on women. And hopefully, get some kind of advice on how not to fuck up my window of opportunity with Wren this weekend.

"All right, Benny. You're better at this shit than me. If I want to seduce a girl, what do I need to do?"

He looks at me like I've lost my mind.

"The slow kind. Obviously, I can get a woman into bed, but I mean the kind where she might actually want something besides my dick. You know?"

The confused look morphs into something curious, if not slightly stormy.

"*Who* are you trying to seduce?"

"No one in particular. Just thinking I might need to switch things up every now and then. Try something different."

"If something different is a bar manager who hates your guts, I don't know that I want to be giving you ammunition.

You know how that will end and it won't be good for you. Or her."

"You all should give the bar manager more credit. She can handle herself. Fuck, I think she could steamroll me if I let her."

"She *can* handle herself. And her two best friends will help bury your body, and their boyfriends will take turns driving the getaway vehicle."

"That's very fuckin' dramatic but thank you for the reminder that my friends would happily betray me for their girlfriends."

"There are far safer options out there for you. Your phone is full of them."

"Yeah, well I have a newly discovered interest in extreme sports, okay?"

"Christ..." Ben shakes his head.

"Don't say anything to anyone, all right? I don't want it getting back to them, least of all her." I'm nervous but I feel like I can trust Ben, out of anyone he might understand. Might give me a break and some advice.

"Yeah. Don't worry. I'm not interested in being the messenger on that one."

"So—advice?"

"I don't know, East. What's your goal here? You telling me you've had an epiphany, and you're into monogamy now? Or you just want a way to trick our friend into your bed?" Ben eyes me warily. "Because I'm obviously not going to help you with the latter."

"Is that what you do with all your cooking lessons and sweet talk? Trick them?"

"No. It's who I am. But you'll also notice I keep it far away from our friends."

"Well, the money and the cars and all of that isn't who I

am. Just things I enjoy. And I get that some women confuse those two things, but if I wanted a woman to look past them and see who I am. How do I get there when the flashy shit is all she ever sees and hates?"

Ben's face shifts a little and he leans back against the wall.

"Are you sure that isn't what this is then? Your ego bruised because she doesn't like the things that normally make it so easy for you?"

"I thought that's what it was at first, yeah. That I just wanted to fuck her, and she wasn't interested, and it bothered me. But... now I'm pretty certain she would fuck me, but only fuck me, and I think I don't like that either."

Ben laughs and shakes his head.

"I think the two of you just make each other unhappy in general."

"Yeah, but I like it. The way she fucking needles me. The way she gets under my skin. And she's so fucking hot when she's mean."

"I think you need to analyze that with a therapist."

"Maybe. Now, are you gonna fucking help me or just give me shit?"

"It's really not that complicated. Just pay attention to her and what she likes. Be honest with her. Have you tried telling her you like her?"

"No." That sounds like the quickest way to losing my balls.

"Then show her if you don't want to tell her."

I eye him skeptically.

"I can't give you a magic formula to get her to like you. You have to figure that out on your own. I'm just saying check your ego at the door and let her know *you* like her. That usually goes a long way."

"Got it."

"And the obvious other thing which you struggle with."

"What?"

"How many girls have you fucked this week?"

"None."

He gives me a look that tells me he doesn't believe me.

"Honest."

"Hell must be cold as fuck right now then. But if it's true—keep it that way. If you act like a fuckboy that's how she's going to treat you."

"I've figured that much out. But it's not like she's gonna forget all the time she's known me. Going to be a dealbreaker you think?"

He shrugs. "Might be."

I let out a breath. "Well, fuck it, I guess. Don't know if I don't try."

"Good luck."

"I'll need it." I smirk, and he gives me a quick slap on the back before he heads out the door.

SIXTEEN

Wren

WHEN WE GET TO THE HOTEL LOBBY AFTER THE DRIVE UP from Denver, Easton heads to the desk and checks us all in while the rest of us just bask in the gorgeousness of it all.

"Do we want to know how much this place costs a night normally?" Kenz gapes at our surroundings and the gorgeous views of the mountains framed by picture windows.

"Probably not. Just appreciate that we're getting the Easton discount, and it fits in our budget darlin'." Waylon kisses the top of her head, and she wraps her arms around his waist.

"We have to find a way to pay him back for making this happen." She shakes her head.

I blink as I turn around, trying to take it all in. I fell asleep in the car on the ride here because I'd worked three late shifts this week in a row and then stayed up trying to get a last-minute paper done. I was running on three hours of sleep, and it was starting to catch up to me.

Easton doles out keys and little folders of information and activities around the resort, and we all agree to meet back up for dinner before we head to our individual rooms. My stomach does a little flip when Easton and I are the last ones left standing in the lobby together. Because now it's real. The two of us, our hateship and a hotel room for the next several days.

"Where are we?" I ask, trying to sound peppier than I feel. Because what I am is tired and nervous and I doubt either of those things is very attractive in the person you're going to be stuck sharing a room with.

"We're on the far side. In the residence wing." He nods his head to the other side of the hotel.

"The residence wing?"

"Yeah. Little bit bigger place. A little more privacy." Something dances behind his eyes as he says privacy.

The flip in my stomach turns into three somersaults. Right. Privacy. If you were going to spend your long weekend fucking the hottest guy on campus in secret while your friends were staying at the same hotel. You might need some.

"Shall we go?" A man appears and starts loading our luggage onto a cart.

My eyes flash back and forth between him and Easton.

"A butler comes with the package." He shrugs.

"A what?" I look at him again.

"It's a nice perk. You'll like it." He grins.

"Okay, Rich Boy." I roll my eyes but I can't stop a small smile that follows.

Our room is not a room. It is a palatial suite, with a bedroom, a living room, a bar area, a huge bathroom, and a massive deck that overlooks the ski lifts with a glittering hot tub in the center of it.

"There is no way my half of this is two hundred dollars, Easton." I gape at him once the butler puts our bags away and gives us a quick tour of the amenities as well as a number to text him any time before he leaves.

"You're right. Your half of this is zero."

"That's not fair. You said I could pay."

"You will." He smirks.

I open my mouth to protest but then I think better of it. Two could play this game.

"Does that make you my sugar daddy then?" I bat my lashes at him.

"God, I hope not. I'd like to make it to 40 before I have to resort to that."

I laugh and shake my head.

"Really though." I look at him as I run my hand over the sheets that must have an insane thread count. They might even be better than the ones he bought me.

"Really. I wanted to stay here. My brother was here last year and was bragging about how nice it was. And I needed someone to come with me if I was gonna try it. So really, you're doing me a favor."

"Uh-huh. If you say so." I sit down on the bed and lay back. "Oh my god, I could just melt into these and fall asleep."

"You can take a nap if you want. I've got some things to do anyway."

"Yeah. I think I better, or I'll be falling asleep at the table tonight at dinner."

"I'll meet you back here before then."

I give him a small smile before he nods and heads out again. Off to who knows where.

SEVENTEEN

Easton

I NEARLY CHOKE ON MY TONGUE WHEN I SEE HER DRESSED up to go out. The dress she has on is delicate looking and elegant as hell, so different from the stuff she normally wears, and I have to assume it's borrowed from Liv. But somehow, despite the fact it's not her usual style or even her own dress, it fits her perfectly. Every curve, every dip, every valley of her body. The sassy as fuck bartender has been replaced by someone who looks like a trust-fund princess who could bring the private club members to their knees with a few bats of her lashes.

"Why are you looking at me like that? Is it bad? Liv loaned it to me, and I don't know about it." She stares down, smoothing the skirt with her fingers.

"It's not bad," I manage to say. Bad for me. Bad for my self-control. Bad for my dick in these fitted pants I'm wearing, but definitely not fucking bad for her.

I take a breath. The effect she has on me. The way she makes all my easy practiced charm go out the fucking window is becoming a real problem. I close my eyes. Remind myself she's just like any other woman I've wanted. It's *fine*.

"You look fucking stunning in it, honestly," I recover my words again.

Her eyes lift to mine, and then rake down my body. I saw the way she looked at me before when I'd gotten out of the shower. She liked what she fucking saw, and she wanted more. For a split fucking second, until she remembered who I was and what she really thought of me. Just like with the kiss. Just like the other night in the car. And I only wish I could get her to look a little harder, see beyond what she thinks she knows.

"Thanks. You look nice. I'm just a little nervous. I don't go to places with dress codes very often, obviously." She gives me a half smile.

"Yeah, well you're lucky for that. They're usually boring as fuck. I have a little faith if Liv picked it though." I return her smile.

"Well that's true. I do trust Liv." She grins as she thinks of her friends, and I know the three of them are always getting into something.

"You ready?" I ask.

"Just gotta get my coat and shoes, and then yep."

Luckily the place isn't quite as far as I thought because I worry about her freezing in the outfit she has on, even with the giant fluffy coat she's piled on top of it. Our friends are in the lobby when we get there and both Liv and Kenz's jaws drop when I help her out of her coat.

"Don't fuckin' think about it," Liam grunts in a low tone as he looks at Wren and then at me.

"Too late for that. You can thank your girlfriend for that by the way. She loaned her the dress," I answer, grinning at him.

"If you ruin this trip by upsetting her or making it so she wants to swap rooms, on a week when I have Liv all to myself, I will hurt you."

"Noted." I shake my head.

"Go fucking easy on him. She does look nice," Waylon says to Liam, but then the traitor turns and looks at me. "But for real. Don't ruin this trip. You think you can handle sharing a room with her without fucking it up, and I want to believe you. But I have similar feelings about my time with Mac."

"Should have just had her stay with Ben and let him bring a jersey chaser." Liam shakes his head.

"Give him a chance..." Waylon sighs.

Ben's busy talking to Chelsea, and I wonder if he's not in over his head with her because she definitely looks at him with those I-want-to-be-your-only-girl eyes. And while Ben may go through less women than I do, and with a lot more endearing qualities than I have, socially speaking, he's probably the least likely of all of us to date anyone. Despite what he says. I'm fairly certain the guy will die a bachelor before committing, where I actually at least entertain the idea once in a while with a regular hookup.

I glance back over at Wren, and she looks so fucking bright. All smiles as she laughs and talks to her friends, and they fawn over the dress she's wearing.

"Definitely going to capture a ski instructor's attention in that." Mac twirls her around once and she grins.

Ski instructor? Not fucking likely. Not after I get my hands on her again and she remembers what I feel like. Except I need to fucking move slowly with her. Give her a chance to care about something other than the sex. But sometimes, with her, it feels like that's all I've got.

———

When dinner winds down, I pull out my phone and send a text message to the hotel's butler service. I'm going to fucking roll the dice hard on this one, with something that will either soften her icy exterior or have her shoving me firmly back into a fuckboy box. Either way, I think it's something she'll enjoy so it's worth it.

I can feel her eyes on me but when I look up they dodge away, back to her friends, smiling like she's focused on whatever story Waylon is telling. She's been doing it all night. Watching me and then trying to pretend like she wasn't. I look down to see her knee bouncing under the table and my fingers itch to run over it, still her nervous habit and tell her how beautiful she looks. But I don't want to push too far. Especially not with our friends here.

So I reach down, putting my hand between us where our chairs touch, extending my pinky finger so it brushes over her knee and down over the inside of her leg. I keep my eyes on Waylon the whole time like I'm as fascinated as she is even though I have no idea what he's talking about now. Her leg stills, her eyes snapping to look at me and then down at my hand. I can see a slight blush rise to her cheeks out of the corner of my eye before she turns her gaze back to Waylon. I glance over at her and there's the slightest little smile, the small upturn of her mouth that lets me know she doesn't hate it when I touch her. And fuck was I going to touch her later.

I brush the tips of my fingers over her one quick time, watching to make sure no one at the table notices before I put them back on the table in front of me, taking a sip of my wine and acting like I'm not thinking about how the woman next to me runs my fucking thoughts lately.

"I've got dinner," I announce when Waylon finishes his tale, mostly because I want to cover her dinner, but I know she won't want me to single her out. It'll throw up all kinds of flags for our friends, and she'll hate it and say I treat her like she's a charity case. If I pay for everyone though, I can take care of her like I want.

"You sure? That was an expensive meal." Waylon frowns a little at me.

"I've got it. No worries." I shrug it off.

I feel her eyes on me again, and this time when I go to catch them, they don't jump away.

"Thank you. That's really sweet of you to do for everyone," she gives me a small but warm smile. One that lights something inside, one that makes me feel like she means it.

"No problem." I tear my eyes away from her though because I can feel Liam's on me, and I don't want to be caught out on this before we even start.

"We're going to go up for a night ride on the lift. Any of you want to go?" Ben asks, his arm casually draped around Chelsea's shoulders.

"There's supposed to be hot cocoa after," Chelsea adds.

"Oh that sounds amazing." Liv gives Liam big doe eyes and that's all it takes for him to concede and thankfully be distracted from whatever he was piecing together about Wren and me.

The table descends into chatter and soon everyone else is agreeing to go, and I see Wren shift uncomfortably again.

"Do you want to go?" I ask.

"Oh um. No I think it sounds a tad too romantic. But you should go if you want." She winks at me in an oddly playful way that causes a little twist in my chest.

"Nah. I was gonna go back to the room for the night, but I'd go if you wanted to have company."

Secretly I'm hoping she says no. I want her to come back to the room with me. I want her alone. But if she says she wants me to I will.

"In case I don't want to be the 7th wheel you mean? That's nice of you, but I'm good. I'm serious though, if you want to go and get some hot cocoa don't worry about me. I can get back fine."

"I'm good." So fucking good because she is going to be sleeping in the same bed as me tonight. In the same room. "The hot cocoa sounds good though. Might have to get some of that."

"Agreed." She nods.

And while she and the girls get their coats back on and everyone says their goodnights, I put in another request to the hotel before we head back.

EIGHTEEN

Wren

By the time we get back to the room, I'm nervous. I don't know why. It's silly. I've been around Easton a million times before. We've been nice to each other all evening. But he's caught me looking at him several times and each time it made my heart skip a beat because of how guilty I'd felt for staring at him. But it's hard not to stare at Easton when he's dressed up like he is tonight. Really, it's hard not to stare at him any day but especially hard on a night like this.

Normally I get to do my staring from across the room at a party or the occasional flick of a look across a table. But here, even though we've only been together a few hours, we're on top of each other constantly. Apparently, stolen gazes cannot be a thing because somehow, he knows when I'm watching him no matter how discreet I try to be.

Once we walk into the main part of the suite it's obvious housekeeping has been in the room with turn-down service.

The bed is neatly unmade, with chocolates on the pillows. A bottle of champagne is on the table with two glasses and there's a cute little towel animal on the edge of the bed. If we were actually a couple and I liked that kind of romance, I think I'd be melting a little. Like I had earlier when I saw him get out of the shower. And that reminds me and gives me the perfect excuse to escape for a bit.

"Do you care if I take a shower? Unless you wanted to take one first?"

"Nah, I had that one when I got back from the gym."

"You went to the gym already? That's dedication."

"I didn't get my run in this morning, and I wanted to make sure. The Combine's coming up."

"Oh, right." I nod. I keep forgetting that even though football season is technically over for them, they're all still running drills and working out like it's mid-season in order to prove themselves at The Combine. Even Liam, who's not participating has been keeping up with them for solidarity reasons.

I go to my suitcase and gather the things I need for my shower, but when I walk into the bathroom, I stop short. The lights are down low. The windows have been partially opened to reveal the view outside. The water has been drawn in the tub. Stretched over the tub is a tray with a bath bomb and chocolate perched on it.

"Um, do you think they got the wrong room? I feel like maybe they got the wrong room," I call to Easton from the bathroom.

"What?" I hear him say, and he passes through the doorway to stand next to me.

"Is this normal? Or did they have the wrong room when they set things up?"

"I ordered it for you."

"What?" My eyes snap to him, and he looks taken aback by the sudden observation.

"I figured it was cold out and you'd want it after we got back. Plus you're supposed to be on vacation relaxing."

"You did this?" I ask softly, perplexed because I didn't think thoughtful Easton existed.

"Yeah. I ordered some hot cocoa too, should be here shortly. If you want to get in the tub, I can let you know when it's here."

I blink at him because I don't know what else to do.

"You ordered a bath and hot cocoa for me?" I say it out loud, like maybe that will help me make sense of it.

"Yes. Although now you're making me feel like that was a bad idea." His eyes shift away from me in an oddly sheepish way for a man like Easton.

"No... I mean, I like it. I just didn't expect it..." I stumble over my words because the whole scene makes me short on them.

"Well hopefully, there's more of you liking things you didn't expect." His signature grin returns and sends little zings of want through me.

He leans forward and presses his lips to mine, soft little touches that make me melt into him. When he finally lets go, I just stare up at him for a minute, just mesmerized by how pretty he is and wondering how I got here. And whether or not I could keep up with him.

"Are you joining me then?" I ask, raising a brow.

He glances at the tub for a moment like he's considering it.

"Nah. Someone's gotta answer the door for room service, and then I gotta set up the next part of the date."

Next part of...

"The date?" I look at him confused.

"Let me have my fantasy and pretend you'd go on a date

with me, yeah? I know you wouldn't be seen with me in public, but I figured we're safe if we stay in here."

The man has had a bath drawn for me on a cold night and ordered me hot cocoa. I would go on a date with him literally whenever he asks. I'm honestly ready to out this whole thing to Liv and Kenz just so that I can tell them what he's done. Ask them if they think the real Easton has been body snatched and replaced with a second Ben who just happens to look like East. Because this kind of stuff? This is not Easton charm.

"Okay," I agree, still confused about what's happening.

"I'll let you know when the cocoa's here." He places a whisper-light kiss against my jaw and then leaves the room.

I turn to the bath, pick up the lavender bath bomb and drop it into the steaming hot tub, watching it roll and unfurl the purple cloudy mist into the water. Trying to figure out what I've gotten myself into.

When I make my way out of the tub, wash my hair and get dressed for the evening—which is an entire ordeal because I have no idea what you wear to bed with your rich fuckboy would-be lover when you're in a suite in the mountains in a hateship—I stop in my tracks at the sight in front of me.

Easton's sprawling on the bed, shirt off with a pair of sweatpants low on his hips. He's leaning back against the headboard, arm bent behind his head as he scrolls through something on his phone. That would be enough to stop my heart on a good day. But he also has a tray of candy and drinks set up, and the movie I missed the other night queued up on the screen across from the bed. The hot cocoa has finally come and is sitting there on a cart too. And now I am very sure he's been taken by aliens or another dimension and replaced with a double.

Honestly, I wish there was a way I could sneak and grab my phone, snap a photo, and send it to Liv and Kenz because someday when I do tell them about this—and we all know I will eventually cave—I want photographic evidence. Otherwise, there is no way they will believe this ever happened. That he is voluntarily hanging out with me and watching a historical romance movie, instead of I don't know, railing me hard over the chair or something. And now that image is in my head and my eyes are back on his body.

I take a few steps toward the bed and he glances up from his phone, smiling when he sees me tiptoeing my way toward my suitcase.

"Feel better?" he asks in a tone so soft it sends a shiver through me.

"Yeah. Warmer. Thanks." I glance up at him as I put my things away.

"Is this the right movie? The one we were supposed to watch the other night? You haven't watched it yet, have you?"

"Yeah, but I don't think you're going to like it much."

"Why not?"

I give him an incredulous little look, but he just raises his eyebrow at me in return.

"There's going to be a lot of thick English accents and pining, and wide shots of the English countryside with voiceovers about how she wondered what he was thinking of at that very moment. That kind of thing."

"And balls? Where they do that little coordinated dancing thing?"

"You're familiar with the genre?"

"My sister went through a Jane Austen phase when we were in high school. I saw enough."

"Jane Austen is not a phase," I say as I climb into the bed next to him, fluffing the pillows to support my back.

"I mean she's good, I think, but after all the pining you would think there would be some banging."

"There was banging. It just happened off page."

"Implied banging isn't the same as real banging."

"Thank you for that expert analysis."

"Is this going to have real banging?" He grabs a handful of M&Ms and pops a few into his mouth.

"Probably. The woman has an affair."

"An affair? Is that what you're into? Cheating?"

"I mean, if her wealthy absent husband doesn't love her or pay attention to her, and he's off having his own affairs..." I shrug.

"Can't they just get divorced?"

"They didn't get divorced back then."

"That sounds terrible."

"Lucky for you, you live in the modern era where you can have as many divorces as your heart desires."

"If I get married, I won't be getting divorced."

"No? You strike me as the type who would need a starter wife, then the wife he has the kids with, and then the younger model he trades her in for." I count them off on my fingers, and he raises a brow at me.

"Nah. If I meet a woman who can convince me walking down the aisle is a good idea, no way I'm letting her go."

"Fair enough. I better get an invitation to that event, because I will need to witness it with my own eyes to believe it."

"You'll be top of the list, Princess."

"Here." He pushes the tray toward me. "I didn't know what your favorite was, so I got a variety."

I take the tray and grab a few things off it, glancing at him as I do. This Easton, the one with none of the usual arrogance, the one just sitting here eating M&Ms and talking historical dramas with me. I might *like-him* like-him. Which sends a flag up at the same time little wings take flight in my stomach.

We watch the movie, but I honestly miss parts of it, too

distracted by him being next to me to care about what's happening on the screen. I'm trying to make sense of this whole night, above all, because when I agreed to this little hateship vacation with him I assumed we'd be having sex. And me taking a bath alone, and now sitting a chaste distance apart from him while we watch a movie is not in line with what I expected the Easton experience to be like.

When a sex scene starts on the screen, the awkwardness of us sitting here like this quadruples because I feel like it's a giant sign pointing back at us. I grab another piece of red licorice and then the sheet, pulling it over me and settling back against the pillows.

"You cold? I can kick the fire on," he grabs the controller for the electric fireplace.

"A little," I admit, starting to wonder if I'm going to have to be the one to make the first move. And then wondering whether or not I should, because I feel like I might get rejected. Maybe he's changed his mind. There is definitely a ton of gorgeous women around town, and he can have any of them, or all of them, rather than be spending his time with me.

His brow furrows and he stares at the fireplace controller, deciding what buttons he needs to push while the couple on the screen gets naked. I slide a little closer to him, trying to close the gap between us, and he glances at me as the fire flickers on, but he doesn't say anything and his eyes return to the screen.

I don't know what the most sexually frustrated I've ever been before this was, but having Easton Westfield half-naked in bed with me while a fictional couple has sex and he acts like I barely exist is competing for first place. And at this point, fuck it.

I turn to him and kiss him. He stiffens at first but then kisses me back, and I use that to get closer, rising onto my knees and running my hands over his shoulders. I'm begging him silently to do anything here to reciprocate. I'm not one of the jersey chasers, and I don't have their talent or ease of grace to seduce a guy like Easton. I'm well out of my league with him. And up until now, he's always taken the lead. Something he doesn't seem to have any interest in doing tonight. Just as I start to pull back though, he pulls me closer and drags me onto his lap until I'm straddling him.

I reach for the hem of my tank top, so I can pull it off and his hands grab my wrists, his eyes coming to mine. A soft pleading look in them that I don't recognize on his face.

"Don't."

"Don't?" I look at him confused.

"I want to go slow," he says quietly as he dots kisses along my jaw.

"You want to go slow?" Apparently, all I can do is repeat his words right now because I am wildly confused by everything he's saying.

"Yes. Slow. Do you normally fuck on the first date?"

"Occasionally," I admit, furrowing my brow as I study him.

"Well, I don't."

I start to laugh until the furrow in his brow deepens.

"We already fucked."

"We weren't on a date when it happened. Now we are."

"And you don't fuck on the first date?" I give him a look begging him to explain what the hell he is talking about.

"Right. I don't fuck on the first date, Princess. So if that's what you were hoping, I'm sorry to disappoint."

"Since when?" I ask, trying not to let too much of the exasperation out in my voice because I feel like he's fucking with me. That or he's really changed his mind. Because Easton is the king of fucking on the first date. In fact I think it's rare that Easton ever has a second date.

"Since I'm on a first date. That's what this is, yeah? What you agreed to when I asked if you wanted to try the hateship out." He honestly looks a tad hurt, and I'm taken aback a little by it.

"I guess it's a date. I didn't think you were serious about that. I assumed the hateship thing was just code for sex. You did say frenemies with benefits."

"No offense, but if I just want another hookup you'd be bottom of the list. Right above Mac and Liv."

"Wow. I guess at least I'm in good company."

"You did just imply I'm a whore."

"I didn't mean it that way. I just meant... you know what? This was probably ill-advised. The hateship thing. We should probably just forget it and try to focus on the project and have fun with our friends."

A stormy look flickers across his face, and something else I can't quite read.

"Yeah. Fuck that." He pauses the movie and turns to me. "I like you. I have fun with you. I want to spend time with you— away from the rest of our friends and without the excuse of a project. And I want you. You know that. I've told you how much I fucking want you. But I don't want this week to just be about that, okay?"

"You don't?" I stare at him, wondering what's happening and how to make it make sense.

"Do you? I mean if you're a secret nympho, you can tell me. I won't hold it against you. I'm already keeping secrets for you, so..." he smiles and shrugs.

I smile, but I shake my head. "I'm just confused. I feel like you're sending mixed messages."

"How so?"

"I mean we're watching a movie and eating candy, yes. But

you're also half naked and we're watching the movie in bed so..."

"We're in a hotel, watching the movie from bed is kind of the thing. And this is me over dressed because normally I sleep naked."

"Of course you do." I roll my eyes and he gives me a tight little smile.

"We both know that's the reason you agreed to this at all. It's not like you think I'm funny or smart." He smiles but it doesn't go to his eyes. I hate it and the prick of guilt I feel.

"You're actually quite funny, and as I'm learning on this project way smarter than I ever gave you credit for."

"And when you think about fucking me, you think 'god, he's so funny I just can't resist him, and the way he can crunch numbers is just so sexy'?" He raises his brow at me.

"I don't know. Maybe." I shrug.

"You know I can see when you look at me, right? Where your eyes go when you watch me?"

"Are you complaining that I objectify you?"

"Maybe."

"Are you feeling all right? Do you think it's possible you've been body-swapped or something?"

He bursts into laughter then, and I can't help but smile back because the man looks positively gorgeous when he's amused. When his laughter slows, he runs his hands down the sides of my arms in a way that lights up little sparks in their wake.

"I'm just saying we've got almost a week. I have a lot of ideas and a range of talents. We don't have to rush it."

I'm gonna add having the campus manwhore tell me I'm moving too fast to my list of life experiences I never thought I'd have.

"Okay." I start to pull away and move back to my side of the bed, but his hands grab my hips and pull me back down.

"I didn't say I was done kissing you though." He leans forward and nips at my lower lip.

I kiss him back, settling in his lap, letting my fingers trace over his shoulders.

"And you can go back to grinding on me again. Just because I'm not going to take you doesn't mean I don't wanna know how needy you are for it."

Fuck me.

Literally, all my mind can manage when the man talks like this.

"If you want to go slow, you can't talk to me like that."

"Oh, I can do both, Princess. I like torturing you."

"You're a sick man."

"And you like it." He kisses me for several more minutes before he puts distance between us again.

"All right. We have to finish the movie."

"The movie?" I ask, still a little dazed from the loss of his mouth on mine.

"I need to know what happens after they fuck. If she's gonna leave the husband and run away with him, or if she's just using him for the sex."

He hits the play button, and I climb off his lap. I curl up next to him and he wraps an arm around me like this is just a normal night for us. When I can think past how confused I am, I feel the little twist and flutter in my chest. Easton Westfield is cuddling with me and invested in a fictional romance, and I'm pretty sure I like it. I'll worry about what kind of problem that is tomorrow.

NINETEEN

Easton

We've all spent the day on the slopes with the exception of Liam and Wren. Liam was sitting it out as he's still doing some PT for his knee, and Wren wasn't interested in learning to ski. I'd tried to talk her into it, but she said she was going to hang out with Liam for a bit and then try to do some reading, and I hadn't wanted to argue with her.

I'd almost stayed with her, in the hopes of getting a few more hours alone, except it would have thrown up flags for our friends because I love skiing, and I had no good excuse not to go. Plus, I don't want to suffocate her. I just can't help knowing that every hour that ticks by is one less I'm going to have with her. It feels like sand in an hourglass running out, and I've already had so little time to convince her to begin with.

So now that we're sitting in the lobby overlooking the slopes having a post-day drink, I'm anxious to see what she's up to.

Having fun?

WREN

Yes. Liam and I did snow yoga and now I'm
getting some reading in. Curled up by the fire.
You having fun?

I smirk at the idea of her sweet little butt curled up on the couch in front of the fire reading a book. And all the things I could do to her.

"Hi! I couldn't help noticing you out on the slopes. You're good. Do you ski a lot?" A curvy brunette sidles up to the bar next to me, and I blink as I realize our friends have mostly moved to the other side of the room, busy pointing at something outside and discussing it while I've been daydreaming about Wren.

"Uh, yeah. It's a hobby when I have the time." I give her half a smile. I'm not interested, but I don't want to be rude. We'd decided to come to a different resort to ski for the day, and the guys had been giving me shit all afternoon about the temptation of ski bunnies.

The weird thing is, as I look at the woman, I don't register that she's gorgeous. That before I might have been very interested in going back to her room for a quick afternoon fuck, but as it stands, I have zero. There's only one woman who makes me want right now, and fuck if it isn't frightening me a little.

"Me too. I love it here. Especially this time of year. What are you drinking?" She eyes my glass.

"An old fashioned."

"I'll have what he's having." She points to my glass and motions to the bartender. Then her eyes flash back to me. "Anything else you're having this afternoon that I might like?"

Fuck.

"Yeah, I gotta get back to my friends. We're all here on a trip together so…"

Her hand goes to my arm, and she leans in a little, her smile widens, and her lashes lower as she slides her eyes over me.

"They won't miss you if you take a quick break, will they?"

I toss back the last of my drink to extricate my arm from her grip.

"Yeah, actually they probably will."

"Well, that's too bad. I could have made it worth your time." She flashes me another look and that's my cue to get the fuck out of here.

"Sorry to disappoint." I stand, grabbing my coat off the chair next to me, and return to my friends.

My phone dings with a message, and I pause to open it. A picture of me talking to the woman at the bar from across the bar pops up.

> WREN
>
> Looks like you are. Just give me a warning if you're coming back here? The yoga instructor was going to stop by in a bit to help me work on my form. He said he could help me with some new positions

I look up and glare at my friends. How are they this fucking fast with selling me out? Not that they know it. They all still looked engrossed in conversation, but obviously one of them is a spy, and I can narrow it down pretty well. When Mac flicks a look over in my direction, I know for sure.

> I'm the only one fucking helping you with new positions. She hit on me. I walked away, which your spy can confirm if you want to ask her

WREN

She just wanted me to be prepared. I'll cancel the yoga instructor then, I suppose...

She sends me a little wink emoji, and I know she's joking. I know she trusts me, and that adds another little spike of adrenaline to my system. Because this girl trusting me is like winning the championship. Like I have a second chance at it, and she thinks I deserve it this time.

"East?" Liv's voice startles me from my phone, and I tuck it away quickly, hoping she didn't see it.

"Yeah?" I look up at her, and she gives me a little smile, and I feel like I'm about to get the mom version of Liv.

"I have a big favor to ask."

"What's that?"

"Well, the rest of us were all talking and we kind of want to do our own thing for the evening. I guess Waylon planned a dinner and stuff with Mac. And Liam and I might do the same. Ben and Chelsea are going to some meet-up thing tonight too. Which kind of leaves Wren alone. It looks like you might have had other plans," her eyes flick over my shoulder to the brunette, a little frown forming before she looks back at me. "But do you think maybe you could keep her company? At least for a little while? I know she's not your favorite person, but maybe it's an opportunity for the two of you to try to find some common ground."

"No problem. I can take her out to dinner or something." I shrug.

"You don't mind?" Liv's eyes search mine, and I hope I'm not giving anything away.

"No, like you said. Opportunity for us to try to get along. We can talk sports if nothing else." I try to give what looks like a half-hearted smile, even though inside I'm grinning like a fucking asshole. Because now I have the perfect opportunity to take her out somewhere for real.

"Just be nice to her, okay? She's really exhausted right now, and I feel terrible that we do so much couple-y stuff without her. I don't want her to be too bummed."

"Oh, don't worry. I'll be very nice," I say before I can stop myself.

It must sound, exactly like I mean it because a little smile flits across Liv's face like she knows something I don't.

"All right. Well, I'm trusting you with one of my favorite people. Remember that."

"Yes, and I know you'd wield my QB like a blunt weapon if I fuck up."

"Look how smart you are." She grins and reaches up and pinches my cheek as I roll my eyes.

———

"Do I have Liv to thank for this dress again?" I ask as we're eating dinner.

"Yeah." She runs her hand over the material absently as she looks at it. "She brought it over tonight. Said that you were taking me out to dinner and knowing you it would be somewhere fancy."

"Interesting." If I didn't know better, I'd think Liv was trying to push us together.

"Fuck..." I mutter when I see my brother approaching our table. And I mentally double that fuck when I see he's got Xavier with him. Tobias is a top receiver in the NFL, and Xavier is on his defense. They make news for everything they do on and off the field, and whatever wild ass shit I can be accused of, they're ten times worse.

"What?"

"My brother is headed this way."

"Tobias?" And the way her eyes light up when she says his name makes the jealousy in my gut churn.

"That would be him." I love my brother, but he isn't the easiest person to be related to. The comparisons never end.

"Oh my god. I don't—I'm not—I'm gonna fangirl out." Her lashes flutter and she grins wide.

"What?" I look at her horrified.

"Your brother is fucking phenomenal," she gushes.

"I feel like you should have told me you had a thing for my brother before we fucked," I grump.

"I don't have a *thing*. I just—"

"East! I didn't know you were up here already. Thought you weren't coming until next weekend."

I stand and grab my brother's hand, throwing an arm around him and a quick pound on the back. I nod to Xavier, and he gives me a chin jerk.

"I came up with some friends. We're staying at the resort I mentioned to you, remember?"

"Oh yeah. The one you wanted the hookup on. How you liking it?"

"It's nice."

"Right? And the views are fucking awesome. Food's good too." He smiles, and then he notices Wren and turns to her. "I'm sorry. I'm being rude. You must be the girlfriend?"

He holds out his hand and she takes it, beaming at him like he's the best thing she's ever seen. I fucking hate it

"Just a friend, but it's nice to meet you." She somehow smiles even brighter and the 'just' feels like a gut punch even though I know it shouldn't.

He grins at her and then lets out a low laugh.

"*Just* a friend, eh? Brother, you are doing something wrong." He glances back at me and shakes his head.

"Oh, no. We're just up here with a group of friends. They're all coupled up though and East was nice enough to take me to dinner, so I didn't feel left out." She smiles, trying to make it sound like I'm the hero in this situation. Even though I'm really the villain because if I didn't have any self-control I'd be dragging her into a dark corner of this restaurant and fucking her up against a wall to remind her which brother she *really* likes.

"Oh yeah? That's nice of him." His eyes rake over her, and I feel my stomach clench. Because it's also rich, considering he doesn't do relationships himself, that he would give me shit for it. He looks back at me, studying me for a second.

"Well, if that's the case you two should come to my party tonight. We've got a big place we've rented and we're having a bunch of people over. Some of the other guys are in town too, taking a break now that the season's over."

"I don't know if we can—"

"Oh, that sounds fun!"

Wren and I both talk over each other, and I feel another little tight pull in my chest that she wants to go. I don't hate the idea generally. It'd be nice to see my brother for a bit even though he does irritate the hell out of me sometimes, and his parties are usually a fuck ton of chaos and fun. It's the idea of taking her there that makes me nervous.

Tobias laughs a little. "Well talk it over and then let me know. I'll text you the address. Some other people you know will be there."

I can guess what he means by that. So can Wren, apparently, by the way her eyes flick over to me and then back to Tobias. She gives him another bright smile, and he grins at her.

"Thank you for the offer," she says in a tone that sounds incredibly flirty to my jealous ears.

"Of course, sweetheart. Hope to see you there." He winks

at her and then he and Xavier nod and finish their exit from the restaurant.

She watches them walk away, all fucking dreamlike. There might as well be little hearts floating in her eyes. Like she's just seen her favorite movie star. I suppose for someone like her who cares almost as much about sports as she does movies, it's not much different.

"He's really nice. I expected him to be an asshole, you know? Given his reputation."

"He was being an asshole," I grumble.

"How?" She furrows her brow.

"He knows we're on a fucking date, and he was practically hitting on you."

"I don't think he was hitting on me..." She looks doubtful, but her eyes trail along the path he took out.

"He was." I take a sip of my drink and stare out across the restaurant.

"Well, we don't have to go if you don't want to. I just thought it sounded like your kind of scene, and I wouldn't mind going if you wanted to," she hedges, but I can tell that she's curious. Given the way she just fangirled out when he came up to the table and how much she loves the game, I feel like a jerk if I don't take her.

"We can go for a little bit, but his parties get wild as hell. More than what you can probably tolerate." I frown, remembering the last party of his I went to and trying to imagine Wren standing in the middle of it.

"Oh yeah? Sounds like a challenge." She wiggles her eyebrows.

I shake my head and smile at her. "Yeah. Yeah. Finish your dinner."

She picks up her fork and gives me a little devilish grin. And fuck, I really like this girl.

We've only been at the party for half an hour and a group of women has already adopted Wren as one of their own. They're teaching her some sort of dance and pouring shots for her, and somehow, I've become the one who's responsible, sipping on the same glass of whiskey and watching every move anyone makes around her.

"So just friends, huh?" Tobias comes up and leans on my shoulder, following my line of sight to Wren.

"I'm not good at relationships."

"That one looks like she is, so what are you doing?"

"You'd be surprised. She's not much for them either."

"And that's the challenge you like?"

"No. I'm not trying to change her. We're just... Hanging out for the trip."

"Yeah, your face when she said, 'just friends' definitely said you were *just* hanging out."

"Just mind your business." I shoot him a sideways glare.

"Sensitive. I see. Want to move to less sensitive subjects like football?"

"You know I don't."

"My season wasn't much better. Some years are just like that." He gives me a swift pat on the back.

"This was my last one. Right before the draft," I counter.

"You'll be fine. You've got the invite to The Combine. You can show them there that it was a one-off. I have faith in you. Besides, I wanna see you on that field across from me. Make our parents sweat over who they're going to root for."

"You know it'll always be their golden boy." I give him a little shake of my head before I take another sip of my drink.

I look up to see Wren doing some sort of ass-wiggling move that makes my mind blank out.

"Oh fuck. She's good at that. Really fucking good. You better go get your girl, or you're gonna lose her to one of these guys." He points to a group of his fellow players whose eyes are locked on her, and I feel the kick in my gut.

TWENTY

Wren

I DIDN'T EXPECT TO FIND MYSELF AT A PARTY WITH A bunch of NFL players and their entourage tonight, but holy hell is it fun. Everyone is so freaking nice, and the drinks taste like candy. It isn't all that wild yet though. I've only seen one couple fucking in a corner, and one person jumping naked into the heated pool, so I'm not entirely sure what East was worried about. Sometimes I think he thinks I'm more delicate than I am.

"Yes, oh my god! You are doing awesome. So much better than I can." One of the girls encourages me as she tries to teach me the dance they're doing.

"Easton. I didn't know you were here." A gorgeous brunette who had been dancing with me suddenly says, and I look up to see her putting her hands on his chest and eyeing him like he's the best thing she's seen all night.

I feel a swell of jealousy. I should have figured that these women would know him. It's his brother's party after all. But it still makes my stomach tighten a little to see it play out.

"Yeah. I'm here with my girlfriend." He points over her shoulder to me, and the description makes my eyes jump up to him.

"Oh! Shit. I'm sorry. I didn't know." She immediately removes her hands from him and looks sheepishly back at me.

I smile and shake my head, letting her know it's okay. And then my eyes float back to his. He smiles but his jaw is tight.

"What's wrong?" I ask when I make my way over to him.

"Nothing." He shakes his head and takes another sip of his drink, but his brow furrows in a sexy way that makes me want to kiss him.

"Think there's somewhere we can sneak off alone?" I whisper and playfully raise a brow at him.

"Considering how massive this place is? Yeah. But I thought you were dancing?" His eyes glance around like he's watching for something.

"I just want you for a few minutes." I slide my hand up his chest, and he looks down at me, studying me for a minute.

Then he takes my hand, threading his fingers through mine and we make our way down the hall, down some steps, and down another hall until it spills out to a large corridor. This basement seems to have a never-ending set of doors and rooms, and I wonder briefly what it must be like to have a space for everything in your own home. To be able to get lost in your own house.

He picks one of the doors and opens it, and it reveals a little home movie theater. Black walls, a huge screen, and couches tiered up a set of large steps make the place cozy. It even has a little popcorn machine and bar at the back.

"Wow. This would make movie nights better at our place." I step in and look around.

He follows me but still looks unamused.

"What's wrong?" I pull him down onto a couch next to me.

"Nothing's wrong."

"Something is definitely wrong. You've been grouchy since we got here."

"I just... fucking don't know."

"Hmm. I can guess." I wrap my arms around his waist and trail my fingers up his spine, and he relaxes the tiniest bit before he goes taut again.

"What?" He looks up at me abruptly, like he's worried about what I'll say.

"Don't take this the wrong way, but you're used to being the hottest, richest, most talented guy in the room. You're used to having all the attention on you. And here... it's a little more divided." I try not to smile when I say it, but my lips waver the tiniest bit, and I bite down on my lower one to try to stop.

"You think I'm that much of an asshole, huh?"

"No. I think you're just used to a certain amount of female attention."

"Maybe... I think the bigger problem is the only female attention I want is divided between me and my brother."

A laugh pops out of me before I can stop it, and it's the wrong thing because the furrow in his brow deepens.

"You can't be serious. Your brother is hot. And his talent is a huge turn-on for sure—"

"This pep talk sucks," he interrupts me, eyeing me like I'm treading on thin ice.

"But you are more talented. He just has more years on you. It's not a fair comparison. And even if I had a choice, you are the one I would pick to take home every single time."

"Why?" He gives me a stormy look, and I can tell the question is a genuine one. I can't honestly believe I have to answer it.

"Because. You're clever and funny. And I like the way you argue with me. The way you don't give up or back down. And I think Liv was right, underneath it all you are kind of a softy."

"A softy? Gee, thanks." He rolls his eyes off to the side and finishes his drink before setting it down.

"I mean that you're sweet when you want to be. It's a good thing. It's a surprising thing, but a good thing." I smile at him, and climb into his lap, kissing him softly.

"I thought you liked me because I was an asshole and good at making you come," he mutters against my lips.

"I like you because I like *you*," I say, kissing him no sooner I say the words because I realize what it sounds like and *fuck,* I have had one too many shots if I'm confessing *that.* It doesn't work though because he pulls away and runs his fingers under my chin, making me meet his eyes.

"You like me, huh?" A little smirk pulls at the corner of his lips, and his eyes dance with something I can't quite read. "Is this a like-me like-me, or like a I'll-tolerate-you like me?"

The way he looks at me makes the butterflies in my chest flutter and twist. I need to be so careful with this man. I need to remember who he is and what he is to me; a friend, a fun time, really good sex, but not an anchor. If I don't remember that, I'm going to get swept away and that's something I can't afford. This hateship is for this trip, while we live in this alternate winter wonderland in the mountains, and I need to remember that.

And I know the perfect way to remember. My hands go to his belt, and I start undoing it and then the button and his zipper, all while he holds my jaw, and his brow goes higher with each step.

"I really like certain parts of you. Certain parts I might even get on my knees for." I try for a vixenish grin, but he just holds my gaze.

"Are you trying to distract me from the fact that you just told me you liked me with a blow job?"

"Is it working?"

"You just offered to put your mouth on me. Something I haven't been able to stop thinking about. What do you think?" He gives me a little grin. "But I don't want you to do something just to distract me."

"I want this." I pull at his waistband and start to lower myself from his lap. "So tell me to stop if you'd rather not."

He loosens his hold on my chin and lets me go, as I try to make the trip to my knees as graceful as possible in heels I don't normally wear. I slide between his legs and pull him out, stroking him once because he's already hard for me. Something that gives my ego a little kickstart, because being at a party like this with so many gorgeous women really puts you in your place. Especially around men like East who can have their pick.

I lick the little bead of precum that forms at the tip and tease him with my tongue before I look up at him again. His eyes search me, looking for something, and I give him a little half smile. His fingers slide along the edge of my jaw and his thumb runs over my lower lip.

"I like you, Princess. A lot," he says quietly.

I have no idea what to say to that or even how to feel, so I take him in my mouth instead. I run my tongue along him and use my hand to help work him over. Because he's even bigger than I remember, and I always feel like I'm out of my depth with him. I glance up and his eyes are closed, a small wave of relief washes over me at not having him watch me for a minute. To just be able to watch him as he rolls his lip between his teeth and a low moan rumbles out of his chest.

If you had asked me if I would ever get on my knees for this man, I would have laughed so fucking hard, and yet here I am. Because I want to be. Because he's oddly sweet to me, giving me things that I don't even know I want until he does. Because our hateship does feel a little real even if I want to deny it. A thought that spurs me on and makes me pick up my pace with him.

"Oh fuck..." he groans as his hands thread through my hair. "Christ. Your mouth, the way you use your tongue like that. My god. You're so fucking good."

He's found his words and they melt through my body, making every inch warm with want for him, and pooling low as I take him a little deeper.

"Fuck, fuck, fuck. Little bird... Fuck. You weren't supposed to know. I call you that in my head sometimes instead of Princess, but I know you hate it when I call you names. Jesus, fuck, I can't think straight. I'm sorry."

I stifle the little laugh of amusement at his stream of consciousness. We can talk about the nickname later, but I think I might like it. I might even like the way he calls me Princess. I might like everything about this man. I use my hand to stroke him a little more roughly.

"Yes. That's fucking perfect. Harder, just like that. Fuck. You suck like a fucking goddess. So *so* fucking good." His fingers tighten in my hair, and I suck a little harder.

His breathing is heavier and his breath stutters as I run my tongue over him again. The sounds and feel of him make me want him more than I think I've ever wanted anyone. I just want to make him come so hard he can't forget it. Can't forget *me*. So I take him even deeper, letting my tongue cradle him in the process.

"Fuck, Princess. You take me so fucking deep, and I can't. I can't like this. You've..." His body tenses under me as the words are ripped from his mouth, and I use my hand to stroke him faster until I can feel him pulse. I feel the warmth of him fill my mouth and taste him on my tongue. I swallow and wipe the corner of my mouth, taking a second to try and right myself.

When I look up at him, he almost doesn't even look like himself. Some combination of stupefied and surprised, his normal cockiness stripped down to the bare bones. He tucks himself back into his pants just before he leans forward and pulls me up into his lap.

"That was so fucking good. Good isn't even the right word. I don't have one. I'm not kidding when I tell you I can't remember ever coming that hard. You fucking kill me." He looks at me like he's never really seen me before.

His hand cups my jaw and his thumb swipes at the corner of my mouth where I'm sure I smeared my lipstick. But I don't care. Just hearing him talk to me like this is all I want.

"Say something. You're too quiet and you're worrying me. What are you thinking?" He studies me like he always does.

"I need you to touch me."

"Need me?" His voice sounds raw like he can't quite get the words out.

"Please?" I ask rising up onto my knees.

It's the only word he needs to hear before his hand is sliding up the inside of my leg, his eyes following it. They flicker over my face before he slides his fingers over the center of my panties, finding them soaked. His breath stutters and his eyes meet mine, a bright but questioning look in them.

"You have to take these off for me," he voices the pained request.

I stand on wobbling legs kicking my pumps off and to the side before I pull the panties down and set them next to the shoes. I slide a leg on either side of him again, straddling him. His fingers climb slowly up my leg again, a tortuously slow pace like he's unsure if he'll get the same reward twice. He raises a brow before he touches me again, and I smile at him. His fingers test me, tentatively, a whisper-light touch on my core.

"Fuck me. You're fucking soaked." He looks at me. "What has you like this? This place?"

"You. Having you in my mouth. The way you talk to me. The words you use. I want you so much."

"Me?" He looks utterly shocked at that. Like I've said the wildest thing imaginable.

TWENTY-ONE

Easton

"Me?" I ask, my fingers just barely skimming her again.

"Yes," she whispers, nodding and drawing her gorgeous fucking lip into her mouth.

"God damn, Princess. You're coating my fingers." I part her and tease her clit with my thumb, and she closes her eyes. "I want to taste you so bad."

Her eyes flick open, a hint of worry in them. "Not now, but I want you to touch me. I need your hands. Need you to get me off. Please."

Fuck. I will do whatever she asks. However she wants. Her words twist me into fucking knots like they always do when she talks to me like this. When she's raw and honest. When she's telling me it's *me* she wants. But I have to know how she tastes. I slide my thumb into my mouth while she watches me. And she tastes perfect, just like I dreamed she would. It makes me want her that much more. Wishing I could have her body in every way imaginable, make her come so hard that she needs me to put her back together again.

"Okay. But first, you gotta kiss me. I want to know what *we* taste like."

Her lashes flutter like she might protest, but she leans in, bracing herself against my shoulders, and I grab her. Pulling her down into my lap and taking her mouth with my own. I'm so fucking ravenous for her that I'm sloppy when I kiss her, my tongue sliding over her lower lip and into her mouth before I pull her lower lip with my teeth. I love the taste of her, the taste of me, of all of it on our tongues. Her sweet fucking body rocking in my lap as she kisses me.

I pull back, and slide my hand back between her legs, cupping her and then swiping my thumb over her clit again as she rolls her hips.

"Oh fuck..." she moans, her eyes closing.

"You take whatever you need. You deserve it," I whisper to her as I slide two fingers inside her, her muscles contracting around them as I do it. I pump them in and out of her slowly as she does it.

"Ride it out. I want to hear every little breath and moan. You're so fucking sexy. Always. But like this... fuck, Wren. I need so much more of it."

"You were right about being good with your hands. I should have let you touch me all those times you threatened to..." she says, nearly breathless.

I smirk at the compliment. "Yeah, well now you know. So use that knowledge to your advantage in the future, yeah?"

"Are you this good with your mouth?" She opens one eye and smiles, in between heady breaths. And holy fuck. This girl. I need her.

"You can ride it whenever you want and find out."

"Fuck. I love the way you talk."

"Yeah? Wait until you hear the things I say when you ride my cock again."

A little breathy gasp escapes her.

"You like thinking about that?" I ask. Because, fuck, I do. I want it. Need it. The second she says.

"Yes," she whispers, her eyes fluttering closed. "I'm so close though."

"What do you need?"

"Faster. Rougher. Please."

"I love the way you say, please." I smile. "Can you do me a favor, if I say please?"

"What's that?" she whispers.

"Say my name when you come. I want to hear you say it like this."

Her eyes flutter open and meet mine. They're heavy and her lids are low. So-fucking-sexy and undone like this.

"Please," I add.

She gives me a little nod as she closes her eyes again, and I give her what she asked for, giving her clit rougher strokes as I pump my fingers in and out of her at a faster pace.

"Oh, please. Just a little more. There," she sighs and then gives a little gasp when I hit her at just the right rhythm.

"Easton... Fuck. Easton... Please," she repeats my name over and over again as her climax hits her. And I just watch her, dumbstruck because I feel something splitting as she says it. Ripping me open in a slow meticulous fashion with each repeat, and I'm asking for it. Craving it until I don't know who she's turning me into.

I watch her come down from the high, her breath coming in more even beats and her eyes refocusing on the present moment. She slides off my lap and curls her legs under her on the couch next to me, and we sit in the quiet for a moment.

"Do you want to go back up?" she asks, at last, nodding toward the party we'd left behind.

"No. I think I'm good."

Any other girl and I'd be dying to go back out. I wouldn't want to talk. I'd want to go party. Have more to drink. Maybe even find another woman. But with Wren, I just want more of her.

"Ah. Okay." She smiles and reaches down for her shoes and underwear on the floor.

"We probably need to get back. It's supposed to snow tonight."

"And we probably need to come up with a cover story that's believable for where we were today." She smirks at me, and I love it.

WHEN WE GET BACK TO THE ROOM, SHE PULLS ME IN behind her and kisses me against the wall, giggling and running her hands over my chest.

"Are you sure? You don't want to rail me over the couch or something?"

"I'm sure. I told you we're supposed to be taking things slow. This is only our second date."

She rolls her eyes. "You're no fun. But fine! Can our second date include some of that chocolate cake I just saw being wheeled into the room down the hall because it looks amazing, and I feel like I need to eat something after all those shots?"

"Yeah, we can get you some cake. I'll order it in a minute." I smile at her because I can't remember a time when I saw her as happy and carefree as she is now. And the ice-cold organ in my chest is ridiculous enough to hope I'm part of the reason for it.

"All right. And you're sure you don't want to take a shower

with me?" she offers, looking back over her shoulder as she takes her coat off. "It can be hands-off."

"We already tried that once. We know how that ended—with me inside you. And again, *slow*, Princess."

"You're so mean. Making me shower alone."

"Hurry, and then I can get one after you before the cake gets here." I give her a soft pat on the butt, and she hurries to the bathroom.

TWENTY-TWO

Wren

WE'VE SETTLED INTO COMPANIONABLE SILENCE, watching the beginning of a horror movie while we wait for dessert. Room service finally rings the door, and he gets up to answer it looking fine as fuck. The long lines of his muscular back dip down to where they meet the top of his sweatpants and the curve of his ass and the way they hug him make me want to rip them off him. Because this is who I am now apparently. At least who I am around him—it's sex and parties and cake all the time. I want to feel guilty for it as my mind drifts back to the bar, and school, and all the things I should be doing, but the indulgence is fun.

There's another blood-curdling scream on the screen, and I look up as East returns to hand me a piece of cake, watching as yet another woman falls victim to the serial killer's knife.

"You'd think they'd learn," I mutter.

But as I take a bite of the cake I'm distracted again. This

cake tastes like fucking magic. Like they stuffed rainbows and stardust inside when they made it and then wrapped it in chocolate ganache and cakey goodness.

"Jesus Christ. If you moan like that, I can't watch the movie," Easton mutters as he sits back down on the bed, watching me as I go to take another bite.

"You need to taste it. It's amazing. Like quite possibly the best thing I've ever tasted."

"Considering you tasted me tonight; I'm feeling a little wounded."

"Okay, rivals the best thing I've ever tasted."

"Better."

"But honestly, I think this might be better than sex. They might not have oversold it with that name."

"I doubt that."

"Taste it." I hold out the plate and fork for him.

He cuts a bite off and slides it into his mouth. And tilts his head back and forth.

"It's not bad. Definitely not better than good sex though. The way you made me come tonight? About a hundred times better than that cake."

I take another bite and look at him. "I don't know. I'd like to believe that, but..."

"I promise you. I don't know why this is hard for you to believe. Haven't you had good oral before?"

"Meh." I shrug. "Every time I've tried it, it just sort of felt vaguely like a sloppy sponge being bandied about down there."

Easton coughs, chokes, and then bursts out into laughter.

"Christ Wren. You've got to stop fucking these randos you keep meeting for hookups. If that's your opinion."

"Please. I would not let some random asshole go down on me. But I've had boyfriends before. Thank you."

"You mean these guys had time and repeated attempts and still couldn't improve?"

"I don't know that it was their fault. I think maybe it's not for me."

"Oh fuck, you can't do that, Princess. You know you can't."

"What?"

"Lay it down like a challenge, when you know how bad I want between your thighs. I'm trying to be good tonight. Do the date thing. I like our little dessert and movie thing we have going." He gives me a pained look.

I laugh and shake my head. "Okay. Pretend like I didn't say anything. Just watch the movie."

He looks at me for a moment longer and then reluctantly turns his head back to the screen.

I try to follow the dialogue between the characters, but I've lost the plot. And now in my mind, all I can think about is what he would feel like. Whether I might actually like it with him. Whether I could relax enough to really enjoy it.

I take another bite of cake, closing my eyes to taste it without the sight of gory blood from the screen, but it's replaced by thoughts of him and his tongue.

"Wren." My name is a rough protest ripped from his throat and my eyes pop open to see him staring at me.

"What?"

"The moaning. *Fuck.*" His pale green eyes are practically burning.

"Sorry. I didn't mean to. It's the cake." I smile at him, but I don't get an answering smile in return. "What's wrong?"

"How bad I want to compete with a piece of cake."

The laughter tumbles through me, and I have to set my fork down with how hard it hits me. "Very funny, East."

"What if we go slow? I'll talk to you for as long as you want first. You can tell me when or not at all. We can see if it's something you like or not," his voice has switched from funny friend I watch horror movies with back to incredibly dangerous man who I can't resist.

"Do I get sex if it doesn't work?"

"I will do anything you want if you let me have a taste of you."

Damn he's good. So good. He has a reputation for a reason though, right? A reputation that is sitting next to me in a luxury hotel suite on 1000 thread-count sheets begging to be used. Except if this goes badly, it is definitely going to sour our hate-ship. Easton has a big ego, but it has recently created craters that are visible if you look hard enough. I don't want to add to that.

"I'm worried if I don't like it, it's going to make things awkward. And I don't want to fake things with you," I say quietly, staring down at the bed.

"I don't want you to fake anything. I won't take it person-ally. If you don't like it, it's fine. Give me a shot? You just eat your cake, slowly. I bet by the end of it, I'll have you wet and then you can decide."

A hard bargain to say no to, so I'm definitely not going to. But I still can't help the whisper of apprehension that runs through me.

"Okay. We can try."

He kneels on the bed next to me and rearranges some pillows while I watch. He's just a mess of muscles; abs, arms, traps. You name it, he has it. Sometimes it's hard to believe he's mortal. I feel another well of anxiety wash through me that I'm going to let this gorgeous man down, so I take another bite of cake.

He smiles and slides behind me on the bed, still on his knees as his hands run under the fabric of the robe I put on after my shower, and he gently slides it off my shoulders. His fingers push my hair to the side, and his lips go to the tender skin at the nape of my neck.

"I know you're trusting me tonight. I hope you know I don't fucking take that for granted. I just want you so much. Want to give you what you need." His lips explore my shoulders and neck as he talks, his fingers sliding over my skin and inching my robe further down. I'm completely naked underneath and nervous about being stripped bare for him again but wanting more from him makes me stupid. Makes me want to give him every little thing he wants.

He pulls the robe down further, and I put the fork down, sliding my arms out of it. His hands still, and I can feel the weight of his eyes on me as he takes a breath.

"Fuck. Every part of you is more beautiful than the last. I need copies of all those photos of you. You think you'd let me have some now?"

"Maybe." I smirk.

"Some day when I've earned it, and you ride my cock again... I can't wait to watch you. We could spend a whole afternoon doing that."

His hand skims down over my breast and his thumb flicks over my nipple. I close my eyes and take another small bite of cake, and honestly, already it's hard to stay focused on it rather than him.

He leans down further, his lips nearly touching my ear, "And I will earn it. Every little thing you give me. Every breath, every moan, every single time you say my name."

Fuck me.

Again, I know the boy has a reputation for a reason but I'm literally not built to withstand this. I'm ready to cave to anything he wants, and it's only been a minute. I reach for the fork again, taking another little bite of cake because I need to buy some time.

"Seriously," I mumble around the bite, trying my best to deflect. "I need to know how they make this frosting. It is a-fucking-mazing. You're missing out."

He lets out a wordless laugh, one that tells me he knows exactly what I'm doing, and he doesn't care. His hands drift down over my spine and around my ribs, kissing my shoulder again.

"Yeah?" he asks. "Then let me taste it again."

I go to cut him a bite.

"No, just the frosting. Just dip your finger in and let me taste it."

I hesitate for half a second before I do what he wants. Because Easton is convincing if nothing else. I glance over my shoulder at him as I offer him the frosting on my finger, and he takes it into his mouth. He sucks the frosting off and swirls his tongue over the tip of my index finger, flattening it and running it over the pad.

I close my eyes and go to pull my hand back, but his fingers tighten around my wrist, his tongue sliding over my finger again. He's very fucking clever because it's nearly impossible not to imagine his tongue working those same patterns over other places on my body.

"East," I whisper at last, and he releases his grip.

"You're right. It's good," he says softly, his lips at my throat again, kissing me and running his mouth over my delicate skin. "But I'd rather taste you."

A little gasp pops out of my mouth when he hits a particularly tender spot on my neck, and his hands dig into my hips as he nips at me in the same spot. I press my thighs together, trying to quell the need for him.

"You need it rougher? Am I being too careful with you?" he whispers the question out loud like he's made a new discovery, his tone low and fascinated. And fucking *hell*. I am fucked.

His fingers thread through my hair and he pulls my head back further, exposing more of my neck to him. His teeth graze me again, and another small gasp comes loose before I can stop it. I can already feel my whole body begging for more of him, more of his mouth, more of his hands, more of him anywhere he wants to touch.

"I can be rough if that's what you need. Is that what you want?"

"I want *you*."

"Touch yourself for me and let me taste."

I slide my hand between my legs, realizing I'm wetter than I thought and bring my fingers up again. He licks them, repeating the same ritual as before.

A gritted, "Fuck," leaves his mouth before he lets my wrist go again.

"Yeah. You definitely taste better. I want that every day if you'll let me."

I close my eyes and take a breath, trying to find the ground again because he makes me feel so unraveled, I can barely think straight.

"Let me try? I'll make the world fade for you for a little while," he whispers.

"Yes," I agree so fast I sound desperate. Probably because I am. That's what he does to me.

He moves the pillows behind me and has me lie back, shifting me up the bed. His eyes rake over me as he slides down, settling between my thighs. And just the sight of him there makes me wetter, makes me want him more.

He kisses a trail over my stomach, beneath my belly button and his fingers part me, gently stroking my clit until I can feel the edges of an orgasm start to form. His kisses trail a pattern back and forth over my skin, coming closer and closer to where his fingers stroke me until he stops abruptly. Moving down and kissing the insides of my thighs instead, his breath is warm against my skin, and the rhythm of his fingers slows.

"Why?" I whimper, and I don't even care how pathetic I sound. He's that fucking good already.

"Because if it's the only time you let me, then I'm taking my time."

"I will let you whenever you want. Just... please."

"Do I get a pinkie swear on that?" he teases.

"East!" I growl at him in frustration.

He laughs, and I briefly imagine whether or not the time behind bars would be worth it before his lips press against my skin again, his tongue dragging over every sensitive nerve ending as he coaxes me back to the edge of my orgasm.

"Fuck! You are so good at that," I mutter, and I know at some point I'm going to regret inflating this rich boy's ego any further than it already is but right now I don't care. Right now, I just care that his mouth is on me, and he is expert-level at using his tongue.

"Swear?" he asks.

"I swear."

"Good."

His tongue works my clit with punishing dexterity, and I fail to understand how everyone before him was so fucking bad at it when he makes it seem so easy. When my body just does whatever he wants, apparently. He takes several long slow licks of me then, dragging his tongue, making me arch off the bed and curl my fingers into the sheets.

"You're gonna let me taste you every fucking day from here on out. Because the way you moan like this, the way you fucking whimper for me. I need it, Princess. I need you like this."

Then he picks up his pace, kissing, licking, sucking, and using his fingers to work every inch of me over. And if I had sensible thoughts at this moment, I would probably be embarrassed by how feral I'm acting under his touch. But anything sensible left my mind the second he put his mouth on me.

"East, please. Please. A little more," I beg him, as my fingers run through his hair.

He does as I ask, and it sends me careening over the edge. Sparks of liquid pleasure blooming and spreading out from my body, until every inch of me feels like I can just melt into oblivion. I almost think my heart stops and melts along with it for a second until I feel it beat again in my chest as I take a deep breath, trying to come back down to earth from whatever astral plane he's put me on.

I wonder for a brief minute—almost out loud before I stop myself—if this is why so many women like rich fuckboys like him. They have nothing to do but sit around and hone their craft, and maybe that's why he's so damn good at it. Why girls don't mind fucking him two at a time, because honestly, he could probably manage it.

I'm still in my thoughts when I realize he's come up beside me, his eyes studying me as his fingertips run circles over my stomach.

"So, at least better than before?" he muses, a little smirk forming on his lips.

"Yes, even better than the cake. You win." I smile back at him.

"Thank god. The shame of losing out to cake might have been more than I could take."

I laugh as I study his face, he's so damn pretty it hurts and it's hard to believe that a guy like him exists let alone any of the other factors tonight.

I roll to my side my fingers going to the elastic on his sweatpants. I give him a flirty smile, but he doesn't answer it, and his hand stills mine.

"No. I meant it when I said I just wanted to hang with you for a bit. I shouldn't have pushed you for more. You just... fuck... you are so sexy, Wren."

When his eyes meet mine, I want to kiss him. I want to confess how much he makes me *want*. How much I think I might really like him despite all the reasons I shouldn't. But I can't make this messy. We have a make-or-break project together. Our friend group doesn't need any drama. And neither of us do relationships, which doesn't leave us anywhere to go. I can't let myself fantasize about what could be in a different reality.

"Are you sure?" I ask.

"I'm sure," he leans over and kisses my forehead in such a tender way I'm a little taken aback by it.

"Okay," I agree, not wanting to argue with him when we're having such a fantastic night.

"Be right back." He hops off the bed.

I watch him walk to the bathroom and I can hardly believe he's real. Hardly believe that any of this is actually happening. But he is, it is—too real. And I desperately need to remember who he is, who I am, because the games we play, they make me forget and I can't afford to forget.

TWENTY-THREE

Easton

THAT MORNING WHEN I SEE HER SPRAWLED OUT ON OUR bed, her hair messed, and a little smile on her face in her sleep, I know I need her. I have no idea how I can convince her to take me seriously, but where there's a will, there's a way, right?

I climb out of bed slowly, doing my best not to wake her, and grab my phone on the way to the bathroom. There are several texts in the group chat discussing breakfast and plans for the day. I'm a jealous asshole who wants more of her time, so I fire off one that says that she's hungover and needs some more time in bed this morning. I promise to get her hydrated and conscious by lunch. Then I send a text to the butler to bring breakfast and hop in the shower.

The food arrives a few minutes after I get out of the shower, and I carry a mug of coffee over to her side of the bed. She stirs, and I press a kiss to her forehead.

"Wake up, Princess," I whisper.

Her eyelashes flutter and she slowly opens her eyes and sits up, pressing the sheet to her chest. I hold out the mug of coffee, and she takes it from me, a lock of her hair tumbling down the side of her face.

"Coffee in bed? You are my hero." She gives me a lopsided grin.

"Anytime you want."

"What time is it?" She frowns because this girl has no chill. The second her brain kicks in she starts worrying about what time it is and what she needs to do.

"Late. But don't worry. I already texted the group and told them you were a little hungover and needed some extra time. I promised to have you patched up by lunch."

"You told them you were going to take care of me? That's gonna ring an alarm somewhere." She laughs.

I know she truly means it as a joke, but it cuts a little.

"I assured them that there would be coffee, electrolytes, and pancakes in your future." I nod toward the table where breakfast is already set up. "You want to eat there, or you want it in bed?"

"I can get up. I just need to get clothes." She sets the coffee down and stands. And fuck with the morning light pouring in through the windows, in nothing but a little lace pair of panties she looks fucking edible. It takes all my willpower not to drag her back down in bed and make her come on my tongue again this morning. But I can be a fucking adult. I can take care of her.

"Here." I grab one of my shirts and toss it to her.

She looks down at it in her hands, and smiles at it. "Thanks."

She pulls it over her head and grabs her coffee, and we sit down at the table.

"Are you hungover? I lied because I wanted you to be able

to sleep in. But I was a little worried after all the shots you were doing last night. I got you a smoothie that's supposed to help with hangovers in case." I nod to it.

"Not too bad. I think the cake helped." She grins as she grabs a few pieces of fruit and puts them on her plate next to the pancakes that are already there, and then takes a few sips of the smoothie.

"You and your magic cake." I shake my head as I drink some of my coffee.

"I mean between the magic cake and your magic tongue; I think I had the best sleep I've had in a long time."

I raise my brow at the compliment.

"Good. You need your rest. Because it sounds like from the group text the girls are gonna run you ragged all day, and then you're gonna have to come back here and let me fuck you ragged. So, I suggest eating accordingly." I wink at her before I look back down at my phone.

A little choked laugh comes out of her, "I don't think I'll ever get used to the way you talk."

"Because I'm honest about how much I want to fuck you?"

"You're very blunt, yes."

"But you like it."

"Yes." A little blush tinges her cheeks as she takes a bite of her pancakes.

"Good. We can play that game later. See how blunt I can be and how hard I can make you blush."

"Okay, stop making me think about sex, or I won't be able to eat breakfast." She shoots me a little warning glare, and I grin at her.

She shakes her head and takes another bite and a long sip of her coffee. "So what are they planning for us?"

"I guess the girls have plans to go on some snowshoeing hike this afternoon. And then they want to have a girl's night and a guy's night. All of us going out and hitting some of the bars and clubs in town."

"But in separate groups?"

"That's what it sounded like. Liv, I think is worried you'll be feeling left out."

"Yeah. That sounds like her. She's sweet like that."

"We should get some work done on the project today too if there's time. I was thinking—what if we do a grand reopening? Once we try some of the things we're planning with the new menu and the broader beer selection. We can reintroduce people to the place. We can get some celebrities to come and push the reopening a little that way."

I can see the wheels and cogs moving as she considers the suggestion, and she nods.

"It sounds great, but what celebrities do you anticipate coming? I mean if we get you guys to come and maybe sign some balls or jerseys, that would definitely get the attention of the college football crowd, but they already know it's a hangout for you all."

"I can ask my brother. He knows a few of the guys who play for the Denver Rampage. If they came it might draw a different crowd."

"Shit, I mean yeah. If he came... people would go nuts to see him. But you think he'd do that? Can we even afford his fee?"

"He's my brother, so yes, he'd do it if I asked."

"I don't want you calling in favors you're uncomfortable with though. And you didn't seem thrilled with him yesterday."

"We have a complicated relationship, yeah. But he's my brother. He'll do it and I don't mind asking. Remember, I want the interview too."

"Okay, let's do it. That's a lot to plan though. We'll have to budget for it and see how quickly we can get the new orders in.

Then pick a date that works... should we time it with the hockey playoffs you think, or avoid them?"

"We'll have to think about it. Maybe not day-of but keeping it during the season might get you a little boost of business after the event. We should put a couple more big screens up too."

"That's going to be expensive." She winces.

"I've got it."

"East, you've already paid for so much lately. This room for starters, and I really feel guilty that I can't contribute more to this bar project. If I had more time maybe I could figure it out but..."

"You contribute more every day than I will by buying some TVs. You're the brains and the passion behind the place. You've kept it going all this time, what, pretty much single-handedly, right?"

"I mean Tom and Tammy help out a lot."

"But running it. I don't guess your grandfather is much help these days with the books and orders and all of that."

"No, not like he used to be."

"So take credit for it. And don't worry about what I'm contributing."

"But I want to pay you back somehow. If the marketing works and business picks up, maybe I can do some sort of repayment plan."

And I know she's proud. I know she doesn't want handouts and help, which makes this hard because all I want to do is help her. Make her life easier. Give her some chance to relax and enjoy things.

"If that's what you want, but honestly, it's just money. I have it, and I don't mind spending it."

"I know. You're very generous. And I appreciate it, a lot. I wish there was some way to show you." She stops and looks up at me, something in her eyes I can't quite read.

I smile back at her and then return my eyes to my phone, pretending to be interested in the stocks information that I have in front of me. But in reality, I want to confess to her why I'm so generous with her. Why I'd give her almost anything she wants.

"Really? I gave you the perfect opening..."

I look up and she's smirking at me.

"What?" I ask.

"That was the perfect opportunity for you to say something about showing my appreciation." She raises her brow expectantly.

"That sounds like a dick thing to say."

"Yeah, but I like when you're a dick." She slides the tines of her fork between her lips and runs her tongue over them.

"Princess, don't fucking tease me this early in the morning. I'm trying to let you recover from your hangover."

"I'm not teasing." She stands up and rounds the table, kneeling down in front of my chair. Her fingers run up my thighs, and her eyes drift up to mine in question.

"This isn't fair. I was gonna drag you back to bed. Fuck you with my tongue for an hour or two, and I told myself not to. To let you eat breakfast and now you're fucking down here on your knees."

"I have to thank you somehow, right? For how good you are to me. For getting me breakfast and coffee. And what a waste of more time alone if we don't use it." She raises her eyebrow and palms me through my sweats, where I'm already hard for her.

"Fuck..." I reach down and run my fingertips along her jaw, and she turns and kisses my hand, running her tongue along the pad of my thumb. "You're not playing fair."

"Just playing your games." She shrugs, and her hands go to my waistband a questioning look in her eyes.

"Fuck yes, but I'm putting you on your back for another

hour after this. I wanna hear you say my name again while you come on my tongue."

"Deal." She smirks as she pulls me out and slides her hand along me, her thumb gently teasing the underside as she licks her way down the length of me.

"Fuck, you are so fucking beautiful. And the way you fucking touch me, makes my heart fucking stop, Princess. It's that good." I thread my fingers through her hair, brushing it out of her face in the process, still messy from having been thoroughly fucked last night.

She grins before she takes me into her mouth, and her tongue swirls around the tip of my dick. And just when she goes to take me deeper, there's a loud knock at the door. She pulls back abruptly and we both glance over at it.

"We could just ignore it," she whispers.

"Yeah... but who would be knocking?" I unthread my fingers from her hair.

Another knock. "Wren? It's us. We've come to rescue you from your hangover." It's Mac's voice at the door.

"Fuckkkkk," she whines quietly, standing up quickly looking like she might combust from panic.

I pull my sweatpants back up and stand with her. "It's fine. Don't worry. You're supposed to be hungover and a mess anyway."

She glances over at me with an incredulous look and then down where my cock is still tenting the fuck out of my pants, raising her eyebrow in question

"I'll start thinking unsexy thoughts. You get back in bed and look hungover. I'll get the door." I pat her on the ass, and she starts moving toward the bed. She grabs a pair of shorts on her way there and tugs them on just as she jumps into bed.

I take a deep breath, readjusting myself and trying to think about things that are gross and wildly unsexy. Anything but her fucking mouth all over my dick... so fucking warm and fuuuc-ckkk. This is going to be harder than I thought.

"Wren?" Mac calls again from the door, louder this time.

"Yeah. Just a minute." She jumps up and grabs my arm.

"Go to the bathroom and fix yourself. I'll get the door." She flashes me a look and then an amused smile.

"Fuck. Okay. Sorry," I apologize and dodge into the bath-room, listening as she opens the door.

TWENTY-FOUR

Wren

I SWIPE MY HAND OVER MY MOUTH LIKE SOMEHOW there's going to be evidence that I've just been getting Easton off and take a deep breath before I open the door. Liv and Kenz give me bright smiles as they hold up a brown bag full of groceries and another bag with what looks like a deliciously greasy breakfast.

"East said he was taking care of you, but I doubt that boy knows how to take care of anyone. So we came over with a hangover care package." Kenz walks past me into the room but stops short when she sees it. "Holy fuck. What is this, the presidential suite? I thought our room was insane. This is crazy. Do you have a hot tub on the deck? And the views. Jesus. Okay, say what you want about him, but his money does buy nice things."

"She is very peppy this morning. Sorry," Liv apologizes.

"Waylon and I got up early and had a massage and then did

the sauna thing. You run out into the snow, then back into the sauna. Then snow. Sauna. It definitely wakes you up."

"Ummm it sounds like it," I say, laughing a little.

"All right." Liv walks to the little bar area near the breakfast nook and starts pulling everything out of the bag. "Gatorade. Alka Seltzer. Ibuprofen. Vitamin pack."

"Coffee and the good cheese and egg bagel sandwich that you like with the Santa Fe sauce on top." Kenz sets the bag next to it. "Although it looks like you already had breakfast."

Her eyes drift over the table where she can see two plates.

"Did East eat breakfast with you?" She sounds surprised.

"Uh, he ate a little before me. I was taking my time getting out of bed. But yes, I had some breakfast. I'll still take the bagel though. It's good hangover food."

"Huh. I really didn't think he'd even be here to help you. I just assumed patching you up meant he'd throw some water and Tylenol on the nightstand before he ran off to fuck some more snow bunnies."

"No. He's been really nice, actually. He got me coffee and pancakes. Even a smoothie thing that's supposed to help with hangovers." I hold up the empty glass for her to see.

"I told you he could be trusted." Liv lets out a little huff.

"Well, I didn't know. I figured he'd have his dick down some chick's throat this morning. You know how he is."

I practically choke on the bite of bagel that I have in my mouth, and I pray to god that he can keep silent behind the door.

"Do you... do you have his shirt on?" Kenz looks me over, her eyes narrowing. I feel panic well up in my gut.

"Not his, no..."

"Then whose? Because you can't tell me that's in your size." Kenz looks it over again. "Did you... did you hook up with someone last night?"

"Maybe?" Why did I just say maybe? Why? *Shit.*

"Did you bring him back here? To this room? Oh my god. You fucking vixen. And here we thought he'd be the one doing it."

"You met someone last night? I thought East took you to dinner?" Liv looks at me quizzically.

"He did, but after we went out. Had some drinks."

"A ski instructor?" Kenz grins.

"Where was East?" Liv asks. And I want to ask her why she is so focused on him in this story.

"No ski instructor. And uh, I don't know. Some women were hitting on him who he knew. I assume he probably went off into a room with them somewhere and did his thing."

"He went off with other women? And left you alone at a party where you didn't know anyone?" Liv's voice raises a little.

"It was fine. I told him to go. He came back and found me later." Lying to your best friends is a maze of dishonesty, and I am *very* lost in it.

"That really looks like a shirt I've seen East wear at the apartment though. Are you sure you didn't accidentally grab his thinking it was the other guy's?" Kenz looks at the shirt again thoughtfully.

"How drunk were you exactly? Are we sure East wasn't *the* guy?" Liv adds.

And I'm wondering if this is a panic attack I'm having because my chest feels like it's on fire, my cheeks feel scorching hot, and I just wish it was all enough to melt me into the floor and stop all the questions.

"I don't think I'd ever be drunk enough to fuck Easton, Liv. Don't be silly."

"Okay. Well, I'm just saying..." She looks me over again, and I need them out of here. Now.

"Listen, I appreciate the hangover care package and you

guys being so sweet. But I really need a shower and a nap if I'm going to be ready for the rest of the day."

"You heard all the plans we have?" Kenz beams at me.

"Yes, it sounds amazing. I really appreciate having a girl's day and night out. It's really thoughtful of you guys."

"All right. We'll let you get some rest. Meet you at 1 in the lobby?"

"See you then." I smile and usher them out of the door, waving as they leave.

When I turn around, Easton's already out of the bathroom. He's grabbing clothes and starting to get changed.

"Oh my god. That was terrifying," I say leaning up against the door and pressing my hand to my heart.

"Yeah. Close call," he mumbles as he throws his shirt on.

"Are you leaving?" I say, a little kick of apprehension in my chest.

"Yeah. I should get going. Meet the guys. I think we're hitting the slopes." He pulls his pants on and I can't help feeling like he's pissed off.

"Oh. Okay... I thought we had some more time. That we could finish what we started..." I start to walk toward him, but he dodges around me headed straight for the door.

"You should finish getting ready, so you can meet them. I'll see you later Wren." He grabs his coat and wallet.

Before I can say another word, he's out the door and gone. My heart sinks hard because I know I've fucked up, but I don't know how to fix it.

———

THAT NIGHT WE'RE OUT AT AN UPSCALE BAR IN THE HEART of the little downtown area. It's a converted theater and the place is swanky as hell. Makes my little sports bar look like a seedy hole in the wall in comparison. The place is packed, and we've managed to get a table on the second floor where we can overlook most of the first floor and people-watch. Which has been interesting since we've already spotted a few celebrities. Although most of them appear to be ensconced upstairs in the top floor VIP balcony area away from prying eyes, a few have wandered down to mingle with us normal folks.

"I can't believe how many are here. It must be half the people in town," I say, looking out over the crowd.

"It's a seen and be seen kind of place I think." Liv takes a sip of her drink, and her eyes drift over a group of people near us.

"The guys are here somewhere, or at least they were headed this way a bit ago. Waylon texted," Kenz adds, looking at her phone and then putting it away.

"Did they all go out?" I ask because I never heard from East, and I was afraid to text him. Afraid that he wouldn't text me back and that it would hurt even more than the way he ran out on me did.

"Yep. They all went." Kenz nods her head along to the music.

"Chelsea didn't want to come?" Liv looks to Kenz.

"No. She said she was just gonna stay in the room. She seemed a little bummed. I really hope she didn't think she could push Ben for a relationship. He said he was worried about it before the trip, but he'd had a conversation with her, and he thought they were both clear on it."

"My guess is he was clear, and she was not." Liv frowns.

"Yeah. I'm honestly surprised Ben hasn't found anyone. He really seems like he'd be the relationship type," I say, trying to reconcile the incredibly sweet guy we all know with the one who seems to break so many hearts by never settling down.

"Seriously. East I can understand. He'll never commit to anything but Ben? I feel like he's overdue," Kenz adds.

And right on cue, my eyes catch on a very familiar figure, surrounded by his friends, his brother, Xavier, and several women, one of whom is hanging all over his arm while he stands and talks to his friends. My heart picks up its pace, and I fish in my purse for my phone bringing it out and seeing that I still have no messages from him. I open the text window, ready to type out a message asking him what the hell he's doing and who she is.

And then I realize how crazy that sounds. I'm gonna what —yell at the manwhore for being a manwhore? Tell him that he needs to remember that he's staying with his non-girlfriend in a hotel room while we have a hateship? I burst out into laughter, and both Kenz and Liv look at me.

"You okay?"

"Yeah, I just saw the guys down there. And Easton's brother Tobias is here."

"The NFL player?" Kenz asks.

"Oh shit, and he's here with Xavier." Liv follows my line of sight.

"I'm going down there." I stand up abruptly.

"Wait! What about girls' night?" Kenz asks.

"Um... Tobias Westfield?" I point down at him.

"That means nothing to me." Kenz, who only knows anything about football because of Waylon, shakes her head.

"He's incredibly talented. And hot. Arguably hotter than Easton." Liv looks to me and then down at the crowd. "You know him?"

"I met him last night." I smile.

"Whoa. Was he the guy?" Kenz asks.

"I didn't say that." I shrug and start walking down the stairs. Because while Tobias definitely wasn't the guy, I am betting his ego is big enough that he would play along. I toss the rest of my drink back and set the glass down, making a beeline for a Westfield.

Tobias sees me approaching, and his eyes flit between me, his brother, and the woman on his brother's shoulder. He smirks and gives me a chin jerk, and I grin at him because we've just made a silent pact to start shit, and I kind of love him for it.

"Tobias! I didn't think I'd see you again."

"Hey, sweetheart." He reaches his arm out and pulls me to his side.

"What made you come out tonight with us commoners?" I smile up at him, pretending I don't even know Easton's there, even though I can feel his eyes burning into me.

"Wanted to see my little brother for a bit longer since you all left early last night." He nods in Easton's direction, and I look up, feigning surprise when my eyes meet his.

I glance at the woman on his arm, and he at least has enough of a conscience to pull away from her.

"Oh, Kenz said you all were gonna be here tonight. I didn't know that you had your brother with you though." I smile at Easton.

He doesn't answer, a little tick of his jaw the only signal that he heard me at all.

"So how long are you here for?" I turn back to Tobias.

"Another day or so, then it's back north." He smiles at me for a moment before his eyes flit back to his brother.

"That's too bad. What are you up to tonight?" I bat my lashes.

He grins wider. "Having some drinks and trying not to get into too much trouble, sweetheart."

I feel my phone buzz in my purse, and I open it.

EASTON

Can I talk to you?

Please?

I have half a mind to ignore it, but then it wouldn't make me any better than him. I take a breath and close it.

"Well hopefully, we can catch up some. I definitely want to talk to you more." I smile at him.

"Of course." He nods, and he releases the grip he has on my waist.

"Do I get an introduction?" Liv questions, finally catching up with me after saying her hellos to the guys.

"Tobias, Liv. Liv, Tobias. I'll be right back."

Kenz looks up at me as I pass her by. "Just gonna run to the bathroom, I'll be back."

She nods, and I move swiftly through the crowd toward an outer corridor. I'm gonna give him exactly 60 seconds to extract himself from that harpy's grip and then I'm gone. I lean up against the wall, crossing my arms over my chest. I almost feel like I might cry. Which is insane. I am *not* going to cry over Easton Westfield. What the hell is wrong with me? I take a breath, trying to clear my head.

"What the fuck was that?" Easton's tone is lethal.

"What was what?" I play naïve.

"You know what."

"I was just saying hi to your brother. Being polite. How's your girl, Easton? Only one so far? Slow night for you."

"I wasn't even talking to her. She just came up and started hanging on me, I was trying to get away from her."

"Right. I believe that."

"It's the truth. Have I ever lied to you?"

"I don't know. Where were you all afternoon?"

"Out with the guys. You knew that."

"You didn't text. You ran out the door this morning."

"Again, I went to meet up with the guys."

"We were in the middle of hooking up when you left."

"No, you were in the middle of telling your friends how you'd *never* be drunk enough to fuck me when I left."

"It was a cover story."

"Was it?"

"Yes, you know it was. You helped me run around and hide things before they came in. You were hiding in the bathroom."

"Because you fucking wanted me to."

"Because it would have been obvious otherwise. I was wearing your shirt!"

"And the fucking scandal if they saw you on your knees for me, right? You'd never live it down."

"We agreed this would be a secret from them. You know how they'll act if they find out. And I won't be the only one getting shit for it."

"Right. So part of keeping your secret is acting like I normally would. And what would I normally be doing if I was out with my guys at a club and a woman like her came up to me?" He leans his hand against the wall above my shoulder, his face coming closer to mine.

I frown because he's right. He was just acting normal. Keeping up appearances without really doing anything wrong. I have wildly overreacted. I feel the heat of embarrassment creeping up my neck.

"You see my point?" He raises a brow.

I give a little nod because I refuse to concede it out loud.

"You don't have to act like you're enjoying it so much. And I still don't want her touching you."

"Why?"

"Because you're—"

I almost say it. The thing that isn't true. The thing that can't be true even if I want it to be.

"Because I'm?" His eyes drift over mine, searching, watching like he always does.

"Nothing." I shake my head.

He grabs my wrist then, and pulls me off the wall, taking me with him at a fast pace toward the elevator. He slams his hand on the button and it's called immediately. He pulls me in behind him, pressing the close-door button as his mouth descends on mine.

He kisses me hard. Punishing strokes, like he's angry and frustrated and tired all at the same time. I kiss him back in equal measure. Not even sure why I'm mad at this point.

"Where are we going?" I whisper against his lips before he kisses me again.

TWENTY-FIVE

Wren

"Somewhere we can talk," he answers, his tone still sharp.

The elevator dings a second later and he pulls away from me, and we turn the corner to see an attendant standing at a rope to this floor. It must be the VIP level because it looks exclusive and extravagant up here. Like they took the theme downstairs and then tripled down on the gold and black luxury.

Easton says something to her and flashes a card and she nods, writing something on the iPad she has in front of her. Then she motions for us to follow, and we're led down a hall to a doorway where she gives Easton some additional information, before she tells us to have a good night.

The second she's gone he opens the door and pulls me in behind him, pressing me up against the wall, his eyes blazing with a dangerous looking combination of anger and lust.

"What the fuck was that with my brother down there?"

I shrug my shoulder. "I just figured if you were going to have fun, so was I."

"Or you just figured if you were going to be jealous, you wanted me to be too?"

"Maybe."

"Well, you fucked up because the idea of you and my brother doesn't make me jealous." His hand slides up my hip.

"No?" I ask because I have a hard time believing that.

"No. It makes me wanna fuck shit up. Burn shit down. And you know me. You know I'll do anything to avoid conflict. So you're gonna promise me you're not gonna do that again." He leans in so close I can feel the heat of his body against mine, can practically feel the irritation vibrating off him.

"I don't know if I can do that," I taunt him.

"No? Why not?" His fingers curl around the back of my neck and his thumb massages the corner of my jaw.

"Just something about him. I can't resist it. He's just so fucking—"

Easton's thumb swipes over my lips silencing me, and his knee goes between my legs, pinning me hard against the wall. A derisive laugh rumbles through him and a smirk that draws up on one side—one that makes him look like he could be the devil incarnate—tugs at his lips.

"Why are you pushing my buttons, Princess?"

I don't answer him. I just stare at him silently.

"You're not gonna tell me?" His thumb swipes back and forth over my lower lip, and his eyes follow it.

"Because I hate you," I say finally.

His eyes snap up, something flickering in his as he searches mine before they harden.

"You don't hate me. You just hate how much you want me. Hate how much you crave getting fucked. Hate how much you like sucking my cock."

The way he talks works on me like it does every time. Making my whole body warm. Making my nerve endings tight. Making my clit fucking pulse.

I roll my lower lip between my teeth and try to look over his shoulder, try to feel and think about something other than him.

"Like the way you sucked me this morning. Trying to play it off like it was gratitude. Like you just want to thank me for everything. But Princess, no one has ever sucked my cock the way you do. Like you love it. Like you'd do anything to make me feel good. I think you'd get on your knees anytime I asked." His lips ghost along my throat, dotting kisses on the way and finally sucking on the tender spot of flesh where my throat meets my shoulder, and a little gasp leaves my lips. "Would you do that for me?"

"Now?" I whisper because I would.

He grins, "Fuck, you would. Wouldn't you?"

"Fuck you," I grit out, realizing that he's taunting me.

"Oh trust me. I want you to, but there are things I want more than that."

"Like what?" I ask quietly.

He smiles again, and then leans in and kisses me. The softest brush of his lips and then a slow, languid kiss that makes me feel like my whole body is on fire.

"Take your panties off for me," he whispers against my lips.

I slide my hands under my skirt, hooking the lace band with my fingers and pulling them down and off without ever leaving his grip.

"Put them in my pocket."

"What? Why?"

"That's where they're going to stay for the rest of the night."

"East..." it's half-protest, half-whimper.

"Use your fucking words, Princess."

"Touch me. Please."

He grins and his hand slips between my legs. He strokes me and his teeth dig into his lower lip.

"Fucking hell," he curses because I am embarrassingly wet for him. So much so that I can feel it slicking my upper thighs as he slides his fingers inside me and strokes.

"You gonna tell me this is because of me again? You haven't even had your mouth on me tonight, and I've barely talked to you."

"Just thinking about you," I admit. "The way you feel in my mouth. The way you fill me so perfectly when you fuck me."

"The way you talk is gonna break me," he whispers against my cheek, his thumb circling over my clit.

"Break you?"

"Make me say things I shouldn't. You make me want things I know I shouldn't. You make me want so fucking much, Princess."

I gasp as he hits my clit just right, and I start to feel the edge of my orgasm hit. He pulls his hand back and kisses me. "Not. Fucking. Yet."

He grabs my wrist and drags me to the other side of the room, where a balcony juts out over the club below.

"Bend over," he grits out.

"What?"

"Bend over. Pull your skirt up and put your hands on the railing."

"Here? Someone could see." I feel the spark of apprehension light up my chest and swarm through me, but I do what he asks.

I hear him undoing his zipper and unwrapping a condom and then I feel him at my back. The warmth of his body against mine as he leans over me. He grabs me by the throat and pulls me up to my full height again.

He brushes his lips up the side of my neck and his tongue teasing the edge of my jaw before he whispers against my ear. "That's the point, Princess. So they can all see my hands on you. They can know that out of all the men you could have in this place it's *me* you want to fuck you. Because you like how I fuck you. How dirty I am. How I give you what you want. You love it so much that you can't even stand to go back to the room before you get my cock. And I want you so fucking much I'll give it to you. You want them to know that; don't you?"

"East... fuck..." I mutter, and he teases my clit with his free hand again, gentle brushes that make me want more.

"That's right, Princess. When I fuck you, you better say my name. Because when we fuck, you're mine. Yes?"

"Yes," I agree.

"Good. Now look down there, where our friends are, where my brother is. You better watch them while I make you come. Make sure they don't look up here and find out how much you like fucking me." His teeth graze the side of my throat before he kisses me one last time. "Now bend over and take my cock."

I can barely think straight when he talks, but I manage to do what he asks. When he slides inside me, I grip the rail because it's so fucking much. So fucking good. And he teases me so well, bringing me so close to the edge, that it's only a minute before I'm coming hard and saying his name between whimpers and curses. He follows me a few moments later.

"Fuck, Princess. You feel so fucking good. And the way your cunt tightens around me. Fuck. Makes me come so fucking hard..." he mutters as he finishes, his breathing ragged and uneven. After he gets rid of the condom and puts himself back together, he pulls me onto his lap on the couch.

His hand wraps around the nape of my neck and pulls me down to kiss him, his fingers threading through my hair as he does it. And the way he kisses me is so tender, so sweet, so opposite of the way he just handled me that it's hard to believe the two men are one and the same. That I get to have both of them in such a short span of time.

"Nothing was going to happen with her. You know that, right?" He looks up at me.

"Yes. Just like you know I would never do anything with your brother, right?"

He nods, and I kiss him again.

"I don't even fucking want to be out right now. I just want to be back at the hotel with you." He kisses me absently on my lower lip and then at the corner of my mouth.

"Me too," I confess, and his eyes flick up to mine, something behind them I can't quite read.

"Wren—" he starts but then my phone starts blaring with a call, and I look down to see it's Liv.

"Fuck," I mutter, noticing I missed a ton of text messages from her.

"Hello?" I answer it.

"Oh my god. I was about to have a heart attack. Where are you?"

"I went to the bathroom and then I ran into East. He was um, showing me the VIP suite up here that he got for us. I'm sorry. I got distracted by all the pretty bottles of liquor. You guys should come up. I'll come down and get you." I make a face at East, and he just shakes his head.

"Oh god. Okay. Kenz and I were so worried," Liv's voice sounds less panicked.

"I'm sorry. I'll be right there."

"Okay. See you in a minute," she says before she hangs up.

"Is that a problem? I didn't know what else to say." I look over East who still looks unsure and a little rattled. I'm guessing he wasn't planning on us having company so soon.

"No. It's fine." He shakes his head, but his brow is still furrowed.

"What's wrong?"

"I just want to fuck you without immediately being interrupted by our friends. I guess that's too much to fucking ask for." He laughs.

"That would be nice." I smile at him. "Let's one of us feel crappy and leave early, okay?"

He nods, and I kiss his cheek before I run off to get Liv.

TWENTY-SIX

Easton

We manage to sneak out early, letting my brother take over the tab while the rest of our friends enjoy the open bar and view from the VIP area. And by the time I get her back to the hotel room, I feel nervous. My stomach rolls and my chest is tight because I'm about to do a thing I've never done before. And there's a high probability that I'm going to get rejected for it and ruin our little hateship in the process. But I don't think I can do another two days like this.

"Oh. I have the perfect idea!" she shouts excitedly from the other side of the room as she tears out of her shoes and jacket.

"What's that?" I ask absently, my mind too focused on what I need to say to her.

"Hot tub and rosé?" She points to the hot tub outside. It's lit up against the night sky with plumes of steam rolling off it, and the mountainside framing it in the distance

"If that's what you want. I think I'll do a scotch though." I need something strong.

"Naked?" She gives me a little devious grin.

"Let's start with something on, yeah?" Because I needed to concentrate, and her body makes that impossible.

"Okay. Back to 'Operation Go Slow' again?" she teases me as she goes into her suitcase to look for a swimsuit.

"Something like that," I say as I walk to the minibar to get something to steel my nerves.

When we get into the hot tub, she looks over at me, a little flicker of worry dancing over her face.

"Is everything okay? If I really hurt your feelings, East, I'm so sorry. I definitely didn't mean to. And your brother even knew what I was up to."

"How?"

"I don't know, we gave each other like a wink-wink, nudge-nudge type thing before I walked up to him. He knew I was just trying to rile you. He saw the girl and saw me and knew I was being a jealous bitch. Trust me."

"Okay," I say, a little relief at hearing that. My brother could be decent when he wanted to be, but he also loves getting under my skin when he can. That's the problem with a family full of competitive over-achievers.

"I'm sorry I'm so jealous. It's just, you're you and it's hard, you know? I know I need to get over it. Especially if we're going to go back to Highland and be normal again. I promise I'll get my shit in order if that's what you're worried about."

I glance over at her, knocking back the rest of my scotch, and staring at the empty glass for a second before I speak. Not that it helps the words I use.

"What if we don't go back to normal?"

"What?" Her brow furrows and her eyes flick up to meet mine.

"What if we keep this up when we go back?"

"How?"

I shrug, "Would you want to?"

She looks down at her glass and then across the deck and beyond, her eyes drifting over the view for a second before they come back to me.

"No," she answers quietly.

My heart tightens and slams against my chest before it falls flat. I'd expected her to reject me, but not so bluntly. Not without explanation or hedging or something. The simple "no" stings like hell.

"No?" I ask because echoing her is all I can manage out loud.

"I couldn't handle the other girls, East. Your lifestyle. Here where you're kinda forced to pick me because we're all alone at a couple's resort is one thing. But out there in the real world? We both know that doesn't go well. Not really. And I... I really like you. I shouldn't tell you that. It ruins the hateship a little right?" She smiles at me. "But I feel like we could be friends. For real. Get through this project—I think together we could do it. Get the first-place nod, get the interview. We're pretty good together when we're not trying to kill each other."

"I feel like the sex is a pretty integral part of us not killing each other." I lean back on the one thing I know she likes.

"I guess that's probably true." Her lips press together in amusement.

"And if there are no other girls? If it was us exclusively fucking?" I hedge another route in with her.

"Exclusively?" Her eyes light up and there's a hint of hope in her voice.

"It'd have to go both ways."

She laughs and shakes her head at me.

"Does that amuse you, Princess?"

"Yes. With your ego, I would think you would understand. It's kind of cute that you have a little blind spot. Maybe that's what makes you so good."

"I'm going to assume that means you'd be exclusive too?"

"Yes."

"Okay. Then we're doing this," I say, my heart fucking beating again with hope at the idea of having her to myself beyond this trip.

"You have to tell me when it's over though. Okay? Give me some warning ahead of time to adjust." She looks at me warily.

"Not a problem, but for the record, I don't anticipate it being any time soon." Because I honestly can't imagine getting enough of her, as frightening as that is.

"It'll be harder to keep it a secret though." She sets her glass on the deck and turns to face me, the lights reflecting in the water and dancing off her face.

"We could just tell them."

"Is it bad that I kind of like it? I mean... I hate lying to Kenz and Liv, but I like that we have a secret—just us. Our own little bubble away from them." She kisses me tentatively and slides a leg on either side of me.

"I mean I can definitely do without their opinions. And I like anything that's just between you and me, Princess."

"And I like sneaking around." She presses a kiss to the side of my neck. "No one else knowing that you secretly like to fuck a girl who serves beer and burgers six nights a week for tips." She laughs and trails kisses down my neck.

"Hey." I thread my fingers through her hair and tilt her head back, so her eyes meet mine. "I would tell everyone if you let me. I told you before, the way you work turns me on. It's hot as fuck that you manage that place on your own. I've imagined you spread out on one of those tables with you in those fucking knee-high socks you wear more than once."

Her lips twitch with amusement and I pull her close to me again and kiss her.

"You scare me to be honest..." she whispers.

"What? Why?"

"This version of you. The way you can be when it's just us..." She frowns a little. "It'll freak you out, but I feel like I should be honest. I think I could end up catching feelings, and I worry that could fuck this up."

"Princess... I've already caught them so don't worry about it."

"What?" Her eyes look bright, nervous as they meet mine, and I worry I've said too much.

"Why do you think I'm asking for more time?"

"You like hate fucking me?" She gives a half-smirk.

"I mean, fuck yes, I do. But... I like *you*. I have no fucking idea what I'm doing. Or where this goes. But I want to see."

She grins and her eyes drift over me, her grin broadening as she reaches my face.

"Me too. I mean, I have no idea either. I'm not good at any of this but..." Her eyes are so soft when she looks at me, that I almost can't hold her gaze.

"We can start with the parts we know we're already good at and go from there." I give her a playful smirk, trying to lighten things because I can feel the thud of my heart in my chest picking up. Feel the way something that must be what falling into a four-letter word feels like cracking away at the ice that's there, and I don't know how to process it.

"I like that idea. Seems like a solid plan." Her fingers slide up my chest and over my shoulder as she leans in to kiss me again, and fuck, this girl has me. And I wonder if maybe, finally, she might let me have her.

TWENTY-SEVEN

Wren

I WAKE UP THE NEXT MORNING TO THE SOUND OF THE phone in the room ringing loudly. I didn't even know there was one, but as it blares through the otherwise quiet room it's very apparent it exists now. Easton is similarly surprised by the way he stumbles out of bed and fumbles over to the dresser the landline is perched on.

"Fuck," he curses as he nearly drops it when he picks it up. "Hello?"

There's a pause on the line, and I can hear a feminine voice through it.

"Yeah. She's here. Sure. One minute."

"Wren, someone's on the line. They say they're your grandfather's aide?"

My heart bottoms out through my stomach, panic and bile welling in my throat because for her to call this line means something bad has happened. Means she *had* to track me down and call me here.

"Hello?" I ask the second I can get the receiver to my ear.

"Wren. Oh good. I was so worried. I've been trying to call your cell, but I wasn't getting an answer. Worried something happened to you too. Honey, your grandfather had a stroke last night. He's in the hospital, and I'm here with him. Wanted to make sure he had somebody he knows. I know you're on vacation, sweetheart, and I hate to bother you, but I have another appointment this afternoon. I hate to leave him alone. Do you think you could come down? I can cancel if I need to. But I was hoping you might have enough time to get here."

"Oh my god. Yes. Of course! Let me just figure out how to get down there, and I will text or call you as soon as I know. I'm so sorry, Sherry. Is he... is he okay? How bad is it? Tell him I love him, and I'll be there as soon as I can."

"They haven't said a whole lot to me, honey. When I found him, he was alert, but he couldn't talk though. So I'm worried for him."

"All right. Keep me posted, and I'll be there as soon as I can."

My heart is pounding in my chest, and I can feel the tears starting to fall before I even know what's happening. I look down and realize I'm still mostly naked, and I need to find clothes. I need to get scattered clothes in my suitcase and then get a car out of here. I grab my phone off the nightstand and open it to realize I forgot to plug it in last night, so I run to my suitcase to get my charger and get it in the wall.

The buzz of shock in my eardrums is so loud I can't hear, and my eyes blur from the tears that are falling. My brain is still half awake, and the dull thud of a headache is already pounding away at my temples. I need water and some of the hangover meds the girls got me, right after I get this stupid fucking phone charged. I can't believe I let it go dead in the night.

I was so fucking stupid. So distracted by drinking, partying, fucking, and being on vacation that I didn't even make sure it was plugged in. And of course, I miss the one time my Gramps needs me. For all I know the bar has burned down too because I wouldn't know that either since Tom and Tammy couldn't have reached me if they wanted to. I try to take a breath, and I almost can't, my throat and my lungs going tight, the echo of my own heartbeat drowning out everything around me.

I swat at the tears falling down my cheeks as I bend to plug the phone in, annoyed that it's another thing slowing down my progress. And I nearly jump out of my skin when I turn around, and Easton grabs my arms.

"Wren!! You're scaring me. What's wrong?" I look up and his face is tense with worry. I can tell he's probably said my name several times before this, but I'd forgotten he was even in the room with me.

I take another breath, my lungs giving just enough that I can get a small one in. Just enough to let me speak.

"My Gramps had a stroke. I have to get back to Denver. I've got to get to the hospital. Oh my god! I forgot to ask her what hospital. Fuck. This fucking phone needs to charge so I can text her. This is a nightmare." A little sob comes out of my chest. And I am not this girl. The one who falls apart. I normally don't mind a good crisis. It keeps me thinking. Keeps me going to have a challenge to solve. But one that involves my Gramps being sick... My sweet old Gramps and my last close family member... I can't face it like everything else. It's just not the same.

"Okay. We'll get you back. Don't worry," Easton says, his tone remarkably calm in contrast to my panic.

"I don't have a car, and I don't know, are there charters or something? A bus? I can't ask Liam to take me back." Most of us, with the exception of Ben and Chelsea, had piled into Liam's SUV to come here because he has snow tires and chains and four-wheel drive. And in the dead of winter, you need them to get up these mountain roads.

"I'll rent us a car. I'll drive you back. Don't worry. I've got you, okay? We'll get you to your Gramps." His thumb swipes away more of the tears from my cheek, and he looks at me thoughtfully.

"You? You can't leave. This is your whole thing. This vacation. And your brother is here. You haven't finished seeing him. And what it'll look like if you take me. They're gonna think it's weird." I start deflecting as I pull back from him and run around gathering my clothes into my suitcase. Because I don't want to be an imposition on him. I don't already want to be falling apart and become some huge disaster he has to help fix when we've literally only just started things between us.

"I don't care what it looks like. I'll just tell them it was the quickest way to get you down there. Just let me help you. I want to help you, okay?" He stops me again and kisses my forehead, bringing my chin up so that our eyes meet.

"Okay," I nod, trying to stifle another little sniffle that makes me feel ridiculous. I have to get myself together.

"I'm gonna call around and get a car brought here. Then I'll call our friends and let them know what's going on. You just focus on getting packed up and ready to go, okay?"

"Okay."

"It's gonna be all right. We'll get you there. I promise." His voice has a firm edge to it. One that's oddly reassuring.

"Thank you." I almost start to cry again, but I bite the inside of my cheek, trying to stop the swell of tears I can feel bubbling up again.

"Of course." He nods and pulls his phone out, starting to look for a rental place.

LESS THAN AN HOUR LATER WE HAVE A CAR AND WE'RE pulling out of the resort. It's funny how well money talks when you have it. I'm insanely lucky Easton and his black card are here to save my ass. I have no idea how I would have gotten home today otherwise. I definitely don't have the money to drop on a rental and making everyone go home would have made me feel awful.

I should have thought about all of this when I agreed to go on this trip. There should have been a plan. A plan *and* a backup plan for something like this happening. I should have had lists. Backup batteries. I should have plugged my phone in. An alarm to remind me.

I send a message to Tammy and Tom to make sure the bar is still doing okay. I haven't heard from them, so I hope everything is still running smoothly but now it feels like everything could fall apart. Like one domino could send my whole world careening out of order.

Because if I have to be at the hospital with Gramps, I don't know who will run the bar, and if he needs long-term care I don't know how we'll pay for it. My mind starts spinning a mile a minute with all the things that I'll have to take care of, and my chest tightens with the weight of it all.

"Wren?" Easton's voice breaks through the fog, and I look over at him. His hand is extended palm open on the console, and I put my hand in his. "It's gonna be okay."

I thread my fingers between his and squeeze.

"You don't know that. You can't know. I don't know," I say softly, watching out the window as the snow-covered mountains whir past through the glass. I'm at least thankful it isn't snowing right now, and the roads are relatively clear. I might actually make it in time to let Sherry get to her appointment. I feel awful that she's taken responsibility for all of this in my absence.

"We'll figure it out. If your Gramps is anything like mine, he's strong. And if he's anything like you, he's a fighter. And we'll get you there soon." He squeezes my hand back.

"Thank you for taking me home. I really appreciate it. I didn't mean to ruin your vacation. I'll pay you back for the rental."

"I've got it. And you didn't ruin my vacation. I just wanted to spend time with you." He brings my hand up to his mouth and kisses the backs of my knuckles.

I'VE NEVER BEEN SO RELIEVED TO SEE MY GRAMPS IN MY life than I am when they finally let me in the room with him. He manages to mouth my name and take my hand with the arm that hasn't been affected by the stroke. I kiss him on the forehead and give him a gentle hug.

"I'm sorry it took me a while to get here, Gramps. I was up in the mountains, and I came as soon as I could. They tell me you got yourself into a little bit of kerfuffle while I was gone though. Got yourself an extra special bed for the night, huh?"

I get a small nod from him, and it makes my heart squeeze tight. He looks so small in the bed, in a hospital gown, hooked up to all the monitors and machines. Even though he's been getting frail in recent years he's never seemed small to me. He was always the strong one in the family. He'd taken care of me and my mom when my dad left. Held my hand when my mom passed away from cancer. Taught me how to pour the perfect beer, make a killer Cajun pasta, handle drunk *and* grumpy customers, the difference between offsides and neutral zone infractions, and every other aspect of running a sports bar. He's always made me feel like I had a safety net to fall back on when times get hard and now I just hope that I can be that for him.

"Well, I'm gonna talk to the doctors soon and find out what we have to do to break you out of here. Might be a bit, but we'll get you back on your feet in no time. I'll ask the nurse if we can get some ESPN or something in here, so you have something decent to watch, okay?" I squeeze his hand, and I can tell he's trying to smile, so I give him a bright one back. Even though it's the opposite of everything I feel inside right now. Because he needs me, and I can do this for him.

The next day Liv shows up at the hospital room door, her knocking wakes me up from the nap I was taking in the chair. I blink and try to stand to greet her, fumbling a little because my back is in knots from being curled up against the wooden arms of the chair. I glance over and my grandfather is still asleep, so I motion for her to go back into the hall, and I follow.

"Hey." I give her a small smile. "Thanks for coming. Did you guys come back early?"

"Yeah. It's only a day early. Liam had a doctor's appointment he was worried about making anyway. And no problem. How's Gramps doing?"

"He's doing okay considering. They have a few more tests to run. Once they get him stabilized, they're going to send him to a rehab facility."

"Well that's good news, right? That they think rehab could work?"

"Yeah. They're hopeful he might be able to talk a bit more. He's still having a lot of trouble swallowing though, and I'm worried for him."

She wraps her arms around me and hugs me tight, and the small gesture makes my tears come again.

"Oh Wren, hon. I love you. It's gonna be okay. I've got your back. And I know your Gramps. He's a badass. He's gonna kick rehab's ass and be back to yelling at the refs on TV and drinking his afternoon beer in no time."

I let out a little laugh, wiping my fingers at my tears. "I really hope so."

"In the meantime though, I was thinking I could sit with him for a few hours. I have a paper to work on, but if he wakes up, I can talk football to him and keep him company. And you can get home and take a shower. Get a decent meal outside hospital cafeteria food."

"Oh. I don't know... I hate to leave him. And that's a big ask for you to sit with him."

"I don't mind at all. I came prepared!" She pats her laptop bag.

"Oh okay. Well, yeah... a shower would be nice. I do feel gross. I wouldn't be gone long though. I just have to find a ride home first. I think the bus route home runs through here—"

"East's in the lobby downstairs. He said he'd drive you home and back whenever you were ready."

"East is here?" My brow furrows.

Something flashes across her face, but whatever she's thinking she doesn't say it. I'm grateful for that. I don't want to have to come up with a lie about why East would care enough to pick me up.

"Yep. He is." She nods.

"Well, that's nice of him. Okay. Are you really sure?" I give her one last look.

"Positive."

"I appreciate it so much. Love you." I give her another hug.

"Take your time. You need a breather. You gotta take care of you to take care of him, okay?"

I nod and grab my purse off the table as she takes my place in the chair. I glance over at Gramps who's still sleeping soundly and blow him a little air kiss before I leave.

"Be back in a while."

"I'll be here." She smiles at me.

When I get to the lobby, East is sitting there in one of the chairs. He looks up when I come off the elevator, his face unreadable, and gets up to meet me halfway.

TWENTY-EIGHT

Easton

WHEN SHE COMES OFF THE ELEVATOR, SHE LOOKS ROUGH, like she's been crying all night and has barely slept. I imagine that's probably exactly what she's done. I stayed yesterday as long as she'd let me, but I hadn't wanted to stress her out by arguing with her, so when she told me to go, I did. But I'd told Waylon and Liam that she was gonna need the girls. That the news wasn't good, and we all probably needed to be back here to help her. 'Cause I know this girl well enough to know that she will run herself to the bone trying to keep everything going and appearances normal at the bar and school while she tries to manage to be at the hospital at the same time. They'd all agreed and come back early. And Liv had volunteered to take a shift at the hospital so we could get her home and get her food and a shower. Now it was my turn to try and get her to take a minute to breathe.

When she gets closer and I see how fragile she looks, how

dark the circles under her eyes are, how far from the girl who was dancing and flirting and teasing me just a few days ago she is, I just want to pick her up and kiss her. Hold her and tell her I'm going to make sure everything is going to work out. That I'll do whatever I can. But I know that her independent streak is a mile wide, and I'm gonna have to handle this with kid gloves if I don't want to stress her out more.

"Hey. How's your Gramps? How are you?" I ask quietly when she reaches me.

"As well as he can be. And I'm fine. In need of a shower and food, but okay. "

"All right. Well, let's get you back home."

"Thank you so much for picking me up. Do you think you could drop me back off here too? I still need to figure out the bus routes to get down here. I will tomorrow, but today if you could, I'd be super grateful."

"Of course. Wherever you need to go. I got you. Tomorrow too, if you want. Where do you want to get food? We can get it on the way if you want."

"Could we stop by the bar? I need to check on things there or I'm going to worry about that too."

"Yeah. We can do that. Car's this way." I nod, and when we get there, I open the door for her, and her eyes lift up to mine and she pauses.

"Thank you. For... this. For being so kind to me. You don't have to do all this you know. I know this made things complicated and weird. Not exactly the fun we were having before and—"

"Wren." I stop her, because the way she feels like she has to apologize twists in my gut. "I don't care about fun. I care about *you*. I'm doing this because I want to. Okay? You always take care of everyone else. Let us take care of you when you need it, all right?"

"Okay." Her eyes flick down to the ground, her face going soft like she might cry.

I run my fingers along her jaw and press a soft kiss to the edge of her mouth. She kisses me back and then slides into the seat, and I shut the door behind her.

I take her to the bar, convince her to eat half a burger and some fries, and get her back to her place to shower and grab a change of clothes and supplies, so she can spend another night at the hospital again. But when I go to drop her off, I can't help but feel like something's changed. She still kisses me, gives me a hug when she leaves the car, and promises me that she'll text me later. But there's just the slightest change in the way she says the words, in the way she presses her lips to mine that makes me feel like it's more than goodnight.

"Wren?" I start to ask her as she walks away, because I want to ask what's going on in her head, the one I know is whirring with all the demands of her life right now. And when she turns back and looks at me, still frail and broken looking, I realize I can't be an asshole. I can't press her for more than she's got. She has enough on her plate without me trying to force her to tell me how she's feeling right now. How she feels about me.

"Yeah?"

"Try to get some sleep, okay? It'll be okay," I say instead because I don't have better words for this.

"Thanks." She gives me a small smile and then turns back to head inside the hospital.

––––––––

UNFORTUNATELY HER GOODNIGHT DOES SEEM TO BE turning into good riddance. Because the next time I hear from her directly about something not project related, and not through Waylon or Liv giving me updates on how she's doing, is a week later when I see her leaving class. And only because I'm following her like a stalker.

"Hey." I hurry to catch up with her as she's moving so fast out of the lecture hall that I almost think she's running away from me.

"Oh. Hey. I'm sorry. I owe you a text. We need to get together about the project."

"It's okay. I've been working on it. I've got stuff to show you, and I've been working with Tom on making the orders for the stuff we'd already agreed on. But I'm not worried about the project. I want to know how you're doing?"

"I'm fine. Just busy. They moved Gramps into a rehab facility, so I've been visiting him, and trying to get through the paperwork for all of that. There are social workers and insurance people. And then the bar and classes. I'm sorry I haven't texted you. I just haven't had a spare moment."

"It's fine. I get it. I just wanted to make sure you're okay. See if there was anything I could do."

She stops then and turns to me just as we reach the edge of the quad. Her shoulders square and her face straightens. And I know whatever is coming isn't good for me.

"No. I'm good. You did so much for me. Getting me back here. Helping me get through those first couple of days. You were really wonderful East. I appreciate it so much, and I honestly can't thank you enough for it."

"Why do I feel a but coming on?"

"But I'm good. Liv and Kenz, they've got me. And I'm good. Really good. Okay?" Her voice wavers the smallest bit.

"I think you need to elaborate on what you mean by good."

"You're going to make me say it? Really?" Her eyes flash up to mine and then over my shoulder.

"Say what?" I can feel my gut sinking.

"East I can't do what we've been doing anymore. I mean we

need to work on the project, yes. And I'm sorry I haven't done enough there. I promise I'll pick up the slack on that. We can find a time to meet—"

"I don't fucking care about the project right now. Just get to what you're trying to say." The words come out much harsher than I mean them. Because I know a brush-off when it's coming. I've doled enough of them out in my life to know exactly what the precursor sounds like.

"But other than the project, I think we just need to go back to however things were before."

"Why?"

"Because I don't have time for anything else. I can't be available for parties and sex and staying out until the wee hours of the morning. I have responsibilities."

"I haven't asked you for any of those things."

"No, but those things are what got me into trouble in the first place. It's why I wasn't here when he needed me. It's why I should have never gone on that vacation in the first place. I don't get to have the life you have East. I have the life I have here, and I have to stay focused on it. Him being sick, it's complicated everything—with him, with the bar, with the finances—fuck... I'm sorry. I shouldn't be talking about it. Anyway, the point is. I have too much on my plate. I don't have the time to give you. I wish it was different."

"I don't want to steal your time, Wren. I just want to be here for you. The rest of it can wait."

She presses her lips together and closes her eyes, staring down at the bricks at her feet for a minute.

"I don't want you to wait. I don't know when this ends. If it ever ends. And I like you. I honestly can't say a bad word about you, East. You were amazing. You have been amazing through all of this. Which is exactly why I don't want to ruin this by complicating it or fucking it up. I'd rather remember it as the fun it was, okay? So please, please just try to understand where I'm coming from?"

"If that's what you need, okay," I say, and it takes every-thing—everything—I have in me not to argue with her. Because I can feel the burn in my chest as I hear the conviction in her voice and know this is over. That she's not going to budge. Anything I say will just make it messy. And the least I can do is not make her life more difficult than it is right now.

"But I'm still with you on the project. I know how impor-tant it is to you. It still is to me too. We'll get together soon. I'll find time next week, and we can finalize the plans for the reopening and make sure everything is set for all the spots we've booked with the local news and radio stations. I've got someone who can help with the online ads too" She immedi-ately goes into business mode and I'm just trying to hang on. Trying to act like all of this is perfectly fucking fine.

"Yeah. Just let me know." I nod, trying to keep my tone even.

"I will. Thank you," her eyes lift to mine for a second, and then she turns to head off to her next class.

Meanwhile, I'm left standing here, wondering how I could do everything I thought was right and still lose her.

TWENTY-NINE

Wren

A FEW WEEKS LATER AND MY GRAMPS IS SAFELY IN A rehab facility, recovering and making good progress. Enough that he can talk some and has ordered me back to the bar and school full time instead of spending all day "pestering" him. He keeps telling me that's the best way I can help him recover; by getting out of his hair and letting the nurses boss him around instead.

I'm doing my best to honor his request, even if I do occasionally sneak in a longer-than-usual visit by convincing him to play a round of Texas Hold'em. I smile as I wipe the bar top thinking of him. There's still a lot of ground to cover with his recovery and some hills that he might not be able to fully climb. I still have a little pit of worry in my stomach every time I think about it, but I at least have more hope than I did before. Which is what I have to stay focused on.

"Two more beers at table six. A cranberry vodka and a gin

and tonic for the girls at table ten." Tammy puts her order in with me and leans against the bar. "How you doin' tonight girly?"

"Just tired. Better than I was a few weeks ago though."

"Well, that's good. You need to get out. Get back with your friends. Have some normal time, you know?" She watches me while I prep the drinks for her.

"I know. They've been good to me, and I owe them a girls' night. I wouldn't have made it without them."

"And what about that boy who was bringing you around here for a bit when Gramps first got sick? The one who keeps coming by to talk to Tom and has been working on your reopening plans."

"He's just a friend. The reopening is that project we're working on together for class."

"Baby girl, he doesn't give a shit about your project. And the only *just* he's tryin' to do is *just* trying to get you out of your panties. Again, I assume."

I can't help but snicker a little and shake my head.

"Tell me what you really think." I grin at her.

"What I really think is that you're wasting perfectly good dick." She levels me with a look and the laughter rumbles through me so hard I have to set the drinks down to keep from spilling them.

"I'm sure it's not being wasted. You've seen him. He can find plenty of other women to assist." I smile as I say it, but the slither of jealousy in my gut tells me the truth.

"Uh-huh. Which is why your face looks like that when you say it."

"This is just my face. And I don't have time to give him what he needs. Between here and school and Gramps..."

"Sweetheart, listen to someone who has years on you. You don't get to be 22 again. Guys like that one don't come around very often, if at all. Don't waste all your chances for happiness trying to give everyone else theirs."

I sigh and look at her and then back down as I finish pouring the gin and tonic. Tammy, for all of her joking, sometimes says things that hit a little too close to home. I slide the drinks toward her, and she gives me a meaningful look before she sashays off to deliver the orders, one that says I'd listen to her if I know what's good for me.

———

I'M MOST OF THE WAY THROUGH MY SHIFT AT THE BAR when my phone dings and I see a message from Waylon. I frown, hoping that nothing is wrong with Kenz.

WAYLON

Are you working right now?

> Yeah. About another hour on my shift. Everything okay?

No. Do you think you could come by my place after? I can pick you up if you need a ride

> Sure. I can catch the rail. It's just a couple of stops. What's wrong? Is Kenz okay?

It's Easton. I think he needs you

SHIT. MY STOMACH BOTTOMS OUT, AND I IMMEDIATELY worry about what exactly East has told Waylon, and whether that information has gotten back to Kenz. The girls will be furious at me for keeping all of this from them and I don't have it in me to have those conversations tonight. I also don't have the energy for Easton. I can't imagine he has anything positive to say to me. We've barely spoken about anything but the project, and whatever friendship I'd hoped we could salvage out of the wreckage of our stupidity has been non-existent. I decide to play stupid when I text Waylon back.

> I don't know what Easton would need from me?

WAYLON

> Things didn't go well for him at The Combine. He's in a bad place. I've never seen him like this. If you don't want to come, it's okay. But I think if you have it in you, he could use you here right now

I can tell from what Waylon doesn't say, that he *knows*. Maybe not everything. But enough that I might as well drop the pretext.

> I'll be over when my shift is up

WAYLON

> See you then

An hour and a half later and a quick rail ride, and Waylon is letting me into their apartment. I glance around, worried Kenz is going to jump out from a corner and lecture me on keeping things from her.

"She's not here. I told her I needed to help Easton with some stuff tonight." Waylon closes the door behind me.

"Are you sure he wants me here? Our last real conversation was not a good one."

"He mentioned. But I still think he wants you."

"What all did he say?"

"Enough to know something's going on between you two. He's very drunk. He didn't volunteer it, just became obvious."

I wince and stare down at the floor.

"Was going on. It's not anymore."

"I imagine that's part of what's got him twisted up then." My eyes flick up to Waylon's, and he frowns. "It's none of my business. But I've never seen him this fucked up before. He's a fucking wreck, so whatever happened between you two, if you go in there—be careful with him, okay? He acts like he's fucking rock solid all the time, but he's human at the end of the day."

"I didn't hurt him on purpose. And I doubt I'm what he's so upset about anyway."

"Mac didn't hurt me on purpose either. Doesn't change the fact it happened all the same."

And *oof*; does it hit me in the gut to hear Waylon say that to me. I stare at the floor for a minute, wishing I'd thought through things more on the ride over. Had a better plan for all this. But all I have is junk food and good intentions. Somehow hoping that can be translated into something that can help Easton. Because as much as we've made a mess of things lately, I do care about him. A lot, if I'm honest. More than I'm going to admit to Waylon.

"I'm not trying to guilt you here, Wren. I just... I asked for you to come because he wanted you. But I want to make sure that's going to be a good thing for him and not make things worse."

"I won't make things worse. I promise. If it seems it's headed that way, I'll leave. Please just... don't tell Kenz that I was here, okay? I haven't told them anything yet, and I'm not ready to."

"I don't like keeping things from her, but you helped me when I needed it. So I'll delay telling her, but you and East better figure things out. Then come clean. I don't want to be in the middle any more than you did." Waylon's brow furrows, and I feel like a giant disappointment in the wake of the look he's giving me.

"Okay," I agree.

"I'm gonna leave in a few to go see Mac, but if you need anything or he does—text me. Especially if things don't go well."

"Will do."

Waylon nods and then disappears into his room. I stand at the door to Easton's, and I can hear music bellowing from the depths of it, and I worry about what that means. I tap lightly on the door, half hoping he's asleep, and I can just leave the food here and go. But he's not.

"Yup. Come in big guy!" he calls and pauses the music, thinking I'm Waylon.

I open the door, and I'm worried that he's already changed his mind about wanting me. If he ever did at all. I can't imagine after our last encounter that he really wants to spend time with me because everything project related we've discussed he's been cool about. Sometimes even cold as ice toward me, despite what Tammy thinks she sees.

His eyes lock on me and his face is an emotionless mask. He studies my appearance and looks down at the bags in my hands. He looks disheveled, fucked up. Like he's been battered around in a sea of bad news, and I just want to reach out and give him a hug. But I stay frozen in place, knowing it won't be well received.

"Waylon said you could use some bar food," I say, wanting to interrupt the oppressive silence and the weight of his gaze.

"Waylon said?" He frowns.

"I guess you mentioned something? Maybe you just needed cheese fries and he got confused." I shrug because if he's already forgotten that he wanted me here this is going to be awkward as hell.

"I didn't fucking think he'd take me seriously. Fuck..." He runs a hand over his face and looks over at the wall.

"Well, I can leave the food and head out again. No problem." I set the food on his desk and take a couple of steps backward.

"No. Stay." He comes closer, leaning over me and shutting the door behind my back.

"Are you sure?" I ask. He smells like a heady mix of scotch and his cologne.

"I'm sure." His eyes rake over my body. "But *you* better fucking be."

"I've got a bacon cheeseburger, cheese fries, and a slice of apple pie." I grab the bag and press it to his chest like it's a shield because I forgot how easily I turn into a puddle in front of him.

"I've got other things I want in my mouth. Things I could eat. You want to hear about them?" He presses closer to me, and I close my eyes trying to remind myself I'm here to take care of him. But *fuck* he makes it hard to concentrate.

I open them again and glance at the half-drunk open bottle of scotch on his nightstand, and then flick my eyes up to his.

"You've had a lot to drink. You're gonna eat food first." I give him a stern look and press the bag harder into his chest.

A little smirk teases at his lips.

"First," he echoes, taking the bag in one hand and my wrist in the other, dragging me back to his bed with him.

I lean back against the wall while I watch him spread the food out.

"Smells amazing," he mutters.

"I told Tom it was for you, so he said he put the stuff on it you like. I don't know how you've managed to bring that curmudgeon around to your side, but he's a fan."

He gives me another little smile as he takes a big bite of the burger. I've gotten more smiles in the last two minutes than I have in weeks.

"Tammy was also singing your praises tonight. Pretty soon I'm going to be chopped liver in my own bar."

"You just gotta talk to them right. Especially Tammy." He grins as he pops a cheese fry in his mouth, and something dances in his eyes.

"You better watch how you talk to her. A cougar like her will tear you limb from limb." I smirk at him.

"I might like it though." He wiggles his brows, and it feels good to be teasing him again. I miss this. Miss *us* when we can be like this.

I sigh, and he looks down at his food, stuffing another bite in his mouth like he wants to avoid the questions he knows are coming.

"What's wrong?" I ask anyway.

He shakes his head. "Just a rough week."

"What made it rough?"

It's his turn to take a deep breath, and he reaches over to the little fridge he has next to his bed, grabbing a pop, and opening it. He takes a long drink stalling for time and just watching him swallow, the movement of his throat has me pressing my thighs together. I should not have come here tonight. Should not be sitting here gawking at him like this. His eyes dart over my face like he knows what I'm thinking, but he looks down at the bed instead of making another comment.

"The Combine didn't go as well as I needed it to. I needed my performance, my times, to be lights out. And it wasn't my best. Between that and the drop... I might go undrafted."

"I doubt that. They're gonna look at your whole year. At

the energy you bring. Your size and the way you block. And that game against Pacific? You had four touchdowns. They're gonna remember that. Everyone remembers that. Not to mention that one-handed catch you made in the last game. That offsets the drop in my opinion."

"Too bad you aren't drafting me then, huh?" There's a bitter tone to his voice.

"Just wait and see before you let it get to you. I've seen the mock drafts. You're in all of them."

"Mock drafts don't mean shit."

"You have back-up plans. You've been doing phenomenal on everything with this project. There's a good chance we get the interview. And even if we don't... your dad, your brother. I'm sure they have connections, don't they? They could probably get you hooked up with a whole host of marketing firms. And you're a genius at this stuff."

"Yeah, the king of the football dynasty will fucking *love* having to call in favors to get his bastard a job." He starts to laugh.

"What?" I ask sharply, not sure I heard him right.

THIRTY

Wren

His lips twist in a half-anguished, half-amused grin.

"Yeah, Princess. That's the dirty family secret we don't talk about. Probably shouldn't say anything, but then you don't want anyone to know about me in the first place, so I doubt you'll say anything to anyone, right?" He flashes a look up at me and then takes another bite of his food.

My heart twists in my chest. I have to fix this, make him understand that's not the way I feel but his statement is so loaded. We need to unravel one thing at a time.

"What do you mean the family secret?"

"I'm a bastard, Princess. My dad had a little mid-life crisis. Went down to Vegas with his friends for a guys' weekend. Tripped and fell into some showgirl. And nine months later she dropped me off on his porch. Well, metaphorical porch considering his house is in a gated community."

"But you look so much like Tobias, and your mom."

"Stepmom," he corrects. "And yeah. That was the lucky part. No one asks too many questions. And Donna was willing to play along. Pretend to be my mom."

"Where's your bio mom then?"

"Who the fuck knows. Probably fucking older rich dudes on The Strip still for all I know. The only thing she gave me was my name before she shoved me back off onto him. She didn't even try to get money out of him or anything. That's how little she gave a fuck before she ran off. Just wanted to make sure someone else took me. Must have thought she was real fucking clever naming me East West, right?"

"Which is why you hate the nickname," I whisper softly, things I've wondered about for a long time coming together. Because I'd always been surprised someone as arrogant as he was didn't like the nickname that was built on the premise of how phenomenal he was on the field.

"Yep. Nothing like having thousands of fans chant the fucking name your bitch of a mother gave you as a joke."

"Is there a chance she just liked it? That naming you was the one thing she could do?"

He gives me a look that says I'm flirting with stupidity.

"And maybe she thought your dad could give you a life she couldn't? Maybe she thought Donna could give you what she couldn't? I think it's a lot to assume that she thought it was all a joke."

"She's never come back to check on me. No calls. No letters. Nothing. You don't need to guess when the silence is that loud, Princess." He shakes his head. "Now can we talk about something more pleasant? How's your Gramps? Waylon said he heard he was doing better. That true?"

I eye him warily, wanting to argue with him about his mom. But it's not my business, not really. He's obviously in a brittle state, and I'm here to make things better, not worse. I'm not a therapist after all. I can't fix that kind of pain, even with good bar food. All I can do is be here, hold his hand, and try to give him what I can offer.

"He's making progress. Talking a little. Telling me to get my ass back to work and school instead of trying to hold his hand. I still hate that he's in rehab though. I wish I could bust him out and bring him back home. But he needs more care than Sherry can give. I'm worried he might need to move into a place more permanently, and he'll be so mad if that's the case. I'm not looking forward to it," I spill my guts because that's the effect Easton has on me. I feel comfortable around him. Like I can tell him the hard shit and he'll just listen and take it in stride without pitying me in the process.

He finishes the last of his burger and wads up the paper, throwing it in the bag.

"Well, I'm glad to hear he's doing better but sorry to hear about the rest. I know you don't want my help, but if there's anything I can do. You know I'm here."

"I know. And I am grateful for that." I try to catch his eyes with mine, but he stays focused on the food in front of him, flipping open the box of apple pie and looking at it briefly.

"I think I'm full." His eyes lift slowly, and he grins at me.

"I've seen you eat before. And I know you like pie. Finish the food. You need something in your stomach."

"Fine but come sit in my lap."

"Why?"

"Do you want me to finish it or not?"

"Fine." I sigh, and I move to my knees to crawl a little closer to him across the bed. Before I get far, he snatches me with one arm, dragging me onto his lap, my legs straddling one of his thighs and his arm pinning me tight against him. His eyes drift over me, his lips pressing together with a hint of amusement.

He uses the little plastic fork I tucked in the box to cut himself a bite of pie and eats it, before he taps it against his lips, smiling at me.

"What?"

"Just thinking about the way you moaned over that cake at the hotel." He grins wider and takes another bite.

"I miss that cake. It was amazing. Definitely the best I've ever had."

"Yeah? Has the cake since then been disappointing?"

"I wouldn't know. Haven't had any."

"Me either."

I let out a choked laugh, and his eyes rise to mine.

"What's funny, Princess?"

"You want me to believe you haven't had any cake? That you didn't run straight to the cake store and get like three different flavors to have in one night?"

He tosses the half-eaten pie aside and grabs his phone, flipping through it and then hands it to me. I take it from him, confused, and look down. It's pictures he took of the photos he had spread out on my bed that first night when we hate fucked our way into this mess. I should be pissed that he took them. That he kept them. But something flutters through my chest at the sight of them. What it means, that he still has them.

"That's the only cake I even look at. Every night. Like I have a fucking problem. Go through the rest of the phone if you don't believe me."

I look at him out of the corner of my eye, and I flip back out to his main gallery. And nothing. Just pictures of food and drinks from the bar. A few of the new dishes we'd come up with for the reopening. A couple from his trip to The Combine. But no women. I flip to his text messages and his messenger app, and there are no girls' names, no suggestive messages, nothing. I look up at him.

"Hurts a little that you didn't just believe me. But now you know for sure, right Princess?" He takes the phone back from me and puts it on his nightstand.

"Why?"

"Don't ask stupid questions."

"I'm not. I let you go so you could go back to... to whatever you wanted to do. So I wouldn't waste your time."

He lets out a little sardonic laugh. "If you remember, I didn't fuckin' want to be let go."

I lean forward to kiss him but just before my lips touch his, he grabs one of my braids and tugs, pulling my head back gently and making my eyes meet his.

"Nah, Princess. I've learned with you we set terms first. You don't get to just walk in here and take, just because I'm feeling low."

"I didn't—" I start to protest, hurt that he'd think I was trying to take advantage of him.

He puts his hand over my mouth and his eyes drift over my face, a smile tugging at one side.

"I missed you. The way you look at me. This little splash of freckles on your nose. These fucking braids. Being able to put my hands on you whenever I want. Did you miss me?"

He doesn't remove his hand, so I close my eyes briefly and give a small nod.

"*Good.*" His eyes glitter with the word. "So here's how it's gonna go. I'm gonna get you ready for me. Treat you like I fucking hate you, talk to you how you like it, so we can get that tight little cunt of yours nice and wet. But when I fuck you? When I put my cock inside you—you're gonna fuck me like you love me. Like you're fucking obsessed with me, and you can't imagine another man ever touching you again. You better make me believe I'm the only one for you. Then we both get what we need tonight. You think you can do that?"

I nod because I can already feel the warmth of his words spreading through my body, touching every little ending and sparking it back to life. Melting the parts of me that had gone cold without him.

He releases his hand from my mouth and lets the hold on my braid loose again.

"Get up and strip for me. Slow. Like you're my own personal cam girl."

I scoot off the edge of the bed, standing in the center of the room, suddenly feeling nervous and self-conscious. Wondering if I can really do what he's asking. His eyes soften the slightest bit when he looks at me like he can read my thoughts.

"You want me to go first? Here." He grabs the back of his tee one-handed and yanks it off over his head, tossing it at my feet and then stands, unbuttoning his pants and pulling them off to reveal a gorgeous expanse of muscle and skin, his cock hard and heavy between his thighs. "That better? I know you like to look."

He lays back on the bed, his shoulders resting against the wall as his eyes drift over me. "Now strip."

My fingers fumble as I grab my tee and pull it over my head, unhooking it as it catches on one of my braids on the way off. I slowly unbutton and unzip the shorts I have on. Trying to pace myself, but I have no idea what I'm doing, and he still has the ability to make me feel nervous.

"Turn around, I wanna see your ass when you bend over to take them off."

I swallow hard as he says the words, doing as he asks, and feeling the answering pull low and tight in my body. I slip the shorts off my legs.

"You listen so fucking well when you want to," he mutters. "Now the panties and bend all the fucking way over when you do it."

I follow his instructions again, nerves fluttering in my stomach as I bend down.

"Fuck... me... The way your ass and thighs look from this angle." I hear a stuttered breath leave his chest. "Turn back around and look at me."

I turn slowly, half afraid that the look on his face might make me crumble. But it's even worse because his hand is wrapped around his cock, slowly stroking as he watches me.

"Now the bra. I wanna see how hard those nipples are for me."

I reach back around to the closures, unhooking them slowly, one at a time, and letting the straps fall down my arms, cradling the bra for a moment before I let it drop.

"Fuck. You're so fucking gorgeous." He closes his eyes and gives himself another long slow stroke before he opens them again. "Touch yourself."

I put my hand between my legs, dipping my fingers in, knowing I'm already wet for him.

"Show me."

I hold my hand out tentatively and a smug little grin forms. Amusement and arrogance dance over his face and then he stands abruptly. His hand going to my throat as he backs me up against the wall, pinning me there. His fingers slide down between my legs, parting me, the pads of them brushing over my clit.

"Look at you. How fucking eager you are. Doing everything I say." He kisses me then, finally giving me what I want most. The taste of him on my lips again and the tender stroke of the tip of his tongue against mine. I roll my hips, trying to get more friction against my clit, silently begging him for it. He slides two fingers inside me, giving me steady firm strokes while he continues to tease my clit with his thumb, and I turn into an embarrassing mess under his attention.

"That why you came over here in such a hurry tonight? Needed me to hate fuck this cunt so you could finally come? Or have you been using the toy I gave you?"

I nod, and he uses his thumb under my chin to push my head up.

"Use your words, Princess. And look at me."

I open my eyes and meet his.

"Yes, I need you, and yes, I've been using it."

"And thinking about me?"

"Always."

He smirks, a little rumble of appreciation rolling through his chest.

"Tell me what you think about."

"Your hands. Your tongue. The way you talk to me."

"Where do we fuck, Princess? In your shower? On your floor?"

"Yes," I breathe as he picks up the pressure and the pace of his strokes.

"And this cunt belongs to me every time, doesn't it?"

"East..." I sigh his name as he gives me more direct pressure on my clit and his hand tightens around my throat.

"Doesn't it?" His tone is hard, demanding.

"Yes."

"The truth is, Princess; it might not all be pretend. I think I might actually hate you a little bit right now. For helping me figure out I had a heart, just to turn around and break it the way you are."

The words cut like a million tiny knives to my own heart.

"East, I'm sorry. That's not what I meant to do," I whisper.

"Oh no. You should own it, Princess. Making me watch you from a distance. Letting everyone else help you but me. That's a special kind of torture."

"I didn't mean for it to be that way." I can feel the tears start to come, and I try to hold them back.

He pulls his hands away abruptly, "Go get on my bed while I get a condom."

I do as he asks, watching as he pulls one out of his night-stand and puts it on. I take a breath, centering myself. Trying to focus on the task at hand.

"How do you want me?" I whisper.

THIRTY-ONE

Easton

"How do you want me?" she asks, her voice just above a whisper. Hoarse like she's on the edge of crying. I've fucked up by saying too much. By telling her too much about how I feel instead of just taking what she's willing to give tonight. I've got to pull myself together and stop being in my head so deep. Stop wallowing in how raw I feel and make this good for her. Give her something we both need right now.

"On your back, Princess. Arms above your head stretched out and arch your back for me. Just like that photo of you I love so much."

She does as I ask, and fuck if it isn't the hottest thing I've seen in my life. Her naked with nothing but her sexy little socks on, doing everything I want.

"Now spread for me," I say as I climb onto the edge of the bed, my hand running down over her knee, over the back of her calf, and kissing the inside of her thigh.

She's spread so wide for me, so fucking wet she's glistening, and I bend to kiss her, sliding two fingers inside and stroking her while my tongue slides over her clit until she arches off the bed for real. Soft whimpers come from her, and she lifts one leg over my shoulder in a bid to get more of me.

"That's right. Let me hear how much you missed my fucking mouth on you."

"Oh fuck... East please, I need you inside me. Please," she begs.

My heart kicks in my chest, hearing her say my name, begging for me again like this makes me feel hope. The kind of optimism I can't really afford but want to drown in tonight.

"Why do you need me, Princess?" I replace my tongue with my fingers, circling her clit, so I can get a better look at the way she's writhing under my touch.

"Because you're the only one who can fuck me right. The only one who gets me."

I feel the answering rhythm pick up in my chest, as I move to give her what she wants, teasing her wet cunt with the tip of my cock as I lean over her. Bracing myself as I brush the hair out of her face and pull her chin toward me. Her eyes open and they go impossibly soft when they meet mine.

"You want my cock? You tell me what I want to hear. You tell me how much you fucking need it."

"I need you East. I need you to fuck me. It's all I can think about lately. What it would feel like to have you again. Please. I want you."

I thrust into her hard, and she gasps and wraps her leg around mine, reaching one arm over my shoulder and letting her nails dig in.

"Oh my god. It's so fucking good," she exhales, running her fingers along the back of my neck.

"It always is with you. This what you've been thinking of when you get yourself off without me?"

"Yes. Fuck..." she whimpers and then takes a breath. "I don't want anyone but you. Just you. I think about what it would be like if we just ran away. If you made me yours. If I was your—"

She stops herself like she's said too much, and she closes her eyes. Biting down hard on her lip. I fucking hate it. I want all of her.

"Finish the sentence, Wren. Tell me. If you were my what?"

"I can't."

"If you were my what?"

"It's embarrassing... Please, East. Just fuck me."

I still inside her and stroke my knuckles down the side of her jaw.

"I want all of you, Princess. I want to make you come, but you can't fucking tease me like that. That wasn't the deal. You promised to give me all of it."

She sighs, and I see it in her eyes the moment she relents. The moment I know she's going to let me in.

"I... I get off thinking about being your wife. Your starter wife. Fuck... It's embarrassing. But now you know. So fuck me. Okay?"

I nearly choke on my own tongue when she says it. If someone had asked me to guess that would have been last on the list. The fiercely independent girl has a kink about being wifed up. And I think I fucking love it.

"Fuck... see..." She sighs and starts to pull away from me.

I stop her, digging my fingers into her thigh and holding her in place. A grin spreading even though I try to stop it.

"You realize that would be a hard fucking thing to keep

quiet. How do you suppose we'd keep being married a secret from everyone?" I tease her.

"East..." She rolls her eyes and then closes them, and I can see a little blush spreading over her cheeks.

"Am I gonna find Wren Westfield carved into one of the tables at the bar?" I smile at her.

A little smile flits across her face before she tries to be serious again.

"Oh, I am. You *are* obsessed with me. I didn't even need to ask you to pretend, did I?" I kiss my way down the side of her throat.

"I never pretend with you. I never have to. It's why I like you so much."

"Like me? You gonna marry a guy you just like? I think you need to raise your standards, Princess," I start to rock into her again, taking her deeper.

"Oh fuck." She lets out a little gasp.

"You just like my cock?"

"No. It's perfect. I fucking love it. I love the way you fuck me, East. So much."

"I know you do, Princess. I can tell." I pick up my pace, fucking her harder and faster and she follows my lead, her breathing and her moaning getting louder underneath me. "I love watching you like this. The way you take me so-fucking-well."

She starts to whimper, countering my strokes with rolls of her hips, and I can feel her tighten around me as she chases her release, and her nails rake my back so hard I know I'm going to find blood when I look.

"I need you, East. I love you, and I need you so much," she confesses, just before I can feel her whole body tense and shudder underneath me.

"I love you too, Princess." I take her mouth with mine as I

start to come hard inside her, fucking her through the last few waves of it until I finally slide out of her, pressing my forehead to her stomach. I feel her fingers in my hair, gently running through. I press a kiss against the soft curve of her hip and then stand to take the condom off and toss it.

When I turn around to look at her, she looks so thoroughly fucked, so satiated, that it makes my heart tighten and strain in my chest. I feel lucky. That she let me give her something she needed, that she confessed so much to me. That she came to me when I needed her.

"East?" she whispers, reaching out for me, and I climb back into bed next to her.

"Yeah, Princess," I answer her.

"How much I want you scares me. That's why I've been distant. Because I know how this ends. How we end. And I'm scared of how much it will hurt."

"How will we end?" I ask, puzzled because I haven't given any thought to it. I've just been focused on the fact that I love her, and she won't let me come close enough to even tell her these past weeks. That I finally have her, and there's hope for us.

"You'll get drafted. Deep down you know you will. I know you will."

"That won't change how I feel about you."

"You say that now. And I believe you when you say it, but you can't know the future."

"Neither can you. Alexi Lalas or some other guy could walk into the bar tomorrow and sweep you off your feet. Steal you away." I tease because in this moment I'm happy, and I don't want to think about all the ways this could be ruined between us.

"East... I'm serious. I want you to understand. I don't want to hurt you. I'm not trying to, but I've lost so many people in my life. I don't want to set myself up for another one. I can't do it. My heart can't take it."

"I understand." I kiss the backs of her knuckles and squeeze her hand in mine. "But I can't take being away from you. I can't take the way you hold me at arm's length and won't let me be there for you. I need you."

She kisses my shoulder and then rests her head against it. "I need you too, but then where does that leave us?"

"I don't know." I kiss her forehead. "But we'll figure it out."

THIRTY-TWO

Wren

FOR GIRLS' NIGHT TONIGHT, WE'RE ALL AT THE BAR SO that Liv and Kenz can try the new food we have planned for the reopening and so they can take advantage of the open bar. Because let's be honest, I'm gonna need them liquored up when I tell them I've been lying to them for several months.

"Oh, this one is good. What is this?" Liv asks, her hand hovering over her mouth as she chews.

"Deep fried salted caramel pretzel bites"

"Sooooo good." Kenz looks at us both wide-eyed as she takes a bite of it.

"And with that beer you picked?" I ask.

"Amazing! I love it." Kenz grins.

"Good."

"So you and East are all set for the grand reveal then, huh? Sounds like it's going to be a star-studded event." Liv raises her brows.

"Yes. I'm ridiculously nervous. Heck even Tom is showing signs of stage fright. I told him whatever he cooks is always amazing, and we'll get through it together."

"That's good."

"I just really need it to be a success. Not just for the project and all that, but I need the revenue. With Gramps maybe needing long-term care, I have to figure out a way to pay for it all." I sigh.

"You'll get there. Somehow, you'll figure it out. And just let us know what we can do to help. Okay? I'm serious. If we have to do fundraisers or bake sales or whatever. We *will* figure it out." Kenz gives me a meaningful look.

"I appreciate it. And thank you for all your help. You guys helping with Gramps and the bar when everything was really going to hell there for a bit," I start to get a little teary-eyed and try not to sniffle but manage to do it anyway. "I couldn't have done it without you."

"Oh, Wren. You don't have to thank us. You've been there for us so many times when we needed help. That's what we do for each other." Liv shakes her head and Kenz tugs me closer to her and gives me a side hug.

"I know, but I just... I don't know what I'd do without you. I don't know what I'm gonna do in a few months when this is all over, and we all move on. How will I live without the two of you around?"

"How will we live without you is the bigger question." Kenz squeezes me tighter.

"Let me get another round of drinks." I stand and head behind the bar.

"Can I have another one of whatever this was?" Liv holds up her glass that had one of the new cocktails I'd come up with in it.

"Definitely. Coming right up."

"Me too!" Kenz calls.

I come back to the table a few minutes later and slide the drinks to them.

"So... I have a little confession to make."

"Uh oh. That sounds ominous. Is this why you're plying us with drinks?" Kenz raises an eyebrow.

"Maybe. Well, that and because I truly am grateful for all the help."

"We know. We love you." Liv smiles at me.

"So... you know that East and I don't always get along but—"

"Oh fucking hell." Kenz curses.

"I told you. Pay up!" Liv grins wide and taps her hand on the table.

"What is happening?" I look between them utterly confused.

"You just lost me 100 dollars." Kenz shakes her head.

"What?"

"Assuming you're about to tell us you've been sleeping with East?" Kenz raises her brow like she has the slightest hope that she could be wrong.

"You bet on whether or not I was sleeping with East?"

"Sort of?" Liv at least has the grace to look sheepish.

"Explain."

"Liv's been convinced for a while that something was going on there. She thought maybe he was wearing you down. And that morning when you came down the steps, I mean we all were having a hard time believing the two of you just slept and nothing happened. But I said that he probably tried, and you told him to go to hell. And Liv said she thought you might be soft on him, and knowing he was hurting..."

"Well, I'm going to lose the 100 on a technicality, but I also have a little confession." Liv swirls the drink in her glass.

"What?" Kenz looks at her.

"I might have gone upstairs while the two of them were fucking and heard them."

"You hussy! Trying to hustle me out of my money when you had hard evidence!" Kenz points at her.

"I mean it wasn't hard evidence. But I heard things crash and then whispering and giggling. So I assumed it wasn't fighting... Not many other options, but I wasn't for sure."

"Still cheating," Kenz admonishes.

"And then when we went on vacation, I was suspicious. And when I asked East to take you out to dinner, the way he jumped on it..." Liv adds.

"And I'm guessing him driving me home and showing up at the hospital..."

"Honestly that was the surprising part. I thought it was you two fucking things out of your system since you're always at each other's throats. But when he looked so worried...." Liv looks at me thoughtfully.

"Yeah. He really stepped up. I was surprised too. I didn't know he could be like that," I say quietly.

"So are you together then?" Kenz looks at me.

"Not exactly. I don't know what we are... You know he'll get drafted. And I have the bar and Gramps. Doesn't really leave us room to be anything." I shrug.

"So it's just fucking then? No feelings involved?" Liv asks.

"Ha... well... it was supposed to be that way."

"But...?"

"But then we might have said we loved each other?"

"Whoa. Whoa. Whoa. Easton Westfield... the Easton we've all seen at parties. The one who never met a sorority girl he didn't want to fuck. *That* Easton said he loves you?" Kenz looks at me.

"Kenz!" Liv scolds her.

"I didn't mean it like that. I just meant like... Listen I'm not judging. I'm with Waylon, so I get it. I just—"

"It's fine. I know what you mean. We all know how Easton is. Or was, I guess. It's fine." I shake my head. "And yes, he said he loves me."

"Damn." Kenz blinks.

"I for one, support this," Liv says matter-of-factly.

"I mean, I think I do too. If you brought that beast to heel, I *am* impressed. And I will be asking for tips." Kenz smirks at me.

We all laugh a little, and I sit back in the booth.

"It's scary though. I don't... I'm not much better at the relationship thing than he is. Most of my guy experience in college is one-night stands too. Or benefits situations. And East is more than that to me."

"You'll figure it out. Just take it one step at a time." Liv gives me a little half-smile.

"If Waylon and I could figure things out... you guys can for sure." Kenz bumps her shoulder into mine gently.

"I really hope so." I sigh.

THIRTY-THREE

Easton

LIAM POPS THE TOP OFF A BEER AND HANDS IT TO ME AS we head into the living room of the football house. I take a long swallow and try to let my head settle. There was too much fucking shit piling up right now between football, classes, and her, and it was all starting to take a toll on my ability to just chill the fuck out. If this was what post-college life was going to look like, I think I might be less excited about it than I thought I was.

"So what's your agent saying?" he asks as we hit the couch where Ben and Waylon are already sprawled out watching a game, eating wings, and complaining about the last play call.

"He still thinks I have a good shot, but I don't know. I'm trying not to get my hopes up." I shrug.

"You'll be in." Waylon shakes his head. "Just a matter of what round you go. And even if you hit free agency, you know you'll get snapped up somewhere."

"We'll see. I just hope the project goes well. I want a back-up plan if shit hits the fan."

"Makes sense. Never know when things can go to hell." Liam gives a bitter smile, glancing down at the knee he blew out this past season.

"Right. You made a decision on that, speaking of?" I look up at him.

"Still figuring it out." He shrugs. "So when's the reopening of Wren's bar again?"

"Next Friday."

"We'll be there," Ben pipes in.

"Yeah and bring a friend, or a few. Wren has more than the project riding on this. Stuff with her grandfather hasn't been great." I take a sip of the beer and Liam's eyes snap to me.

"You guys have been spending a lot of time together." He looks me over like he's assessing something he regrets not noticing before.

"Yeah, *a lot* of fucking time," Waylon chokes back a laugh.

"Why is he saying it like that?" Liam's points his bottle toward me. "Please fucking tell me you didn't."

"I plead the fifth," I deflect, avoiding his gaze by staring at the TV.

I guess I couldn't avoid this much longer. She'd told me she was telling Liv and Mac, so it was only a matter of time until he found out anyways. Although I was kind of hoping Liv would tell him, as he was less likely to give me a lecture then and I suspected she would have my back on this.

"No one else is worried about this?" Liam looks around at Ben and Waylon.

"Just tell him." Waylon raises his brow at me.

"Fuck... I told you not to go there. That it would end badly for all of us if you did," Liam groans.

"Yeah, well I went there a while ago and you all have survived so far."

"And why weren't we informed of this? Or am I just the last one to find out?"

"You're the last because I knew you'd rip my fuckin' head off for it, and it wouldn't have changed my mind anyway."

"So how long have they known?"

"A few weeks."

"More than that." Ben looks at me.

"He knew before me?" Waylon sits up, looking at me like I just punched him.

"I needed fuckin' advice. We all know Ben is better with women than the rest of us. Plus I didn't tell him so much as he guessed it."

"We could all fucking guess. You've been telegraphing that shit for months," Liam grumps.

"Yeah well, you're one to fuckin' talk." I level him with a look.

"So what's the story now then? So I'm aware of what I should be fucking worried about."

"We're... I don't know what we fucking are."

"Sounds promising." Liam gives a tight smile.

"She has a lot of stuff on her plate. She's worried about me getting drafted and leaving. We've got this project to finish. I'm giving her space."

"She needs space from you already?"

"You know how she is. She likes her independence."

"Right. And how's that working with your need to fuck a different girl every week?" Liam asks flatly.

"I'm not fucking anyone else."

"How the fuck did she get you to agree to that?" Liam's brow furrows in disbelief.

"She didn't. I just haven't. Don't want to."

"Holy fuck." Liam stares at me wide eyed.

"I told you I'm fucking capable. I just needed someone who could keep up."

"And Wren can—you know what? I don't fucking want to know." Liam sits back again.

Waylon and Ben both burst out into laughter.

"Good. Because I'm not fucking sharing details with you either."

"I, for one, am happy for you." Waylon holds up his beer and tips in my direction.

"I am too. I just hope it works out." Ben gives me a half smile.

"I mean I'm fucking happy for them. I'm just trying to figure out when the fuck hell froze over."

"Thanks for the vote of confidence. Now can we go back to watching the game?"

THIRTY-FOUR

Wren

I RUN THROUGH MY CHECKLIST FOR THE THIRD TIME THIS afternoon as Tom, Tammy, and a few of the other servers who are here early run around getting everything ready. I know we're prepared, that we've all spent the entire week making sure that every single detail was taken care of, but I can't stop worrying there's still something I've missed.

"I promise you've got this," I hear my favorite voice behind me just as large hands wrap around my waist.

I turn to give him a kiss, but when I see him my jaw nearly drops as I take in the sight. He's wearing a perfectly tailored suit and tie, his hair is freshly cut and styled, and his green eyes are bright, a designer watch on his wrist and a wicked little grin forming at the fact I'm gaping at him.

"Wow," I whisper as I run my fingers down the black tie he has on.

"Did I just render you silent, Princess?"

"Just trying to find the right words for all this."

"You could use the ones I love to hear you say." He brushes his lips over mine.

"Which are?"

"*Fuck me.*" He smiles against my lips and then takes my mouth with his, kissing me hard as he pulls me tight against him.

"Definitely one of the things I was thinking, but not quite sufficient. How have I never seen you in a suit like this before?"

"You never come to the games or watch the pressers apparently. I wear them when they make me."

"Clearly, I missed out."

"That's all right, Princess. I'll make sure to wear them more often for you. You can get a better look at this one later when you fuck me in it," he whispers only loud enough for me to hear.

"Don't start. I have to stay focused." I grin and kiss him one more time.

"All right. Put me to work. What do you need done?"

"Can you make sure all the tech stuff is in order? I checked it last night, but I just want another set of eyes on everything."

"No problem."

"Did we get all the RSVPs we needed on your side of things?" I ask, following him back to where the controls are for all the screens and speakers.

"Yep. We're all good to go. Tobias and the rest will be here. The Rampage guys are bringing a couple of game balls and game-worn jerseys with them for the raffle, and Tobias said Xavier decided to come at the last second. So we'll even have an extra on hand," he answers me as he checks everything.

"Oh wow. That's amazing. You thanked your brother for me right? Is there anything we can do for him?"

"I got him a bottle of his favorite tequila and a couple

cigars. He'll be happy. Anywhere people are gathered to worship him is a place he likes to be."

"Huh. A family trait." I smirk, and he flicks me a look.

"Watch your mouth, Princess."

"Or else?" I raise a brow, giving him a teasing look.

He sets the control down and turns to me, glancing up to see if anyone can see us where we are before he grabs me and drags me against him.

"Are you trying to get fucked right here? Cause if you think I won't, I will. I don't care who sees. You're the one who'd have to explain that one to your employees."

"East..." I protest, because he's hard to resist when he's like this. The man always makes me want to do stupid things. It's a talent of his.

His hand slides down my back and over my butt as he kisses me softly. When he pulls back his eyes drift over my face and a little smile forms on his lips.

"Don't tempt me then. I'm trying to be on my best behavior today."

"You'd better be, for both our sakes." I dot a quick kiss to his lips. "All right. I'm off to do a final check on food and the tables."

It doesn't take long for the whole place to fill up. There's a wait at the door and the small lobby area we have is overflowing. A few people are even willing to brave the cold and wait outside or in their cars for a table to open up.

Between the guys bringing in the college fan crowd and Tobias, Xavier, and a few of their friends from the Rampage, the place is packed with people vying for autographs and photos, but luckily most of them are staying for food and beer as well, which means even I've had to put my apron on and help serve tonight. Not exactly the plan, but definitely a challenge I can handle. As I head back to the kitchen, I notice East even has his jacket off and his sleeves rolled up helping Tom plate up orders.

"You look so fucking sexy like that," I grin at him as I lean over the prep table.

"Don't break my focus, Princess," he whispers, giving me a meaningful look. "I don't want Tom to fire me on my first day."

I grin and dot a kiss to his cheek.

"Everything going okay out there?" he asks.

"It's going really well so far. I just hope people waiting to be seated don't get too cranky."

"I sent Tobias out to talk to people. Do a little PR for us."

"That's nice of him. I really feel like we owe him more than tequila for this. Maybe we should take him out to dinner or something?"

East grunts in response so I don't push my luck. I grab the orders from my table and spin my way back out to the main room, running the food out and getting refill orders on beers and drinks.

By the time I stop for a break and look up, I see East sitting with Gramps and Sherry at one of the tables where Gramps is holding court. Sherry and I had managed to convince the folks at the rehab to give him a few hours out of the facility for the event, and I haven't seen him so excited in ages. He's still weak and needs a wheelchair to get around, but his speech has improved dramatically and it warms my heart to see him getting to talk to so many people.

I walk over to the table and sit down next to Gramps, rubbing his shoulder and giving him a big grin.

"Your Gramps was just telling me about what it was like when he opened this place." East smiles at me.

"Oh yeah? He loves telling that story." I glance over at Sherry who has probably heard it fifty times by now and she smiles at me.

"It's a good one. Ages like fine wine. Just like your grandmother did," Gramps grins.

"She was really beautiful. I miss her."

"Me too, kid." He looks at me thoughtfully.

I lean my head against his arm and squeeze.

"You having fun tonight, though?"

"Yeah. Few of my guys showed up." He grins again. "And your guy here is letting me talk some football with him. Told him I've seen him play a few times."

I hadn't said anything to Gramps about who East is to me, and it feels strange to hear him called "my guy" but I look up at East and he smiles like he approves. My heart squeezes a little in my chest that the two of them are getting along, and East made a point of coming over to talk to him.

"I had to meet the guy who made this place happen. I told him it's my favorite place to come watch games and relax."

"He does love the cheese fries, almost as much as you, Gramps."

"That's why they're on the menu. Classic. People think it's the wings. But it's the cheese fries that keep 'em comin'."

We all have a little laugh.

"Okay Gramps, I gotta get back before I'm missed. But I wanted to come say hi. If I don't get to see you when you leave, I love you. And I'll come by tomorrow to visit, okay?"

"Sounds good, kid."

I lean over and give him a quick hug before I hop up again, noticing that Tammy is signaling for me, and one of my tables already looks like they're in need of refills.

When we finally close the place down and get everything in some sort of order, it's nearly three in the morning. While I probably should be collapsing into a heap on the floor, I have a buzz as we run the final numbers. It blows every other night at the bar completely out of the water. I jump up and down and kiss East on the cheek.

He grins. "Fuck. Pretty damn good. We also had some news folks come by."

"I know. I did a few quick interviews. The paper, a news station and a local blog. Told them all about the place and Gramps. If we get some free press from this, that will be amazing!"

"We'll get it. Now we just have to track how this trends. Hopefully it gives you a sustained boost for a while."

"I hope so." I let out a little sigh. "You want a drink?"

"Yeah, I think I could use one. This shit is not for the faint-hearted. I don't know how you do it day in and day out."

"You get used to it," I say as I pull a bottle of whiskey out and give us each a generous pour. "But you really pulled this off, you know?" I slide the glass to him.

"I didn't do that much." His brow furrows.

"Don't be modest. You did a lot of it. I was all spun up with Gramps and you picked up all the slack. With the menu, the orders, and running all the numbers. Not to mention all the marketing contacts you pulled out of thin air. I'm gonna have to tell the professor I was a slacker and you deserve the real credit for the grade." I take a long sip of the whiskey.

"You weren't a slacker. You helped, and you were taking care of your family. That's why we're partners. Give and take, Princess."

"Still. I should have done more to help you. I really appreciate it though. Everything you've done for me." I feel a little well of tightness in my chest, like I might lose a tear or two if I can't hold it together.

"I'm just glad you let me help. It's okay to admit you need help sometimes, you know?" He runs his fingers along my jaw, and I lean into his touch.

"Sometimes," I acknowledge and then smile a little. "Especially when the help comes in a suit and is incredibly fucking sexy."

I close the gap between us and pull on the knot in his tie that's already come loose, as he takes the final draw off his whiskey.

"Don't tease me, Princess. I told you how much it turns me on to watch you run this place and that's all I've been watching for hours. Like slow fucking torture."

I smirk at him and grab his hand, dragging him with me to a table and pulling a chair out.

"Sit." I nod my head toward the chair and he gives me a skeptical look in return. "Trust me. You'll like it."

I pull his tie out of its knot and off his neck, and wrap it around his eyes, tying a loose knot at the back of his head.

"Princess, I trust you but you're making me nervous." His hands drift over my hips.

"I just want to thank you for everything you've done for me. I owe you since we got interrupted the last time."

"Oh yeah? You gonna get on your knees for me but not let me watch? That's cruel."

"Well, I don't have my usual uniform on tonight. So you'll have to imagine it. This will help," I whisper against his ear. "You gotta pretend like I've got my hair in braids, my socks on and nothing else. Remember? Wet and desperate for you like I was the other night."

"Oh, fuck..." he groans, leaning back in the chair as I kneel down and start undoing his belt and pants.

THIRTY-FIVE

Easton

"ALL I COULD THINK ABOUT TODAY IS HOW LUCKY I AM TO have you. How good you are to me," she says the words softly as she starts to stroke me.

I'm so fucking weak for her when she's like this. When she says all the things I've been dying to hear her say for so long. All the things I imagined she might say for months.

The moment she puts me in her mouth I almost come out of the chair, it feels so damn good. The way she sucks me—using her mouth like she's trying to make sure I know exactly how much she appreciates me. I reach out blindly, my fingers finally connecting with her cheek and I brush over the soft curve of it as her head bobs back and forth, taking me in steady strokes as she builds up my need for her.

"Fuck me, Princess. You're so fucking perfect. You make me feel so fucking good," I whisper into the dark.

She offers me a soft moan in return as she takes me a

little deeper, and the vibration of it sets all my nerve endings on fire. I shift forward involuntarily, trying to get more of her and then pull back, scared I'm going to hurt her. But she doesn't flinch, doesn't stop, just sucks me harder; moaning and sliding her tongue over the length of me like I'm the best thing she's ever had in her mouth. I know if she keeps going like this, it's not gonna be long until I fall apart.

"Oh Princess... fuck... you suck me so well. You're so fucking good. So *so* fucking good. But I need inside you. Come up here. Take those panties off and ride me."

She pulls away from me and I hear her standing, the sound of cotton brushing over her skin, and the feel of her hair against me as she bends over to take them off. I pull a condom out of my back pocket and put it on, fumbling a bit with my lack of sight but still managing it.

"You look so fucking hot like this," she whispers. "Definitely think I have a thing for you in suits."

"How wet are you? Need me to tell you how much I hate you first before you fuck me?" I smirk.

She takes my hand and slides it between her legs, and I brush my fingers over her. She's so warm and so unbelievably wet for me, I can't help the little groan I make when I touch her.

"You like sucking my cock that much?"

"Yes, but that's not the main reason tonight."

"Oh yeah. What's got you so fucking desperate to be fucked tonight?"

"Who you are underneath everything. What a good heart you have. How lucky I am that you let me see it." Her lips brush against mine, her teeth grazing my lower lip as she straddles me and guides me inside her.

"Fuck me," I mutter when I fill her, her tight wet cunt

clenching around me. Her breath dances over my lips as a little sigh leaves her.

"You're so good. So very fucking good, East. Everything about you is so perfect." Her hand slides up my stomach and over my chest, coming to a rest over my heart. "And in here, you're the best man I've ever known."

My chest goes tight and I'm lost for words as she starts to move. I've never wanted anyone the way I want her. Every other woman I've ever known pales in comparison. The way I *need* her. I know in the depths of my fucking soul that I'm lost on her for good. The way she touches me, the way she talks to me, the way she *sees* me—I know she's *my* fucking person.

"Wren..." I manage to say, pulling the tie off my eyes and running my fingers along her jaw to bring her eyes to mine. Hoping she can understand what I can't find the right words to say. What I might be a little scared to say even if I could. A little flit of a smile curves over her lips, her eyes going low and soft.

"I know." She presses a gentle kiss to my lips. "Me too."

I wrap my arms around her then as we both go quiet, the sound of her breathing filling the air around us as she takes what she needs from me until she finally comes apart in my arms, saying my name and telling me how much she loves me. I follow her moments later, spent and wrecked all in one go.

THIRTY-SIX

Wren

OTHER THAN THE WEEK I FOUND OUT MY GRAMPS HAD A stroke; this has been the worst week of my life. It's been a combination of good and bad news that's put me here. News that makes me so happy for other people, and so sad for myself. News that I just have to learn to accept.

Like the fact that Easton was drafted by Cincinnati and has to report there in just under two weeks. Or the fact that our project went absolutely amazing, and the bar's revenue is still up and holding at 20% above average, but our presentation still only got second place which meant no interview or shot at the summer internship I was desperately hoping for.

Then there was the current moment, where I was sitting in a conference room with the elder care attorney we'd hired, Gramps, and a pile of paperwork our accountant and the senior living facility Gramps is supposed to move to is sitting like a wall of problems in the middle of the table. I'm doing my best to smile and stay levelheaded as the attorney walks us through a sea of legal jargon and technical information they have to provide while I wonder how the heck any of this makes sense to anyone.

I glance over at Gramps, and his furrowed brow and the straight line of his mouth tell me he's about as amused as I am right now. He wasn't thrilled with me either—that had been possibly the lowest point this week, rivaled only by finding out for sure that I was going to lose East. Gramps and I had fought for the first time since I was a teenager.

He was insistent that he could move back into his old apartment above the bar. But the place has no elevator, and he still needs a wheelchair to get around. He kept trying to convince me he could get out of it any day now, if we would all just get out of his way, that he could still make the stairs no problem. Except the doctors had been clear about what would be safe for him. Even if he could make them once, the chances that he could make them regularly to go to the grocery store or get to doctor's appointments, was highly unlikely. And a fall at his age could mean the worst. There had been yelling, tears, and a whole lot of disappointment on both sides of our argument, and I still felt a little heartsick over having it with him.

"So can you just give it to me straight? I want to know how much this place is going to cost a month."

"Well, after you pay the initial deposit which they're estimating will be about 30K, then it will be about $5,575 a month. That goes up though if you opt in to having the laundry services, extra snack options, and/or the pill organization and distribution services. And as you age into needing additional care that fee will also go up. So you'll want to budget more like 7 to 8K a month for this."

"Age into additional care my ass..." he mutters to himself, luckily not loud enough for the attorney to hear.

"I'm sorry, we need 8K per month for that room? It's just a room. It's not even a full apartment," I say, sounding desperate to my own ears.

"That's unfortunately the going rate for a facility. You can eventually qualify for government assistance, but he'll need to spend through his assets first."

"He doesn't have that many assets though," I say tapping my finger on the bank statement that shows he only has a few thousand left in the bank after all the doctors and care bills he already has had to pay.

"Which is why it's important we liquidate the biggest one as soon as possible. You'll need it to even pay the deposit on the facility."

"Liquidate?" I ask, a pit forming in my stomach.

"You'll need to sell the building where his apartment is currently located."

"The building? But that's where the bar is. That's our main source of income."

"Don't panic. You may be able to work out a deal with the new owner that you continue to rent that space back from them so that you can keep the bar open. A real estate agent can help you frame the listing that way so you'll attract buyers willing to come to terms with you."

"Rent it back to us? We don't make enough money there to pay rent." I feel the tears clawing at the back of my throat as I stare down at the pile of paperwork. I have a sudden urge to burn it all or toss it out the third story window across from us.

It's unbelievable that someone worked their whole life, carefully spent their money, saved, and then at the end of it was reduced to absolute fucking poverty just trying to get care. I'm furious. But the attorney is only the messenger, and getting upset is only going to rile Gramps and make him return to the idea of moving back into the apartment.

I look over at him again and he looks pale, upset, and rattled just like I am. I reach over and rub his back.

"We'll figure it out," I say softly, and he just shakes his head. I have a feeling we're both fighting back tears right now.

"Please don't worry or panic. This is a very common issue, and my firm is very familiar with navigating it. That's what we're here for. We'll help you get through this."

I'm sure they would, to the tune of several more thousands of dollars we didn't have.

———

THAT NIGHT I'M OUT TO DINNER WITH EASTON AT A restaurant downtown that he wanted to go to, trying my hardest to stay upbeat despite everything.

"Don't like it? Want to see about ordering something else?" He points to the food I haven't eaten.

"I'm just not that hungry. It's been a day," I sigh, taking another small bite of the ravioli. It tastes amazing but I just don't feel up to it.

"We could have stayed home."

"No. We wanted to try this place and I wanted to spend time with you." I give him a little smile but worry colors his features.

"If this is because of the draft, I told you we'd figure it out. I'll pay for you to fly out—whenever you want, every week if it works in your schedule."

"I know. And that's part of it."

"And the other part?"

"I really didn't want to ruin dinner talking about all this," I sigh.

"Talking about what's bugging you isn't going to ruin anything, Wren. It's what I'm here for. So tell me what's going on?" He sets his fork down, taking his drink and leaning back in the booth to watch me.

"We went to that elder care attorney. And you know Gramps is already fighting me on this whole thing. Well, we found out how much it's going to cost today."

"Yeah, how much?"

"Eight thousand a month. I nearly cried right there in the office."

"Fuck. That is a lot." His eyes go wide. "How do people afford that?"

"It'll be less initially if he doesn't take all the options and can do some things himself, but I don't even know that he can. He also can't afford the deposit, so the attorney told me we'll have to liquidate assets."

Easton's whole face goes hard. "They're gonna make you sell the bar?"

"The whole building. With the apartments upstairs." I try not to cry, because that's the last thing I want to do in this restaurant. It's upscale and posh as hell, and I doubt a lot of people cry in here unless it's out of happiness for actually getting a table. "She said we can frame the listing in a way that says we want to rent the bar back, but you've seen the numbers."

"Yeah, no one is going to want to rent to you at the price you could afford. Not for the size of the restaurant and the location. What they could get on the market... But if your upswing continues, maybe in a year."

"We don't have a year. He needs a big chunk of money just to get in and reserve his spot at this place."

"I suppose if I tell you that I'll front you the money, you're going to tell me you don't want it." He gives me a doubtful look.

"Absolutely not." I want him to know I mean it. I hope he hears me. Because my heart and my pride could not take a five-figure hand out from him. "It's way too much. And it still wouldn't help with the monthly fees. He'll have to sell the building. But I'm devastated about the bar, especially after we put so much work in it and things are promising."

"I know. Fuck, that definitely sucks, Princess. I'm sorry. Maybe there's still hope though. Don't give up just yet... see what the attorney and the real estate agent can come up with, okay?"

"I know. I'm just trying to prepare myself for the worst. Especially after we lost out on that interview."

"It was bullshit. We definitely deserved first place. We even had better numbers."

"Yeah. And if he thinks it's easy to market a bar near campus, I'd like to see him try it someday. It's harder when there are so many options and everyone has a favorite already."

"I mean, the fact that you kept it open so long through everything says a lot about how good you are at the job. How well you made the lack of big budget marketing work. Honestly, fuck that professor." Easton gives me a little smile.

"Yeah. Fuck him for not recognizing our talents." I smile back, because even though this week has been hell and today has been particularly brutal, it still helps to have someone like him in my corner. Rooting for me. Fighting for me.

THIRTY-SEVEN

Easton

"You going somewhere?" I ask when I show up and see Ben looking dressed up.

"Yeah. I'm headed out to an art thing."

"Date?"

"No. Just going by myself."

"What?" I stare at him like he has two heads because while Ben is a far more sensitive soul than I'll ever be, I didn't exactly picture him wandering art galleries alone in contemplation.

"I'm... It's..." He trips over his words, and I raise a brow in response.

"You all right there?"

"I'm going to see someone. Not see them, like talk to them see them. But just, check on them. From a distance."

"That... sounds a lot like stalking." I try to stifle the amusement I know is showing on my face.

"I'm not stalking her," he grumps at me defensively.

"Whoa."

"She's just a friend of my sister's. She's had a rough week. I just want to see if she's okay."

"But you don't want to talk to her?"

"No. She won't recognize me."

"How do you know?"

"Because I do. Why are you interrogating me anyway? Don't you have better things to do?"

"I need your help."

"With what?"

"With Wren."

His mouth flatlines and he gives me a look.

"I don't know who else to go to. The girls won't want to meddle on my behalf and Liam and Waylon are useless. You're the closest thing to the girls."

"You're not selling this."

"I just mean you're better at the relationship side of things."

"I haven't had any more relationships than you."

"Right. But you're better at the romance thing. At the talking. At the nonphysical side of things with women. Is that better?"

"Slightly. You're bad at asking for help. That's part of your problem."

"I'm fucking aware."

"If you want the advice now, you'll have to go with me."

"Fine. Although this sounds fucking terrible."

"You could use some culture."

"You sound like my mother."

"She's probably right. That's the first tip. Listen to the women in your life. Even if you don't agree."

"I'm going to regret asking you for help, aren't I?"

"Maybe. Let's go." He grabs his keys and heads out.

———

WE GET INTO THE ART GALLERY WHERE THERE'S SOME sort of photography exhibit opening tonight. I follow Ben's lead as he walks around. He looks nervous in a way I've never seen him before and he scans the crowd occasionally like he's looking for the mystery woman.

"This seems like a lot of work for a friend of your sister's. You love your sister that much or this girl mean something to you too?"

He looks at me, his eyes searching me for a minute like he's trying to decide if he should answer before he does.

"Both."

"Did you fuck her? Date her?" I'm intrigued. Ben occasionally tried someone more steady like he did with Chelsea on the couple's trip we took, but inevitably it ended when she wanted more and he didn't.

"Neither."

"Neither?" I ask, a little incredulous.

He stops abruptly in his tracks, and I follow his line of sight to a corner where two women stand. Both tall, one with short black and red hair and lots of tattoos, the other with long brunette hair, splashed with plum-colored highlights and pale skin. They're both beautiful in an offbeat way. Not that either of them compared to Wren. Then again, no one does.

"Which one?" I know Ben normally goes for blondes but he also loves his heavy metal and punk music, and I could definitely see him with a chick with tattoos and colored hair.

He looks at me warily.

"I'm not gonna do anything. I mean, I think we should go talk to them. See if she recognizes you, but I'm not going to tell her. Don't worry."

"The brunette..." His eyes drift over her.

"She the one that got away?"

"She's the one that doesn't know I exist."

"Why not?"

"Because I'm her best friend's little brother and she's the type that always has a boyfriend."

"Hmm. That does put you at a disadvantage. I thought you said she had a rough week, though, she seems happy enough."

"She and her fiancé split up. For good this time if my sister's right."

"So what are you waiting for? Go be the rebound."

"She's not the rebound type, and she's out of my league anyway."

"Oh fuck that. Everyone is the rebound type if the person is right. Let's go. We're at least gonna talk to her." I start walking in their direction.

"No. East! Fucking fuck. Do *not* tell her who I am." He whisper shouts at me as he hurries to catch up.

"I won't. But I'm not being a creepy fucking weirdo about it standing back here in the shadows with you either. Just talk to her. You won't know until you do."

I shake my head and cross the short distance between us.

"Hi." I look down at the tattooed woman's docent tag. "Joss is it?"

"Yes."

"You work here?"

"I volunteer here." Her voice has an edge to it.

"We were just wondering if there was a best way to see the exhibit. An order, or maybe a tour or something?" I ask, looking to her friend, the one Ben's so obsessed with.

And I get it, especially now that we're closer. She's pretty, her eyes a pale aqua that make it hard not to stare. Eyes that flash over me, find me wanting, and then land hard on Ben.

"Yeah, follow us. We'll get you a pamphlet and I can give you a little head start on the tour," Joss answers me.

"Are you together?" Ben's girl asks us, her eyes floating between us. I narrow my eyes at her name tag as it's partially obscured by her hair.

"No. I mean, yes. We're here together. As friends. Just thought we'd do something different tonight." Ben trips over his words and I give him a *what the fuck* look. This guy normally has the kind of game I'm jealous of, and watching him flail like this is something to behold.

"Oh, I just meant if you needed anything else." She looks between us and then to Ben again. The guy is fucking clueless if he thinks she wouldn't fuck him, because her eyes are currently raking over him, pausing over every detail she likes. All of it despite how weird he's being.

"Yeah, actually while Joss helps me get these pamphlets... I know he had a couple questions about those photographs."

"What?" Ben looks at me.

"You know, the ones over here." I point randomly as we start walking. I give him another pointed look, trying to give him a lifeline and he just manages to look starstruck. I have to bite the inside of my cheek just to keep from laughing.

"The ones of the mountain scenes? I love those. Some of my favorites. The abandoned cabins and mines?" She looks to him again.

"Yes, those," I answer when he continues to be rendered silent.

"I've hiked up to a few of them. Have you ever been up to any of the abandoned mining towns?" She looks at me briefly, but her eyes return to Ben.

"I haven't had the opportunity. Football takes up a lot of free time." I shrug, and Ben shoots me a look.

"Oh, do you both play football?" She studies him, waiting

for an answer, and holy fuck, it's like this guy has completely lost his ability to speak.

He never does answer. Instead he pulls his phone out and looks at it and then at me. Like he's checking the time or has a message that's urgent.

"I actually need to run. Did you want to come with, or did you want to stay here?"

I stop short and blink. I'm watching him melt down in real time, and I'm not sure anyone would believe me if I told them that Ben failed this badly at even talking to a woman.

"We can go... Joss? Is that your name? Joss, I am really sorry. Thanks for the help though. I will definitely come back and finish the tour another day."

"You're welcome." She raises a brow at me and gives us both a skeptical once over.

"And thank you too—I didn't get your name?"

"Violet."

"Violet." I smile and then look at Ben, still silent as a grave as he stares at the ground in front of him. "Thanks, Violet."

When we get back into Ben's car, I bust out into the hardest fucking laugh I've had in a while.

"What the fuck was that?" I look at him, and he looks utterly shellshocked. Like he has no fucking clue what just happened either.

"I told you I didn't want to talk to them. You fucking insisted!" He looks like he's about to go full pout mode on me.

"Okay, fair. I didn't realize how serious it was. She's your literal kryptonite, huh? But you realize she couldn't stop looking at you. If you could have strung a few words together, turned on your fucking Casanova act just for a few minutes she would have been going home with you tonight."

"I don't want her to go home with me." He huffs.

"You don't?"

"I don't want her like that. I want... Never-fucking-mind. You don't fucking get it." He stares out the windshield.

I look at him and suddenly realize we're two sad fucking losers in the same boat. We can get all the women we want so long as it's for a night or two. But when it comes to winning hearts and minds, it's an entirely different set of skills, ones we apparently both come up short on.

My laugh fades into a sigh as I stare out the windshield with him.

"I get it... That's why I wanted to talk to you. Because you always seem to have the right thing to say or do. I could use the help. Guess it doesn't work when it's your heart in the fucking vice, huh?"

He glances over at me, shaking his head. "It's a crush I can't quit. I don't know what's wrong with me. Trust me, I've tried."

"Well I'm serious when I say that she couldn't stop looking at you. I think it was because she was into you, but maybe she recognized you?"

"Doubt it. Last time she saw me and knew it was me was when I was a teenager. Before the growth spurt and all that."

"Saw you and *knew* it? Is this stalking bit a regular thing then?" I can't help the amused smile that returns to my face.

"It's only the second time. Just when my sister mentions something's happened. I tell her I'll check on her."

"I see." I raise an eyebrow.

"Let's not start with the judgment or we'll be going back and forth all night." He levels me with a look that tells me to fuck off.

"Well I'm not judging. But I do need your advice."

"You and Wren having problems already?" He turns toward me.

"Not exactly. Life is just... hitting her hard right now, and I want to help but I don't want to overstep or piss her off. She's so independent and I don't want to try to take that away from her. But watching her struggle, knowing I could make it easier... It's fucking hard to do."

"Can you tell me what's going on? Without breaking her confidence, I mean?"

"I can give you the highlights..." I say and start to explain the situation to him.

"Fuck, that is rough."

"Right. And, the thing is... The signing bonus would let me buy the building. I already have an agent ready when it goes on the market. I know she might be freaked out about it, but it would give her time and choices. Plus, I just want her to know that this move to play in Cincinnati doesn't mean my feelings are changing. I want her. Just her."

"That's a hard sell when you are who you are."

"I know, trust me. I fucking know. But... she knows I love her."

He stares at me for a minute, and I give him a look.

"Sorry, I just never thought I'd see the day you'd say you were in love."

"And I'd never thought I'd be helping you stalk a woman, and yet here we are."

He rolls his eyes and shakes his head, a little grunt coming before he speaks again.

"Buy the building. It might freak her out, but even if it does, she'll get over it and be thankful she has the choice. And you'll have shown her you're invested. It's what I'd do."

"You sure?" I feel the worry well up in my gut again.

"No. You can't ever be sure, and you know her better than I do at this point. But it's what you think will help her most, give her choices—so follow your gut."

"All right. If she dumps me when she sees it though, I'm coming here and outing your stalking act."

"I'm not stalking her. It's only been twice!"

"That's how it starts." I smirk.

"Fuck! I shouldn't have let you come." Ben starts the engine and we start to head back toward home.

"For real though, good luck with her. I hope you get your words back and get a chance to use them."

"Thanks, I think."

THIRTY-EIGHT

Easton

To celebrate the end of the year and the fact that both Waylon and I were drafted, Liv is throwing a huge party at the girls' house. By the time I get there, it's already spilling out into the backyard, the music is loud, and the kegs are flowing. Wren's actually gotten a night off for the evening, and I'm thankful because I need some time with her. Time alone away from this crowd. Because in a week I have to report to my new team in Ohio, and I don't have much time left to convince her that we can make this work.

She grins at me when she sees me, setting her drink down and throwing her arms around my neck to kiss me. I press my lips to hers, loving every chance I get when her perfect body is pressed up against me like this.

"Now we can really celebrate." She glances up at me with a look that would melt any wall I had left around my heart.

"Can we go upstairs for a few minutes?" I ask quietly.

She gives me a little wicked grin, assuming it's because I want a quick fuck before I have to play party host. And here's to hoping the reality isn't too disappointing for her.

"Always." She smiles.

I don't correct her assumption because if she knew what I was really doing, I don't know if she'd come up with me. Instead I just follow her up the stairs, and into her room, setting my bag on her bed when we get there.

"What's in there?" She gives me a curious look.

"Some things we need to discuss."

"That sounds ominous. I hope fun things..." She looks at me warily.

"Depends." I give her a half smile. "I hope it's good."

"Okay... you're making me a little nervous, though." Her eyes flit over my face like she's trying to find answers there.

I unzip the bag and pull out the large manila envelope inside, my fingers practically shaking as I hand it to her. I don't get anxious very often. Even at important games I'm usually able to keep the rattling of my nerves to a minimum. But with her, it feels like everything that matters to me is on the line. I'm just hoping I did the right thing.

"What's this?" She looks at the envelope, her brow furrowing.

"Open it."

Her fingers fumble at the clasp but she manages to undo it and pulls the paperwork out. She stares at it for a long minute. An interminable amount of time while I wait for her reaction. Her brow furrows and she blinks. She pages through the paperwork. Looking down at the paper and up at me a few times before her eyes turn up slowly to meet mine.

"This is a copy of the deed to the bar. Purchase documents."

"Yes."

"How do you have these?"

"I bought the building with my signing bonus. Or part of it anyway. And it's yours if you want it."

"You what?" She blinks rapidly and I can see the tears forming in her eyes.

"Don't cry. Please don't cry. Please don't be mad at me. I just... I know how much it means to you and your Gramps. I know you were ready to do what had to be done, but I wanted you to have the choice. You can still sell if you want, but this way you have more time to decide what you want to do. How you want to do it."

"You bought the building for me? Why? Why would you do that?"

"Because I fucking love you, Princess, and it's something I could do for you. To give you choices. You deserve to make your own choices instead of always being pushed in one direction or the other by what's happening around you. I want to see you make things happen the way *you* want them. If I can help with that, then I'm going to."

"Easton you shouldn't have done that. That's so much money. I have no idea how I'll ever pay you back. Even with the extra revenue from the bar, it'll take years." Tears start to fall down her face and I reach out to wipe them away.

"I don't want the money. It's a gift. You've given me so much just in the last few months. It's the least I could do."

"Given you what? A pain in your ass? Lots of bitchy stubbornness?" She laughs through her tears. "Easton, I don't know how to make this up to you. I'll figure out a way though."

"There's nothing to make up. I'm serious, Wren. I just want to see you happy."

She puts the papers down on the bed and wraps her arms around me, crying softly into my chest and I wrap my arms around her, pulling her tight.

"There's more though..." I say softly.

"More? How can there possibly be more?" She dabs at her tears and looks up at me.

"The bar is something for you. This is something more for me."

Her forehead furrows and her lashes flutter, and she pulls away from me a little without removing her hands from me. I reach back into the bag and pull out the two jewelry boxes inside, holding them for a minute as my chest goes tight before I set them down on the bed. One smaller box first, and then a longer one.

I feel her fingers dig into my sides and I watch the confusion on her face spread.

"What's this?" She asks, her voice whisper soft.

"Open it. The small one first."

"East..." she looks at me out of the corner of her eye.

"Just open it. Please," I say, my heart twisting in my chest because the way she looks I'm almost sure now what the answer is going to be.

She picks it up and opens it, slowly, and gasps a little when she sees the ring sitting inside.

"This isn't... I mean. You're not... Right?" She looks up at me, searching my face for answers.

"I want you to come with me. I know you said we just have to accept that it is what it is. But it doesn't have to be."

"East you can't be serious. You have a whole life ahead of you. There's so many new opportunities for you and I will just hold you back from them."

"I'm very serious. You're the only thing I want. The only person I want with me. I don't need opportunities or choices. I made my choice the second I realized you actually fucking loved me. Having someone like you—so smart, so fierce, so fucking independent look at me and actually want me? Choose me? Love me? I'm not stupid enough to pass that up."

"I do love you; you know how much. But, East, we're young and I know, I know I said I fantasized about being your starter wife but I... I can't do that. I told you before, having you and then having you ripped away from me. I can deal with you going away now. I know that's what's happening. I prepared myself for it. But if we did this, and we got there and then you realized you wanted more..." she trails off as worry stains her features.

I know she's just trying to be smart. Be a realist. Do what she thinks a wise person would do. I know she's trying to protect us both from making mistakes and getting hurt. But I also know that I don't want anything or anyone but her.

"I've told you. You're it for me. I'm sure of it. Do you trust me?"

"Of course I trust you. More than anything. I believe you when you say this is what you want East, I just also know that people's minds change. I've seen it. The chance that I'm enough for you, long term... it's not high. I'm just trying to be realistic."

"Or just trying to push my buttons..." I try for levity.

"I'm not trying to push your buttons." She looks up at me, concern flitting over her features.

"Then maybe you think there are better options out there than me?" I give her a little half smirk.

She laughs. "Yeah. I'm going to find another guy that even remotely compares to you. Who loves me like you do, who fucks like you do. One that buys bars for me and rides in like a white fucking knight every time I have a problem. I'm sure I can just wander down to the store and bump into one."

I raise my eyebrow at her.

"What?"

"Exactly. So don't be fucking stupid. Put the ring on."

"Did you just call me stupid?" Her mouth opens a little, like she's shocked I'd call her out.

"You're acting fucking stupid if you think I'm going to find someone like you again. Someone this fucking smart, gorgeous, driven. With this insane fucking body that you have, and a mind that rivals it. And that fucking mouth... don't get me fucking started. Plus, you're right, no man is going to worship you like I do. No one will ever come close to the way I would spend the rest of my life making sure you got any and every fucking thing you wanted or needed. We were fucking made for each other, Princess. You want to fight it, we can. I'm very fucking patient when it comes to you. But we both know it's gonna end. With you up against that wall, my cock inside you and this ring on your finger anyway so you might as well give in now. Unless that's the way you need it go. If you need me to convince you, I can."

She looks at me and then down at the ring, rolling her bottom lip between her teeth. She pulls it out of the box and holds it up to look at it. It's on the tip of my tongue to tell her I'll get her a different one if she doesn't like it, but then her eyes snap to mine.

"Make me." She grins.

THIRTY-NINE

Wren

A WRY GRIN CROSSES HIS FACE BEFORE HE GRABS ME AND hauls me backwards, up against the wall. He lets my feet touch the ground but keeps me pinned there, his lips going to my neck, kissing his way down and back up again. His eyes are heavy as he looks at me, but he pulls back, pausing and studying my face.

"What are your objections? You might as well tell me so I can knock them down one at a time. And don't give me any fucking shit about other women or wanting something more. You're it for me, so move on to the next one."

I love that he knows me well enough to know that I'm going to be worried about a whole list of things before I can agree to this. That I'm going to have to think through all the details before I can say what he wants to hear, and that he's patient enough to work through them with me.

"What about the bar?"

"It's up to you. Sell it. Keep it. If you keep it, you'll have to hire someone else to manage obviously. In the meantime I think Tom and Tammy would have it pretty well covered for you. We can fly you back and forth, though, if you want. Could fix one of the apartments upstairs up for you and it could be your place while you're here checking on things. I assumed you'd want to keep it at least short term even if you did want to sell it so everyone could find other work first."

"Yes, definitely."

"And?"

"And I guess those are good options. Would be hard but doable."

"All right, next up..." he raises a brow at me, waiting patiently.

"What about Gramps?"

"He comes with us. I already looked in Cincinnati and found a couple of places that have a good reputation not too far outside the city. There's one that looks even better than the one you were thinking of here. Low patient-to-staff ratio, lots of extracurriculars, and even a lounge where they can watch games."

"He'd like that. But still... That's a big change for him."

"True. And again, if he doesn't want to come, or you don't think it's right, we'll fly you back here as often as you want to spend time with him. I'll pay for it, so don't worry about the cost. Even if it's every week."

"I'd have to talk to him, see what he wants to do. I just worry about him."

"I know you do. You talk to him, or we can both talk to him. That way you have someone to throw under the bus if you need it." He winks at me, and I smile in return.

"I think he'll get it. I know he'll want me to follow my heart.

He's been telling me for a while I need to find a nice boy." I laugh at the thought of Easton in that role.

"Something funny, Princess?"

"You being a nice boy."

He smirks, and his eyes drift over me, his lashes lowering.

"Oh, but I am nice to you. I make you feel so fucking nice..." His fingers drift under my shirt, brushing over my stomach and then back down to my pants.

He leans back and starts undoing them, pulling them off of me slowly and then reaching for my shirt, guiding it up over my head while I help him. He tosses my clothes down to the side, his own clothes following them to the pile at his feet a minute later.

His fingers run over me, sending little sparks of awareness through me everywhere he touches. He looks lost in thought for a few moments before he glances up at me again.

"The time for objections is running out, Princess. What else you got?" He mutters as he pulls a condom out of the pocket and stands to put it on.

"It's a big change for you. Moving there. A new team. Lots of pressure. New ropes you're going to have learn... What if I'm just in the way of all that?"

He lets out a little huff and shakes his head. "Those are all reasons I need you there. You help me stay centered. You bring out the little bit of good I have in me. I'll need all that to get through it."

"East..." I sigh, my hand drifting over his chest and my eyes following the path over his skin. "We could do all of this without a ring."

"We could. But it would just be wasting more time. I don't want to waste anymore when it comes to you. We belong together and I don't need to spend time fucking around for months or years pretending I'm still figuring it out."

His fingers slide under the band of my panties and he drags them down over my thighs and legs until they hit the floor at my feet. He looks up at me smirking, and then his hand slides its way back up the inside of my leg as he stands until he reaches the tops of my thighs. He uses his fingers to part me, stroking me long and slow until he gets the soft moan out of me that he's looking for. His other hand goes to my throat, pinning me back and tilting my chin up until my eyes meet his. He watches me while he slides his fingers inside me, curling them slightly as he moves them in and out at a tortuous pace, his thumb stroking roughly over my clit until I'm raising up on my tiptoes, gasping a little each time he brings me closer to the edge.

"Yeah. You like that. I know. Because your sweet little cunt here knows it already belongs to me. It has since the first time we fucked. And you know what else? Give me your hand," he rasps, and he temporarily lets go of my throat to bring my own hand up around it, sliding his over mine and holding my finger-tips to my pulse. "You feel that? The way your heart beats like that? Because it beats for me, Princess. Only *me*. I love the way it feels under my hands, under my lips. Knowing how fucking much you want me every time I touch you."

"Fuck, East…" I give him a desperate look and he lets my hand fall away under his, and then tightens his grip just the little bit more I need. The way he holds me making me feel like I'm his and I'm safe. I don't have to think. I don't have to worry. I don't have to plan. I can just *be* with him.

"You just gotta know when to concede. Recognize when your body knows what your mind hasn't caught up to yet. You lost yourself to me a long time ago. And I already belong to you, Princess. So if you want me, you put the ring on." His eyes burn into me, challenging me to try to lie and say that any of it isn't true.

He's right. I want him. Need him. I would have never guessed it would be him before, but now I can't imagine anyone else. I'll give him whatever he wants to feel like this every day—seen, loved, wanted. I take the ring, sliding it on my finger and a little grin forms on his lips, spreading as he stares at it.

"Look how well you fucking listen, Princess. So fucking well. Now you get what you want so much." He grabs me, picking me up and sliding inside me as he pins me against the wall. "Fuck me. You feel so good. We gotta make this fast. I'm too fucking wound up from knowing you're fucking mine now."

"Good. Take me hard. Like you did when you hated me," I whisper.

"Fuck, Princess. The only thing I hate now is that I didn't convince you to fuck me sooner. That we could have had more of this."

"I know. I'm stubborn." I grin and kiss him as he starts to thrust into me, until the feel of him is all I can focus on.

"Yeah, I've fucking noticed. It does make it that much better when you come for me though. And you're gonna come fucking hard for me right now, Princess. Now that you know you're gonna come for me every fucking night."

Then he takes me hard and fast. A punishing pace and I brace myself against him and the wall, rolling my hips to try and take more of him as he fucks me harder.

"You coming close for me Princess?"

"Yes…" I breathe, feeling the roll of it start to hit just right, hitting every little nerve ending I have.

"Put your nails in my back. I want to know how good I make you feel."

I do as he asks, coming as I say his name. Him following me while he tells me I'm his and then sliding us both down to the floor where we collapse, our breathing rough and heavy. He takes the condom off, tying it and leaning over to toss it in the trash. His fingers run up my thigh until he takes my hand, studying the ring and leaning over to kiss it.

"I love you. More than fucking anything." He looks up at me, giving me a meaningful look.

"I love you too." I press a kiss to his shoulder.

FORTY

Wren

After a few minutes I feel like I can breathe again and as I look up I see the other box, the longer one, sitting there still unopened.

"Wait, so what's that one then?"

"Open it." He nods to it.

I reach for it and manage to get one corner with my fingertips and drag it towards me. Opening the box to reveal a long silver chain inside.

"It's beautiful, but does it mean something?" I look to him, searching for more information.

"I thought that if I managed to get you to agree to the whole thing... I figured you'd probably want a long engagement. That you might want to keep it to yourself. And I'm okay with that. If you don't want to tell people. You can do it when you're ready. But I want you to wear it. I thought you could put it on that. It's long enough it'll keep it hidden." He's so stoic, so thoughtful as he says it, that it only makes my heart twist harder that he thinks I still want to keep him hidden.

"Get dressed." I nod to the pile of clothes we've scattered everywhere.

"What? Princess, you fucking wear me out. Like I'm gonna have to skip the gym on days you need fucked like this. I need a breather."

"Get dressed. It's important. You can rest after. Please?" I give him my best pleading eyes and he sighs and relents, standing to put his clothes on.

I don't know that I'll ever get over the view of him naked either. The idea that it's going to be all mine. Signed, sealed, delivered. Officially stamped and recognized? My heart starts racing in my chest again just thinking about how fucking lucky I am.

I start putting my clothes on too, combing my fingers through my hair and trying to make it less of a mess, but he'd done a number on it. I smooth out my clothes and then turn to him. He's dressed but still looking at me like he's not quite sure. I take his hand in mine and open the door.

"Princess, you still got your ring on. You wanna leave it up here?"

"No. Come on." I tug on his hand and take him downstairs with me.

The party is in full swing now, people literally everywhere, and definitely the biggest crowd we've ever had. When people see him, they start shouting his name and telling him congratulations on being drafted. A few people trying to stop him while I keep tugging him along to the dining room. I grab a chair from the dining table and stand on it.

"Everybody I need your attention!!" I yell. "Listen up. Please!"

I clap my hands loudly and a few people start to quiet

down but there's still a dull roar. Easton grabs the chair next to me, standing on it.

"Everyone shut the fuck up!" He yells in a booming tone that takes the entire room down to a dull whisper. Then he gestures to me, looking a little puzzled and unsure but still more than happy to follow my lead.

"I just have a quick little announcement and then you all can go back to the party. I promise this won't take long." I look for Liv and Kenz because I want to make sure they hear it from me, even if I am doing it in an unorthodox way. I spot them on the far side of the living room with Waylon and Liam, both looking at me like I might have lost my mind. I'm about to double that feeling. "I just want to say my boyfriend here, your favorite tight end, just asked me to marry him and I said yes. Because he is the best fucking thing that has ever happened to me, and I love him. So you know, drink an extra beer or something to celebrate." A laugh bubbles out of me as I see a few shocked faces and several impressed ones.

I look over at him and he's smiling, the most arrogant self-satisfied grin I have ever seen him have, but with the tiniest hint of something else at the corner of his eye. He mouths the words "I love you," as he looks at me.

"Holy fucking shit! Hell fucking yes!" Waylon holds his glass up high and a moment later the whole fucking party erupts into cheers and clapping.

Easton steps down off his chair and pulls me off mine into his arms and I wrap my legs around him, kissing him for a long minute before he sets me down on my feet again.

"I fucking love you, Princess."

"I love you too." I grin at him, threading my fingers into his as people start to come up to us to congratulate us and ask questions.

Liv and Kenz thread their way through the crowd and

come screaming up to me, wrapping their arms around me and hugging me tight.

"Oh my god. Congratulations!" Liv smiles.

"I am so happy for you!" Kenz grins.

"Yeah, well given the look on Waylon's face right now, I think he just got an idea he likes." I laugh as I hug her.

"Oh god. Don't start. I can't think about that. Right now I just gotta be in awe of your ability to take that man and turn him all the way fucking around." Kenz looks up at him over my shoulder as he talks to Liam, Ben, and Waylon.

"He's really, *really* good to me. I know he hides it well, but he is such a good person on the inside. He even bought the bar and gave it to me as a gift." I feel like I might cry from how happy I am. How lucky he makes me feel.

"He what?" Kenz looks at me wide eyed.

"I knew he had it in him." Liv grins. "That's amazing."

"There are so many things to figure out now. I'm a little overwhelmed." I give them a look and take a deep breath.

"But you're happy?" Liv asks me thoughtfully.

"Happier than I've ever been, honestly. I think I might kinda get your point about finding the right guy now." I smile at her and the two of them hug me tight again.

Easton looks back over his shoulder at me and shakes his head at the three of us, grinning and winking at me. The warmth that blooms in my chest at having him at my side makes me feel like I could face anything—do anything, and the knowledge that it's a feeling I'm going to have for the rest of our lives makes me feel like I've finally found a new home. One with him. Surrounded by our friends.

EPILOGUE

Easton

"Fucking finally." I lean back against the door as we get to our hotel room after the wedding reception. I could give a fuck less about everything that happened between her saying she was mine and getting her back in this room alone with me. But for her sake, I played along with all of the pomp and circumstance required for the day.

"It really did drag on forever. I think there were still people drinking when we left." She looks back over her shoulder at me as she slips out of her shoes.

"Open bars will do that to people." I smile and run my fingers down her spine where her skin is exposed by the open back of her reception dress.

"Your uncle was hilarious though. I think I'll like seeing him at the holidays." She smirks.

"He's one of my favorites. You know what else is my

favorite? This fucking dress. You look fucking gorgeous, Princess." I slide an arm around her and kiss up the side of her throat as she runs her fingers down my side.

"Princess?" She holds up her wedding ring for me to see, and fuck if I don't love seeing that reminder. "I think I got upgraded to queen today, don't you?"

"Princess, queen... I'll fucking call you goddess as long as you let me worship between your thighs every day." I spin her around and take her mouth with mine. She goes soft for me, letting me have her tongue and pressing closer to me, her hands wandering down to my belt.

"You can have me whenever you want me," she whispers.

I still her hands as she starts to go for the zipper on my pants. "Oh no, you don't get my cock yet. First, you're gonna pull that dress up. Take those panties off and sit up on the bed."

Her eyes flash to mine, a little smile forming and disappearing as she does what I ask.

"Right here on the edge and spread your thighs for me." I press her knees apart as I kneel down until I get the view I want. "Look how fucking wet you are. You been pressing these thighs together all day wishing for this haven't you."

It's a statement. Not a question. I know she has. I've been getting looks from her all day. Little whispered confessions about how much she wants me. How much she couldn't wait to leave the reception and have me inside her. I'd been taunting her too. Telling her while she ate her cake how much I couldn't wait to see if tonight's version was better than the first.

"East, as much as I want you... it's late and we have that early brunch with our friends, and then our flight. We could just have a quickie in the shower. We have our whole honeymoon ahead..." She looks at me thoughtfully as her fingers run through my hair.

"Always so fucking practical." I kiss the inside of her thigh. "But I need to taste my wife, Wren. If you need persuading, I'm happy to do that too."

I lean forward to slide my tongue over her, but her fingers catch my chin, and she tilts my face up to meet her eyes.

"Compromise? Turn the water on in the shower, and you have until it gets hot to get me ready for you. Because I've been thinking about you fucking me in there all day too." She nods toward the bathroom.

This is why I married this woman, and one of the many reasons she has me wrapped around her little finger. I give her a small smirk and make a quick detour to turn on the water before I'm back on my knees in front of her again, kissing my way up her thigh.

I part her with my fingers and slide my tongue over her clit, teasing and sucking it in intervals until she's nearly edging off the bed. Soft little moans coming out of her while her fingers run over my shoulder, up my neck and through my hair as she spreads wider for me.

"Fuck, East... you're going to make me come before we ever make it to the shower."

"And?" I pause to ask.

"I want the first time I come as Mrs. Westfield to be with you inside me. The whole wife fantasy, you know. Please?" Her words come out in little bursts and stutters between gasps as I work my tongue over her.

"Fuck..." The word rips out of me like a growl because I like the sound of that too much even if I do want her coming on my tongue. "Get up and get that dress off then. Or I'll rip it off, and I like you in it too much. You're gonna have to wear it on the honeymoon for me again. Let me fuck you in it."

She shakes her head as she gives me a sly little grin,

working the buttons at the back of the dress as she asks me to get the two she can't reach. I strip down with her as she works out of it and the rest of her lingerie underneath, and a few moments later we're in the shower.

"Remember when you let me in the shower with you that first night?" I ask as she bends for me, bracing herself against the tile as I slide inside her tight little cunt.

"Yes," she answers as her fingers slide over the tile, pressing against it as I start to move.

"You gonna finally admit the little soap routine was for my benefit?"

She lets out a tiny laugh in between the gasps and moans I'm working out of her as I take her deeper.

"The soap routine was just me taking a shower—the bending over in front of you—*that* was for your benefit."

"I fucking knew it."

She looks back at me, a smirk on her face. "You get your shot to seduce Easton Westfield, you take it. And look how well it worked out for me."

I feel the familiar warmth spread through my chest as I shake my head at her, grinning as I slide my hand over her hip. That I get this fierce woman—the only one that has the ability to crack my icy fucking heart and make it beat—is still a novelty every single time I'm reminded of it.

"Fuck, Princess. I love you so much. You're so fucking perfect."

"I love you too, East. You and your mouth are the best thing ever."

"Good. Now you better come for me, Mrs. Westfield."

A laugh tumbles out of her before it's cut off by a soft moan, and it's the best sound I've ever heard in my life.

Ready for Ben's book? Get it here!
Want to know what's next and get sneak peeks of
future books? Join the newsletter.

ALSO BY MAGGIE RAWDON

Pregame (Prequel)

Play Fake

Delay of Game

Reverse Pass (Coming March 2nd!)

ABOUT THE AUTHOR

Maggie loves books, travel and wandering through museums. She lives in the Midwest where you can find her writing on her laptop with her two pups at her side, in between binge watching epic historical and fantasy dramas and cheering for her favorite football teams on the weekends. She loves writing about dirty athletes and has a soft spot for characters who banter instead of flirt.

Join the newsletter here for sneak peeks: https://geni.us/MRBNews
Join the reader's group on FB here: https://www.facebook.com/groups/rawdonsromanticrebels

instagram.com/maggierawdonbooks
tiktok.com/@maggierawdon
facebook.com/maggierawdon

ACKNOWLEDGMENTS

To you, the reader, thank you so much for taking a chance on this book and on me! Your support means the world.

To my Street Team, thank you so much for your constant support and your love for this bunch of friends.

To Kat, thank you for your constant help, support, and patience. You helped me move mountains with this book, and I will never forget it!

To Deb, thank you for working through the holidays to help me make this one a reality!

To Lindsey, thank you for always holding my hand and giving me feedback on my characters and constant support and encouragement.

To Justin, who would be horrified to know this is how I put all that fact-checking about the minute details of college football to good use, for always being a font of knowledge and willing to patiently answer my questions.

Made in the USA
Las Vegas, NV
29 December 2023

83667561R10164